P.S.

Be My Angel

notionpress
.com

P.S.

Be My Angel

BAMAN TADIWALA

notionpress.com

Notion Press

Old No. 38, New No. 6

McNichols Road, Chetpet

Chennai - 600 031

First Published by Notion Press 2015

ISBN 978-93-5206-487-8

Dedication

This book is dedicated to all those people, who are still loyal to their bae even after their break-up.

Acknowledgment

This book was written when I was facing the toughest part of my life, although during this writing period, a few people helped me by continuously motivating me to complete it. All the people whom I thank below are more than my soulmates, who really care for me.

I don't have any real sister in my life, but Heenal, Aastha, Rishu and Prachi filled that void and never made me feel alone. I love you, girls!

Dhruvesh Patel, Amay Desai and Vrund Shah, my besties, who were able to see my tears, deep inside my heart. Love you, guys!

Zubin Macwan and Evangelin Samuel for gifting me a wonderful childhood as my best friends!

Vraj Patel, Arpit Patel and Haard Shah, my best buddies, who made me laugh in our computer classes!

Ashwini Soni, Netri Trapasia, Prutha Kothari, Rahul Ravichandran, Ujjwal Makwana, Neel Talati, Parth Shah, Harshil Joshi and Arnold Mecvan, my buddies, who always make me believe that life isn't beautiful, but that they are there to make it beautiful. Also special thanks to Mahima Trivedi for allowing me to use her poetic quote in this book.

My deep respect and thanks to my teachers. They always treated me as their son. Without their blessings and wishes, Baman is nothing. Love you all!

Special thanks to my Guru, Pratibha Madam. She was the only one who inspired me to believe in myself when I was left with emptiness!

I would love to thank my father, Percy Tadiwala, who always gave me chances to prove myself. He is the best father in this world. My mom, Tanaaz Tadiwala, for always loving me more than herself. I'm blessed to have a mother like her. My nana and nani, Cyrus and Mehroo Dadachanji, who gave me shelter in their house, after I left my own house due to frustration during my tough days. They made me believe in love again, and thus, this novel is in your hands today. My late dada and dadi, Dinyar and Freni Tadiwala. Yes, they are smiling from heaven today, because I've made them proud.

Finally, thanks to the NOTION PRESS team, for maintaining their patience and showing their faith in me.

Prologue

Tera haath sey haath chhodna!
Tera sayo ka rukh modna!
Tera palatke phir na dekha!
Nahi maaf karunga mei,
Jab tak hai jaan,
Jab tak hai jaan!

Location:- Kamatibaug, Vadodara
Date:- 13th April 2015
Time:- 3:00 pm

Why am I here? The sun is burning over my head, yet I am sitting alone on this bench. Yes! Perhaps this is my destiny now, or perhaps not!

'JEE 2010', also known as 'Joint Entrance Exam', has taken my remaining self confidence away from me.

Is it necessary that a brilliant student should always remain brilliant?

Though four years ago, my story was completely different. Those days I was well known as 'The Bhavam' and now, people only know me as 'the ex-bf of Preksha'! Just give me a break! This thing is annoying! Why do these people address me by her name? She cheated me, she ruined me, and that's why, like a fool, I am sitting here in the garden, wondering why she left me.

"I shouldn't have loved a girl who just used me for nothing. But why do I still have mixed feeling for her? When I think of her at any instance, she comes before my eyes. Why so? Do I still want her? If yes, why?" I asked my invisible friend, looking up at the skies.

As always he listened to me, but didn't reply.

"Yes, you won't say anything, I know. But now I feel that whatever she did was correct. Why should she love me anymore? Maybe I am not as cute as her current bff. I am definitely neither hot nor sexy, but, yes, she is gorgeous. Therefore, she deserves the best," I intoned, looking up towards the skies.

People who were passing by looked at me, thinking that I had surely gone insane.

"Look, people might think that I am a fool. But no girl can love me. Then how could she love me? Indeed, love is such a strong word to be used for a person like her," I said, again looking up at the skies.

No reply!

I stood up and started taking heavy steps towards the forest part of the garden, which hardly anyone visited. Why was I going there? The reason was simple; I wanted to explode. I rushed towards the grassy meadow and fell on its lap, crying madly, due to my heartbroken memories of Preksha.

"Why me?" I asked.

No reply.

Tears were still falling from my eyes on the green grass of the forest garden. In no time, I heard someone's footsteps behind me. Initially, I ignored it, assuming it was a dog. The noise stopped for a moment, and then again, it resumed. When I shifted my attention, I saw a beautiful middle aged woman, with a gentle melancholy over her face.

"Boy," she said.

I wiped my tears and stood up in front of her.

"Yes, lady," I replied.

"Are you okay, son?" she asked.

I smiled and said, "Thank you, mam; it feels good when someone asks me that."

She also smiled in return, but said nothing.

"Sorry, but I don't know you!" I exclaimed.

"I don't know you either, but I can surely say that you were crying here because of a girl," she said.

"They only give tears, even if you make them smile thousands of time," I replied.

"That's not the case always. If you give love, in return you only get love," she explained.

"Sorry, lady, such universal sentences are not apt for the universe in which we survive," I said.

"Then where are they applicable?" she asked.

"I don't know. Maybe at some place where the love is true," I said.

"How can indubitable love transpire when true men don't exist?" she argued.

"No! All men aren't like that!" I exclaimed.

"Exactly! You have answered your own argument," she said, and smiled.

I smiled as well, after hearing her convincing response to my one sided argument.

"I am not smart like you, sorry," I said.

"I will tell you one thing," she suggested.

"What?" I asked.

"Forget her and move on!" she replied.

I started laughing madly when I heard her practical solution in the impractical world.

"Why are you telling me these universal facts, which are not applicable in real life?" I asked.

"I am not telling you; I am just stating the truth. Have you ever tried to move on?" she asked.

"No introductions, and I am discussing my personal hell with you," I said.

She laughed, and said, "My name is Tanishq."

"I guess that is the name of the jewellery shop, isn't it?" I asked.

"Boy, you are funny! I feel sorry for your ex," she said.

"It's not her fault. I realize now that I wasn't made for her," I said in a low tone.

The lady impinged and asked, "What was her name?"

I felt strange now. Before today, I had never seen that lady. Who was she? I got my senses back and realized that I was just blabbering to a totally unknown lady.

I decided to end the talk, and so I said, "Lady, I need to go now."

"You can call me Heenal; that's my real name," she replied.

"Bhavam," I said, and signed off.

"Damn it! Who was she?" I asked myself as I was leaving the garden.

But then I convinced my mind not to concentrate on that short incident because it was not as important as the passing semesters.

I was a student of KSU, fourth year, Textile Engineering. I had to pass my coming examinations in order to sustain myself because I had already performed badly in previous semesters.

The reason was simple; I was trying to move on.

Sometimes I think, *break-up is a process.*

For soft hearted guys like me, it generally takes six months to realize that we are single now. It takes six months more to come out of that feeling, and in this way, one whole year gets wasted.

The same thing happened to me. My first year was a waste due to such a process. The fourth year was now on the verge of ending, and this time I was determined to score well, excluding all the distractions from Preksha, as, indeed, her memories!

To go forward, I had to erase her memories.

I again looked up and asked my invisible friend, "At least tell me how to erase her from my mind, because she isn't going from my heart and soul."

No reply again.

"You play very well with me," I said, looking up.

I went outside Kamatibaug and started searching for my vehicle.

"Look at my mental situation. Once upon a time, I was a scholar who remembered everything, but now I have even lost my presence of mind," I said to myself.

I had forgotten where the hell I had parked my vehicle, because Kamatibaug was such an enormous place, and there were always issues related to parking.

"What shall I do now?" I asked myself.

My mind instructed me to walk to my hostel. KSU hostel was not too far from Kamatibaugh, just a brief 10–15 minute walk.

I again looked up at the skies and said, "I am happy because, when I ask my mind, it replies to me sometimes. But you never reply to me. Do you even exist?"

I knew there was no reply coming, so I plugged in my headphones and started walking with a song to support my heart which was still broken, due to the break-up with my girlfriend, Preksha. Of course, now she was my ex-girlfriend.

I reached the college gate but it was closed. Why was it closed so early? I looked at my watch, but the time was just 6:00 pm. I wished I had a room partner, but my parents had never supported that. At such times, room partners help you, but I had no one because my father was a renowned personality, and he could arrange a private room for me in the hostel where I had to stay alone, isolated from all the other students.

Once I asked Dad why he was doing this, and he just said, "Live up to your standards. You don't deserve to share and stay with these hopeless and aimless guys."

Was he worried about my studies? Never! He was just worried thinking that I would get spoiled if I was in close contact with other students. How could I change his ideology? I wish I could tell him that if I could still stay loyal to my ex-gf, how could I spoil his name by doing wrong deeds? As always, I made up my mind and accepted the situation.

Now there was an issue as to how to get in. I went to the guard who was standing there and asked, "What is the problem? Why are the gates closed?"

"There is a new rule now, don't you know it, boy?" asked the guard.

"Which rule?" I asked.

"Instead of bunking, do visit the collage someday. There is a rule now for the science faculty students, that no one will be allowed to enter or exit the hostel gate after 6:00 pm," he said.

Just opposite our science faculty hostel, there was a hostel of the commerce faculty and next to us, there was a hostel of the arts faculty. I looked at them and found that the gates of those two hostels were open.

I pointed in that direction and said to the guard, "Then why are they open?"

He said, "This is only for the science faculty, not for commerce and arts."

I shook my head in disbelief and requested him, "See, Vrajen Kaka. I didn't know about the new rules. I request you to open the gates for me."

He looked at me with a deep emotion and took out the keys from his pocket and opened the door. As soon as he did that, I came inside.

"But this is the first and last time I am doing this, mind it! " he said.

"Thank you so much. You are very kind." I said with a blink of buttery emotion.

"I did it just for you. Do you know why? Because you are the only exceptional kid in this college who has never fought with or abused me, like the other creeps," he said.

That brought a smile on my face and I looked up at the skies and said, "See, someone still respects me."

"Wait a minute, son, I need to ask you something. Four years have passed since you have been here. I don't see you hanging out with other guys, no girl friends either. Forget about girl friends; I don't think that you even possess a single friend who can help you," he said.

"I have a friend, but don't know why he never speaks," I said.

"Then solve the issue, and he will talk," replied Kaka.

"He is busy solving the issues of the rich and the scholars. He has no time for simple people like me, even though he is my friend," I added.

"Seems to be a unique friend! How far away from you does he stay?" Kaka asked.

"I don't know his address," I replied.

"Then you are a bad friend; you should stay in touch with him," said Kaka.

"But Kaka, I have searched for him everywhere, but I couldn't find him," I said.

Vrajen Kaka took out his HTC desire 820 G and said, "You tell me his name, and we will find him here via Facebook."

I started laughing.

"Why are you laughing, pig?" he asked.

"My friend doesn't use Facebook, although he knows the correct password of everyone," I said.

"Is your friend a kind of a hacker or so?" Kaka asked.

"Yes, a big hacker of problems, but no solutions," I said.

"What is his name?" Kaka asked with a doubt on his face.

I smiled and said, "You know him, but you aren't his friend. You just follow him, that's it. I don't follow him, but I am his friend."

"Boy, now you are making puzzles for me. Get to the point," Kaka said.

"Don't pay any heed to my blabbering, Kaka. Let me go inside now," I said.

"You are impossible, but tell me your name?" Kaka asked.

Wow! Today, everyone seemed interested in knowing my name, earlier that lady, and now Vrajen Kaka.

I replied, "One day when I do something cool, my name will be respected, and so you will automatically come to know it."

Wish Vrajen Kaka could understand that the friend about whom I was taking was none other than GOD.

Woh khuda bhi kesa hai?
Mei roj usse fariyad karta hu,
Aur woh roj muje ansuna karta hai...

Chapter 1

Location:- My hostel room

Time:- 7:30 pm

My private room was at an isolated place which only Vrajen Kaka knew. So I had no disturbance from seniors, as well as juniors.

As always I went to the room and avoided putting the lights on.

Since years now, I had started liking darkness. I washed my face, opened the window and started enjoying the touch of the cold dark winds.

My situation was getting worse instead of improving. Even while feeling these winds, I was able to sense the presence of Preksha's grip. Why so? I wanted to control my tears, but again I just cried loudly.

I was alone. No one to hear!

"It's okay if I cry, but there shouldn't be a single drop of a tear in her abysmal eyes," I said, looking at the twinkling stars.

They were twinkling, indicating to me that they had accepted my wish. I closed the window because I was almost out of my mind.

For the last four years, I had developed a habit to write in my diary on a daily basis. I wrote about the events which occurred throughout the day and kept a note of it. My diary included each and every event of my life, starting from the beautiful 'relationship day' to the worst 'break-up day'.

31st was the only date in the month which made me happy, because that was the day Preksha had accepted me. The 24th of every month used to make me upset because that was the day Preksha left me after our break-up. All such salt and pepper talks were comprehended in my diary. I didn't have much communication with anyone, so there was no issue that someone would read my personal diary.

The clock showed 8:00 pm, which symbolized that it was time for dinner. I was always excited about dinner because that was the time I could see my college mates. Some of them were good friends of mine.

There was a routine menu as always, including rice, dal and one vegetable with alternate rotations on either of the days.

The cool studs of the college used to fight daily with the canteen cooks over the awful food, but again we had no option but to sit and eat. So as I took my food, and sat at my table, my good friend, Dhruvesh, approached me saying,

"BC, today also the same stuff."

"This is what written for us, mate," I replied.

"But it's horrible, dude! I can't eat dal and rice every day," he replied.

"They say that they change the menu on a daily basis," I said.

"They are the biggest assholes in this college. There are seven days in a week; on the first day, they serve us steamed rice, and on day two, they provide jeera rice; on the third day you can find some sprinkled onion on that jeera rice and they say it's called onion-pulao, while on the fourth day, they add turmeric power to that pulao and serve us calling it yellow-rice. Then on the fifth day, the yellow-rice gets converted to khichdi and on the sixth day, they add some vegetables in that khichdi and tell us that they have prepared masala-rice. On day seven, they add all the remaining vegetables in that masala-rice, fry it in the oil and say that it's Chinese rice. We aren't too foolish to understand such a gamble going around in the canteen," said Dhruvesh angrily.

"Now we can't even go out to eat because of the new rules," said Vrund, Dhruvesh's friend!

"Dal is also not tasty," I muttered.

"Tasty? I call it horrible, and I wish I could pour it on the head of that nasty cook," said Dhruvesh.

"Try the vegetable," said Vrund.

We all looked at the vegetable and were confused, wondering what the hell it was!

"I have never seen such a vegetable ever in my life!" averred Dhruvesh.

"What's it?" asked Vrund.

I tasted it and said, "It's spinach."

"Spinach? But that is green in colour and this looks as black as coal," argued Dhruvesh.

"We again have no option but to eat roti because that will be the only thing prepared without an error," said Vrund.

Dhruvesh took the roti and said, "Roti? Really? Really? I think it is a biscuit."

As always, the roti was also too hard to eat. I had no complaints, but my friends had.

"I am just fucked off with these daily meals; let's complain to the dean about this matter. How long can we bear it?" suggested Dhruvesh.

"But what does the dean have to do with the food of the hostel?" I asked.

Without knowing anything, Vrund interrupted, "Yes, we will go. Bhavam, you can accompany us."

"I will just accompany you guys, but say nothing, because I am alright with the food," I replied.

"Really?" asked Dhruvesh.

"Eat what you get. People struggle even for such meals," I said and left.

"Whatever! I am gonna put this matter in front of the dean tomorrow. Those who want to support can join me, and the rest can shut their mouth and eat the lateral shit provided," said Dhruvesh, taunting me.

After that bold statement by Dhruvesh, they all left for their respective rooms. I knew that, the next day, Dhruvesh would rake up the useless issue in the college.

Our batch was not interested in studies at all, but we had unity in whatever we did, so regardless of anything, Dhruvesh was going to get much support from the whole Science faculty. After all, the students were really fed up of the food provided.

We had to be regular in college, of course, in terms of attendance. Once the attendance was taken, those who wished to study were allowed to stay in class, while the rest bunked college.

The prime locations for bunking in our city of Vadodara were Kamatibaug (which I generally preferred to share my sadness with nature) followed by Seven Seas, Sindh-road, Rasalpur, CCD and many more.

Next day…

"Now I am going to the dean; is anyone coming?" Dhruvesh asked in a loud tone so that each and every student of the class could hear him.

Immediately, 15 students got ready, and later on, the girls had the same issue. So I had no option left in front of me other than joining the group, because I knew that if I remained isolated, I would be tortured by my own mates. To be honest, torturing was not bearable for me. After the attendance, all the students suddenly stood up.

"What happened?" asked Dr Umar, our Physics Professor, with surprise and a tinge of fear.

"Sir, we are going to solve an issue related to the daily torture which we are facing in the hostel," said Dhruvesh.

"What kind of torture?" asked Dr Umar.

"Sir, you don't stay at collage; so it is better you stay out of this and allow us to do what we want," said Vrund.

"I won't allow you to go unless you tell me what the issue is!" protested Dr Umar.

"It's a personal issue," said Aastha from the group.

"Yes, if it's a personal issue, you can solve it after this lecture. I won't allow you all to go anywhere," said Dr Umar in a loud tone.

Dr Umar was a smart but very cunning personality. All the students disliked him and barely respected him. The reason was simple! Firstly, he failed most of the students, and secondly, he always set the toughest Physics papers. All the other professors in our faculty were lenient, barring Dr Umar, but the students were also not any less. Dhruvesh and group decided to play a short prank on him.

"Sir, we have a doubt, said Dhruvesh.

"I will answer only if it is related to Physics," replied Dr Umar.

"Well sir, did you go through a love marriage or an arranged marriage?"

"That's none of your business," responded Dr Umar.

"Okay, Aastha also wanted to ask you something," said Dhruvesh.

"Sir, all the girls want to know if you fought with your wife today!" remarked Aastha.

As soon as she asked this, the whole class started laughing and clapping. Even a sad soul like me giggled.

"What the hell! What do you mean by that?" asked Dr Umar.

"Sir, a married man is usually angry only because of his wife," said someone from the class, maybe from the back benches.

"Who was that?" asked Dr Umar desperately.

"Mrs Lajvanti," said someone from the back.

"What? How do you know my wife's name?" asked Dr Umar in surprise.

"Excuse me, sir; they are quite angry with the current issues in the college. So if you don't allow us to go, they will continue commenting on your personal life," said Dhruvesh.

"Shut up! I know how to handle you all. Remember I have 70% of your marks in my hand," warned Dr Umar.

Dhruvesh stood up from his place in anger, threw his bag down, lifted his collar up and went near Dr Umar, responding in a polite manner, "We respect those who respect us, sir. And please don't bring our marks into this discussion, sir."

"Of course I will," he said. "That is the only thing which will bring your attitude back on the floor. These numbers are interrelated with your attitude, child," he added.

"Number one, I am not a child. Number two, our marks won't represent our attitude. Your thinking is not proper, sir," replied Dhruvesh.

"I don't need to explain that to you. You had better know the consequences, if it happens," threatened Dr Umar.

"But I can explain to you that our attitude doesn't determine our marks," said Dhruvesh.

"I give you only two minutes," said Dr Umar, glancing at his wrist watch.

"Suppose anyone says that you don't teach proper physics, and that is because of your triple XL size, would that make any logic, sir? Secondly, you are renowned for failing us, so will it be proper to assume that you get rid of your personal frustration on our answer sheets because of disputes with your wife?" replied Dhruvesh.

As soon as he completed his speech, the whole class blew whistles and started clapping. My God! For a moment, Dr Umar was stunned by the witty explanation. He was holding the duster in his hand, and he threw that at Dhruvesh in such a way that it fell in front of his legs.

"Oh! That was like real projectile motion," commented Dhruvesh.

"Stupid!" abused Dr Umar. "Don't you have any respect for your professors? You don't fear for your marks; wait, I have one more punishment waiting for you. I will suspend you, forever. And once you are suspended by KSU, no other college will give you admission!" replied Dr Umar sternly.

After saying so, he immediately left the class, and we didn't know where he was going.

"He looks hyper. I hope he wasn't serious about suspension," said Vrund, looking at me.

Aastha approached Dhruvesh and said, "Go quickly, idiot, or he will really suspend you."

"He cannot suspend me like that." replied Dhruvesh.

I went near him and said, "You don't know him. A few years back, he suspended one student."

"On what basis?" asked Aastha.

"I don't know, but Kaka once told me that Dr Umar placed an ultimatum in front of the dean, giving him two options. Either the student's suspension or his own resignation. Since the college needs him, the dean could not afford to lose a brilliant physics professor like him; so without any option, the dean had to suspend that student," I said.

When I had completed my say, Dr Umar vigorously entered the class in anger alongside the dean of our science faculty. We stood up and said a formal good morning to the dean.

"You all are experts in changing your behavior just like camouflage," muttered Dr Umar.

"Who is Dhruvesh Patel?" asked the dean.

Dhruvesh rose, with his head up, making eye contact with Dr Umar.

"I will be talking to you, so you can look at me," said the dean.

Dhruvesh shifted his attention and looked at the dean, but said nothing.

"As you can see guys, Dr Umar is quite frustrated with this class, and especially you, Dhruvesh," said the dean in a soft voice.

Wow! For the first time we realized what respect meant. We had never seen the dean before, but he was talking in such a polite and kind manner, which fascinated me.

"I apologize to you, sir, for the inconvenience." replied Dhruvesh politely.

"Don't go by his words, sir; he has two faces. He was talking trash with me a few minutes back," said Dr Umar.

"Umm…will you excuse us, Dr Umar? My mom has taught me not to interrupt when two people are talking," said Dhruvesh, which lifted everyone's eyebrows because it was a direct insult to Dr Umar, and quite frankly, the worst one!

"Wish you had learnt some discipline from your father, but no, he must be just like you, totally characterless!" replied Dr Umar which annoyed each and every student.

Now this was really getting very personal.

Dhruvesh bent down and grabbed the duster in his hand, and was about to throw it in anger at Dr Umar, but the dean came in between and separated both of them, saying, "Please, this is a college, not your personal property. Behave yourselves."

"Sir, please stay out of this. I can't spare a person who calls my father characterless," said Dhruvesh in a loud tone.

Vrund and all immediately approached him to console him, trying their best to make him calm, while, on the other hand, the girls went near the dean and explained what exactly had happened.

As always, I was away from all these. I was sitting on the last bench and writing in my diary. I was a neutral person in this matter because what Dhruvesh initially said to Dr Umar was wrong. However, what Dr Umar later on commented about Dhruvesh's dad was very immature!

"You saw that, sir?" said Dr Umar, pointing at Dhruvesh.

"Suspend him and end the matter!" he added.

As soon as he said that, all students were shocked and protested loudly, "Ayyeeeeeeee..."

The dean interfered and said in quite a harsh tone this time, "Shut up!" and all were quiet.

"I can't suspend anyone like that, Umar sir," said the dean and we were relieved.

"Okay, it's fine! Then I think that this college needs a new physics professor," proclaimed Dr Umar.

"Sir, I request you on a personal note not to end the future of any child like that," said the dean in a mild but clear voice.

"He has already ended his career, sir. Ask him any one simple question from this book, and he won't be able to answer it," responded Dr Umar.

We all stared at Dhruvesh but now he was looking down.

"Enough is enough! This child has crossed his limits; eventually all of them misbehaved with me, but what was done by this guy was horrible," said Dr Umar.

"Dhruvesh, go and apologize to him with full respect; otherwise I will be forced to obey his orders," said the dean.

"Yes, first apologize, and then I will see whether to forgive you or not," said Dr Umar arrogantly.

Dhruvesh lifted his eyes again and said to the dean, "Umar sir doesn't deserve my apology, but I apologize to you for wasting your precious time."

What was Dhruvesh doing? If he didn't apologize, he would be thrown out, and then no other college would accept him.

"All right, now get something straight! Suspend him or I am giving in my resignation," insisted Dr Umar.

It was a horrible situation. Why was Dhruvesh showing so much of attitude? If he had apologized, the matter would have ended there, but no! He had to impress the girls and he thought that he would become a hero by arguing and staying stubborn.

Yes, maybe Preksha used to like guys having an attitude like Dhruvesh, and I was too calm and simple. I still don't have my personal vehicle and these guys have expensive bikes. If I wanted, I too could demand my personal vehicle, but now for whom? I didn't have a girlfriend and I also didn't wish to make one, because it only brought pain.

"He will be thrown out; let's do something," said Vrund.

"Go on, say something in his favor and your internal marks will be deduced," I replied.

"But he is our friend; we can't stay quiet," said Vrund.

"I told you guys last night, eat whatever is served. If you had kept your mouths shut, this would not have happened," I said.

"Yes, but now what?" asked Vrund desperately.

"I don't know, ask these girls. Maybe you will be able to find someone to at least talk with you," I said, and again began to write in my diary.

"What the fuck are you writing continuously in this diary?" he asked.

"I am not writing a fuck, so don't worry," I said.

"Then what? Because I know you aren't a scholar, and so you are definitely not writing formulas or boiler's equations," he said.

When he used word 'scholar', it brought an electric shock in my heart because once upon a time, even I was a scholar. Girls used to like me because of my intellect and smartness in studies, but now everything was over, since Preksha had left me. After my break up, I hardly concentrated on my studies because that never worked for me again. So I used to visit Kamatibaug and find some peace for myself, writing in my diary and talking with my only good friend, God.

I looked up at the skies and said in my memory, "I told you, only scholars and rankers survive and get respect, but you always encouraged me to do something unique, but now I am an average student."

As always he never replied to me.

Though I was lost in my recapturing, I still heard a loud voice saying, "You are suspended, Dhruvesh."

He had tears in his eyes, and so did all the students too. At last he was loved by all. It was a bit expected too. All the students were now in deep silence. For the first time ever, we saw tears in his eyes, which was a rare sight.

Dhruvesh lifted his bag and went near the dean, and said, "This is the price which I am paying for raising my voice. It's fine. I am out of here, but before going, I need to tell you something. We are daily tortured here in terms of food; just look once at the quality of the food being served. I am sure you will dislike it."

"Nothing is bad in the food; everything is wrong with your tastes," said the dean.

"If your lovable daughter had been studying here, she would also have told you the same. Would you reply her in the same manner then, sir?" asked Dhruvesh.

"Enough is enough now," interrupted Dr Umar. "You had better get lost now," he added.

"Yes, I am going. I don't want to study in a college where a professor is more powerful than the dean," said Dhruvesh, while leaving the classroom.

All were stunned. Yes, Dhruvesh was suspended and this was an evolution. Evolution of silence, I guess! I was sure about one fact. From now on, no student would dare to do anything against the norm.

Chapter 2

As soon as Dr Umar completed his lecture, all students escaped from the class through the window at the back, again following the *bunking system*.

I carried my bag, which had a few Physics notes and my diary, and decided to go to the place where I always felt at peace; Kamatibaug.

On the roadside I saw two couples enjoying 'panipuri'.

I glanced up at the heavens and said, "She too loved panipuri and I could never give her a treat. Maybe that's why she left me. But I wanted to give her innumerable treats in future, but she couldn't ever understand my feelings."

A small beggar, hardly five years old, was wandering outside the street of the garden. Maybe he was hungry, so he went near the couple, who were eating panipuri and demanded food. The boy insulted that poor beggar pathetically, while his girlfriend enjoyed the fun.

I was stunned to see that scene and again looked up at the skies saying, "Fuck your creation! The guy who can never respect the feelings of that small kid can never love and respect his girlfriend, whom he calls 'baby'. That girl is also blind enough not to see the truth. And yes, that's your justice too. You sustain the fake love of those people who don't respect their inferiors."

"It's like that only," said a feminine voice from behind.

When I turned around, I found the same lady who had met me yesterday in the garden.

"But why?" I asked.

"You look at him first; tell me how he looks!" she remarked.

"I think he is all right," I replied.

"Well! Now look at the girl, and tell me how she looks," she again said.

"Pretty!" I exclaimed.

"So here you can see, the guy is handsome and the girl is pretty. So they are one, on the basis of external attraction. So they can never understand the heart of that small child," she replied.

"It's the reality. If you are the best, you get the best; otherwise you will be compared with the rest," I said.

"Yes, you are right, but we do have an option to make the REST the BEST," she said, smiling.

I smiled too and said, "You are full of positive energy, I guess!"

She laughed and replied, "I am full of energy."

"So tell me something about yourself. You met me yesterday, but I was in a hurry," I said.

"Hurry to get to your girlfriend?" she asked.

"Never. I am single," I replied.

"Don't joke," she said.

"Joke? I am telling the truth," I said.

"Singles don't come to the garden alone with the memories of their ex-gf," she said softly.

"How do you know that?" I asked in surprise.

"I have passed your age. So I know everything," she smiled.

"Then why are you here?" I asked.

"My love promised me he would come here, but he hasn't arrived yet," she said.

"So how long have you been waiting for him?" I asked.

"Five years," she replied and I was shocked.

"Five years?" I asked in surprise.

"Yes, he asked me to come here and said to wait," she answered.

"But five years?" I again asked.

"Yes!" she replied.

"You mean that you have been coming here daily for the last five years?" I again asked.

"Yes, I am waiting for him and I am sure, he will come one day. After all, he promised me that," she said.

"Do you have any idea that you are being cheated?" I asked.

"Don't you say that, boy! I have trust in him and he will surely come," she said.

"One who hasn't shown his face for the last five years, and then suddenly comes in your life, symbolizes that he only needs you for his satisfaction," I said.

"He can never use me," she replied.

"Which century are we living in?" I asked.

"21st century!" she replied.

"Oh God! I mean to say you can't trust anyone like that in the 21st century," I said.

"That is applicable to you, college kid. Not for a mature person like me," she said.

"Okay, tell me, are you in a relationship with that guy for whom you are waiting?" I asked.

"Eww! Relationship is such a weird word, dear," she said.

"In the 21st century, the union of two bodies is called RELATIONSHIP, while the union of two souls is called BONDAGE. So I am not in a relationship with him; I am just bound to him," she replied and I was speechless.

After a few minutes, I broke the silence, saying, "What's his name?"

"What's her name?" she asked, smiling.

(*That's how girls turn tables.)

"Preksha!" I replied in a soft tone as her name was enough to make me weak.

She placed her soft hands on my palm and said, "You still love her. But you should accept that some things are just not made for us."

"I know she will never come back to me, but my heart will take a long time to accept that fact," I replied.

"Maybe God has created someone better for you than her," she said.

I smiled and said, "Maybe God has created someone better for her than me. I take it that way."

"You should love her enough to let her go," she said.

"I loved her and that's why I respected her decision to let her go away from me," I said.

"What actually forced her to go away from you?" she asked.

"I have no answer to that question," I said reluctantly.

"That means you don't know why she left you?" she asked.

"No, I don't. So I assume random reasons for her having left me alone," I said.

"That's so childish. But I can tell you the real reason why she left you? But you have to keep your heart strong enough to listen to that," she said.

"I hope it's convincing," I said.

"I will tell you the truth and *the truth is always convincing, though hard to believe*," she said.

"Okay, tell me the reason. Why did she leave me?" I asked. "I am still in search of that answer," I added.

"First of all, you answer my questions without questioning me, will you?" she asked.

"Okay!" I said.

"Look up, can you see that butterfly?" she asked.

I looked up and replied, "Yes."

"Cool! What is the work of a butterfly?" she asked.

"To fly freely and to go from one flower to another flower," I replied.

"Why does it not stay at one flower for a long time?" she asked.

"Because once it takes the fragrance, its work is over, and so it goes to the next flower for again taking the fragrance," I replied.

"So do you think that no other butterfly will come to the same flower used by the previous butterfly for taking fragrance?" she asked.

"No! It is not possible. Other butterflies will surely at least sit on the flower," I replied.

"Wow! You got such a good sense of humor. Then why are you not able to understand the reason for your break up?" she asked.

"But wait, that isn't my answer," I said.

"I will explain. Here assume you are the flower and your ex-girlfriend is the first butterfly. At first she takes the fragrance of love from you, but later on, she is not comfortable, and so she leaves you and goes to the next flower. Now at present, you assume that you are useless, but indeed you are not! You are a flower, so the next butterfly will come and again take the fragrance of love from you. It's your duty, boy, to make your fragrance of love so powerful that your butterfly doesn't leave you," she replied.

I was lost in her excellent reply. I always blamed myself for not being perfect but now, I realized that Preksha wasn't the perfect butterfly either.

I looked at the lady and said politely, "Thank you, lady, for making me realize the fact."

"No need to thank me, and stop calling me lady. I am just a few years older than you. So you can call me by my name," she replied.

"I forgot your name," I said.

"You are such a dumbo!" she exclaimed. "My name is Heenal," she added.

"Nice name!" I said and she smiled.

"Bhavam, you are such a nice person. You can keep any girl happy," she said.

"But who will that girl be?" I asked.

"For that you have to wait, because you only said that the best thing goes to the best, but correct things come to the correct person at the correct time," she replied.

She was motivating me. For the first time after my break up, I was sensing some positive energy around me.

"Before my break-up, I was a scholar. Then I lost my dignity. How do I get it back?" I asked her.

"Oh! I was never a scholar, so I can't say anything about that. But as you say that you were a scholar, it's better you ask your conscience that, and you will surely get your answer," she said.

Her counterclaims were so beautiful and logical that they were making me more inspired.

"You have given me a reason to live again," I said, thanking her.

I took out the packet of cigarettes from my pocket and placed it in her soft hands saying, "I daily smoke after my break-up, and you know the foolish reason why I was taking it? Because after my break up I never had the guts to end my life. So I thought that by consuming cigarettes, my life will come to an end, which never happened, because I am still alive," I said.

She took those cigarettes and threw them in the dustbin, saying, "Promise me that you won't ever smoke."

It brought tears in my eyes as I nodded.

"Listen, I don't have any sister. So can I be your brother? I promise I don't have any wrong intentions," I said.

She looked at me with pitiful eyes, suggesting something, and said, "Sure, you can be my little brother. But promise me that you won't forget me."

"I never promise more than I deliver, but I always deliver more than I can promise," I said.

We both smiled and then she said, "Everyone can make mistakes. Yes, even I made mistakes. Life didn't come with instructions."

"Although I don't use technology, my friends do, and I can assure you that you have spoken the above lines from some Instagram post," I said, and she began laughing.

"I am caught!" she said naughtily, and smiled.

"Well, I need to go now, otherwise the college gate will be closed and I will have to stay on the streets tonight," I said.

"By the way, in which college do you study?" she asked.

"KSU!" I replied.

"It's the best college in the city," she said.

"I know, and very strict too," I said.

"I have studied arts in the same college; so don't worry! I will tell you the secret road which joins the arts faculty with the science faculty," she replied, blinking her eyes.

"Woah! Please tell me," I said hesitantly.

"Enter the arts college gate and reach the auditorium hall. It's common among all three faculties. After reaching the auditorium, go to the back of the theater and turn left, and that will take you to the science faculty, while turning right will take you to the commerce faculty," she said.

"Are you serious?" I asked incredulously.

"If you don't believe me, try it today," she said.

"Yes, I will try. I still have some time left and if it doesn't work, Vrajen Kaka will surely spare me again," I said.

I went my way now and Heenal was still sitting, waiting for her love to come and meet her.

"Thank you for making me realize that I wasn't worthy of Preksha, and neither was she worthy of me. So it's better we got separated. Keep her happy and now I will determine to keep myself happy," I said, looking up at the shallow yellowish afternoon sky.

I decided to make my sad life a bit adventurous, and therefore, I diverted my steps towards the arts faculty. In terms of construction, the arts faculty looked more ordinary than ours, but the main thing which it inculcated was freedom to students!

I entered the arts faculty and there was a guard at the gateway, but he didn't stop me. The whole campus was surrounded by a number of students which mainly included girls. I was not able to see very many boys, because they didn't normally want to take arts. None of them paid attention to my entry, and that was what I wanted.

Firstly, I wanted to enjoy that sight, because I had never seen students in my faculty, talking and enjoying themselves. So I stood at one of the corners and watched the whole scene.

All sorts of weird abuses, and non vegetarian jokes were clearly falling in my ears, from the nearby boys' group. I had to find the auditorium, so I went near the guard and asked him, "Excuse me, can you tell me where the auditorium is?"

I was so nervous that, for a moment, I thought that he would catch me but instead, without asking any further questions, he showed me the way and I got directed towards it.

Wow! So lucky were the arts students! There was no one to question them on where they went and whom they met.

For instance, if they looked at our faces, they would surely have said that the science faculty was a *faculty of depression*.

I went towards the auditorium. As I was proceeding further, the number of people were becoming less. Suddenly the weather changed, as the dark evening became darker. The black clouds surrounded the yellowish sky and the strong winds took guard. In no time, the weather had completely changed. Suddenly the rain began to fall heavily and all the students rushed inside their hostels. I was on my way and had no option except to continue.

The rain had increased its speed. I was able to see nothing in front of me, although I kept walking because I had to reach my hostel in a few minutes.

All of a sudden, I dashed against a heavy object. I screamed and fell on my knees. When I looked up, my eyes got stuck to the vehicle with the number plate - **4651**. I had indeed dashed into one of the vehicles.

The person who was driving the vehicle immediately came and asked me if I was well.

"Are you okay?" said a beautiful voice, as someone placed a palm on my shoulder.

When I lifted my head, my eyes got a glimpse of a cute and pretty face. I got up immediately and said, "Yes, I am alright."

(*When you see a pretty face in front of you, all pains tend to go away!)

"Actually I need someone to help me. My vehicle is jammed in this mud puddle. Will you help me?" she asked humbly.

How could any guy reject a beautiful girl asking for help?

For a moment, I looked at her; she was fair as milk, her charming face was as cute as the full moon and in the rains, she looked even more beautiful. She was short but attractive.

I shook myself and brought my senses back, and said, "Don't worry; I will take your vehicle out of this puddle."

I looked up at the skies and said in my mind, "Don't create a scene in front of her; otherwise I won't talk to you."

"I applied my maximum energy, but it's not moving a bit, as it's totally jammed," she said.

"Don't worry; I will do it anyhow," I replied.

"So sweet of you!" she smiled.

I applied my maximum energy, though the tire didn't move at all.

"See, I told you," she said in a low tone.

"Oh! Why are you panicking? When I told you that I will do it, I will. Have some trust," I said.

"Woah! You are like a *Never Give Up* type of a guy, haan?" she asked.

Instead of replying her, I just preferred to smile.

I went aside and brought two flat stones. I placed one of the stones near the front part of the tire and other one behind the tire.

"Aah, sorry, I don't know your name, but please pull the vehicle from your side now and I will pull it from the back," I said in a shy tone.

"Yes, sure, and my name is Ashwini," she said.

She began to pull the vehicle from her side and I applied force from my side. My physics worked. The wheel came on that flat stone and I immediately applied more force and the vehicle was out of that puddle.

"Wow, you did it!" she exclaimed in delight.

"Yes," I said shyly.

"Just wow! But how?" she asked.

"Are you a science student?" I asked.

"No," she replied.

"Then you won't understand," I said smiling.

She laughed and said, "Thank you so much, but what are you doing here?"

"I want to go to the auditorium," I said.

"Okay, all right, thank you so much for the help," she said.

"My pleasure," I replied.

"I need to go now, as it's very late! Bye bye," she said and sat on her vehicle.

I just looked at her, because she was something different. Immediately she stopped and turned back.

"What happened? Is the tire in the puddle again?" I asked, smiling.

She laughed and said, "No, no. Actually I forgot to ask you your name."

"My name is Bhavam Sharma," I said.

"I am Ashwini Soni," she said.

"I know," I said.

"How do you know my name?" she asked.

"You only said, remember?" I replied.

"Acha? I don't remember. See you. Bye," she said and went away. I looked at her till those four digits of her vehicle disappeared. Yes, the rain had stopped. Was it a situation specially created for me? I didn't think much more about it, and without any delay, I entered the auditorium.

As Heenal had instructed, I went near the theater, and then directed myself backstage. Here I was able to see two doors, one on the left and the other on the right. I opened the left door and it had a very narrow passage. After walking for ten minutes, I was able see myself at the backside of some huge building; later on I realized that it was, indeed, my hostel only. I was very happy. I reached my room, and for the first time, turned on the lights and said to myself, "Thank you for this beautiful day."

That day I didn't have my dinner because happiness had taken its place. After my break-up, this was the happiest day for me. I sat and wrote the whole incident in my diary. From now on, I decided not to shed a tear remembering Preksha, because it only stopped my progress. I decided to remain happy, stay cheerful and once again try to become a scholar.

I prepared my rough time table for my studies and started my work-out to inspire myself to become the best.

Chapter 3

Location:- My hostel room
Time:- 2:22 am

I suddenly got up from my sleep as I was feeling very uncomfortable. Something was paining within my stomach, and the pain was slowly increasing.

"Now, there's some more excitement for you!" I looked up and groaned.

Last night I had not eaten my dinner, so maybe my digestive system was searching for food, and I assumed that that was the only reason for my pain. I felt like vomiting. I went and brought out everything, and after that I felt good.

But why did it happen? I had not eaten anything like junk food. I had thrown away my remaining cigarette packets, as I had promised Heenal not to smoke anymore. I realized that my body was addicted to cigarettes, and so when it didn't get its smoke, it resulted in this. I accused myself for having developed the hobby of smoking, as it had partially damaged my health. Thank God for Heenal, who had come at the right time and saved me.

From the medicine box, I took a pain killer which, at least, provided me a deep sleep. Guess what? When I opened my eyes, the clock read 9:12 am!

Yes, I was late, in fact, very late for college. I hurried and without having a bath, I literally ran for my classes because I knew that against my name, an 'absent' had already been marked. If my parents were told, it would create huge trouble for me.

(*God has given Engineers one specialty. Although they wake up just a few minutes prior to the lecture, they can still attend the lecture at the correct time.)

"May I come in, sir?" I said, knocking at the door of the dean.

He nodded and I went in. Wow! His office was not less than a five-star honeymoon suite.

(*I questioned myself. "Why the hell had the word 'honeymoon' come to my mind?"

My mind answered me. "I was still half asleep.")

"Actually sir, I have been marked absent today," I said.

"Yes, so why the hell are you here? Go… come tomorrow. Your parents will be told regarding your absence," he said.

"But, sir, I stay at the hostel and I was not well, I got up late because last night, I suffered from a severe stomach ache," I said.

"Are you giving this reason to a nursery principal?" he asked.

"No, sir, I am telling the truth," I said.

"Any proof?" he asked.

He wanted proof, and I was fully charged again. So I decided to pull his leg.

"Sir, one request," I said.

"What?" he questioned angrily.

"Empty your table fast," I said in a desperate tone.

"But why?" he asked enquiringly.

"I feel like vomiting again," I replied, even more desperately.

He took off his spectacles and said, "Boy, if you are acting, it will be really bad for you."

I was also fully charged, and so I placed one hand on my mouth, indicating that I was about to vomit. Seeing me do this, he stood up from his place and said hurriedly, "Hey, stop. Get out of here. I understand you are ill. I won't report this to your parents.

Now get out of here! Don't you dare dirty my precious cabin."

After he said so, I was relieved. However, I had to complete the rest of the drama, I placed both hands on my mouth, and again when he saw me doing that, he stood up on his chair, because he assumed that I would vomit. So without troubling him more, I went out of his cabin and pretended to vomit, so that he would feel that I was, indeed, a sufferer.

As soon as Dr Umar completed his lecture in our class, all the students escaped the class through those windows; again that same bunking process!

"Bhavam, where were you?" asked Vrund.

"Actually, I wasn't well, so didn't come," I said.

"Yes, what other reason will you have? You don't have a girlfriend; so naturally you won't drop a class for her," he said.

I ignored that and decided to leave. He stopped me and said, "You have a good reputation amongst the girls, dude. Can you help me?"

"Do I have a good reputation? Really? But I never communicate with them," I said in surprise.

"Then try to talk. They are all flirts, dude," he said.

"But I don't like those type of girls," I said.

"That's also correct. So which type of girls do you like?" he asked.

"Why should I tell you?" I said.

"That's also correct," he said.

"And come to the point. I don't like loose talk," I said firmly.

"Can you impress a girl for me?" he asked.

I laughed and said, "I can't impress a girl for myself; how can I impress her for you?"

"You know that girl really well," he said.

"Okay. Who's she?" I asked.

"Some say she's your ex; her name is Preksha," he said.

My gloomy face suddenly turned serious.

"Look, dude, don't get angry, but she's beautiful. Any guy can fall for her, and personally, you aren't fit for her. She deserves a cool and funky guy like me, not a sensible and sweet person like you," he said.

"How do you know her?" I asked with an edge to my voice.

"Social media, dude. She is famous on Instagram, where she has more than 5000 followers, and wow, each and every uploaded image of hers is sexy! I am in love with her beauty," he said.

"I am not in touch with her for the last four years," I said.

"Why not?" he asked.

"I don't use social media anymore," I replied.

"That's awful, mate. If you are doing all this, just because of her, then you are making a very big mistake," he said.

"What do you mean?" I asked.

"Look, she doesn't care what you do and think about her. She even doesn't pay a fuck to what people says. She lives off her friends, and do you know what they say about her?" he asked.

"No, I don't," I said.

"They say that Preksha is a girl who can sell her best friends too. This is what one of her close friends told me," he said.

Vrund was not lying. It could be true because if she could leave the person who loved her like anything, she could do anything.

"Yes, but I don't love her anymore, so do whatever you like! It's your life and it's her life too; so let her live," I said.

"Yes, but come back on social media, dude. It's very odd if you aren't connected socially with any person in the 21st century," he said.

Vrund was right. I had my Facebook account, but I deleted it after Preksha left me. I had not yet created an Instagram account.

"You are right. I will think about it," I said and left.

Preksha! Wow, now she was a famous personality. The whole college knew the fact that I was her ex-bf. It was such an annoying thing.

Again her name was pulling me down. I wanted to smoke but I realized that I had promised Heenal not to smoke anymore. I wanted to talk to her, so I went to Kamatibaug, because I knew that she would be there.

I reached the place where she sat daily, but I couldn't find her. I searched for her, and went near the grassland, but couldn't find her. Where was she? I thought that her boyfriend must have come and so she had left.

I was sad. I wanted her presence, because she was my only source of inspiration.

"Where are you, sister?" I asked, looking up at the skies.

No reply came.

"It's useless talking with you, God, but at least once give me a glimpse of her. I need to find out a solution for what is troubling me," I said.

Again there was no reply.

I sat on the same bench and put my head down, wondering where she was. In no time, I could feel a soft touch on my shoulder. It brought me energy. I knew it would be Heenal, and there she was, all in white. She was looking even more beautiful in white that day.

"Where were you?" I asked desperately.

"I cannot be there for you 24 × 7," she replied.

"At present you are my air, I want you everywhere," I said.

"Woah! Nice poetic lines, and very meaningful too," she said.

"I needed to ask you something!" I said.

"Carry on; I am your answering machine, little brother," she said.

"I told you about Preksha, but she isn't still out of my mind. I know she isn't my girlfriend anymore, but when I heard her name today, my heart started beating. Why is this so?" I asked.

She lifted one heavy stone from the ground and asked, "What if I hit you with this stone?"

"Are you mad? I will get injured," I said.

"What will happen if you are injured?" she asked.

"Nothing great, but I may be out of action for a few weeks," I replied.

She looked at me and said, "Perfect. The same thing goes for love, my little brother. When the stone of 'cheating' and 'break up' hits your relationship, you are injured mentally, and as you said, you are out of action for some time. But that doesn't mean that you won't recover.

The pain which you are going through when you hear about her is not because you still love her; it's because you are trying to move on," she added.

Wow! Another brilliant explanation had touched my heart.

"She seems to be my fear, I guess." I said.

"If she is your fear, than face it. That's the only way. Even to make a sword effective, we have to rub it with stones," she said.

"Heenal, how can I fully exclude her from my heart?" I asked.

"It's very difficult thing for you; so I won't tell you," she said.

"No. Please tell me," I said, urging her to tell me the way.

"But do you promise to accept it?" she asked.

I nodded.

"Forgive her," she said. "Forgive her for everything she did against you. Forgive her for every pain which she gave you. Once you forgive her, you will automatically forget her," she replied.

"She used me and you tell me to forgive her?" I asked.

"She didn't use you. Yesterday only I said that she wasn't comfortable with you, so she left you for good. So now it's your duty to show some maturity and forgive her. She will be equally happy to see you move on," said Heenal.

"It's very difficult, but how do I show her that I have forgiven her?" I asked.

"Very simple. You said that you aren't socially connected. So get connected and communicate with her. I am a girl, so I know what girls think," she said.

"What do they think?" I asked.

"I can't tell you everything. Just follow what I say! Take out your mobile," she instructed and I did so, and placed it in her hands.

"Why have you kept it in my palm? Have you gifted it to me?" she asked, smiling.

I shook my head and took the cell phone back in my hand and said, "Sometimes you girls are just impossible. I placed it in your palm because you asked for it."

"You are an idiot! I said it for you!" she exclaimed.

"Now will you tell me what to do?" I asked.

"Stop looking at me and create your Facebook account," she said.

I did so. I created my Facebook account. Woah! I was seeing the face of Facebook after my break-up. It felt really good from inside.

(*Facebook is the best face you can ever see after a break-up.)

"Now send the friend request to everyone in your college," she said.

"I know that," I replied in an arrogant manner.

"Girls also!" she said.

I smiled and, in return, she smiled back.

"Now create your Instagram account fast," she said.

"I will create that later on, not now," I said.

"But why later on?" she asked.

"Correct things at the correct time," I said blinking my eyes.

"And don't get stuck to it for a long time; it's injurious to health," she advised.

"I know that, thank you," I said.

"Okay, I need to go now; see you soon, little brother," she said in a

soft tone.

I was lost in my mobile, so didn't pay attention to what she said. After a moment when I looked up, she wasn't there. I knew she had left.

The first thing which I wanted to see was Preksha. When I typed the letter 'P' in the search toolbar, my heart again started to beat. But then as Heenal said, I had to face my fear. I allowed my heart to beat and when it was normal, I continued typing her name. We had many mutual friends, so searching for her was not a big issue. As soon as I completed writing the word 'Prek', the search dialog box dropped down her full profile. I fingered my thumb on 'Preksha Chahal' and I was able to see her.

Wow! I was seeing her after such a long time. I clicked on her profile picture, to see her properly. She looked more beautiful after she left me. She had completely changed. Now she smiled without showing her teeth, which she used to do earlier. Nevertheless, she had a pouty expression in all her photos, one which

I tried to mimic, because it gave her more than 750 likes on her profile picture.

Had she lost her smile or had she changed? I looked at her other photos, but in none of the pictures was she showing her teeth. Maybe she was a different girl now. From *'beautiful girl'* she had converted herself into *'sexy bitch'*. I never used such words for her, and she described herself as such in the comments.

Her current Facebook status was – "You want to be the priority, but you are not showing your importance."

When I scrolled my thumb down, I saw another interesting status which read – "This is me, a little high, a little low, a little pretty, a little bitch, a little mature, a little in love; yes it is me, made of many little things."

Yes, this status actually suited her; she was, indeed, made up of many little things. I had to ignore it, but I could not because everything was perfect in that status, except the word 'bitch'. Why was she addressing herself as a bitch?

I didn't like that, because she wasn't a bitch.

I know, she had used me but still my eyes were not able to read the word 'bitch' for her. But it made no difference to her because she was going to do what she wanted. Keeping my heart strong and brave enough, I sent her a friend request. Wondering if she would accept my request or not, because she had more than 1000 friends on Facebook!

It had turned cloudy. I realized that it would rain again. A drop of water felt on the screen of my mobile, and it reminded me of the incident which had taken place yesterday with that beautiful lady. I immediately wrote 'Ashwini Soni' on my search dialog box and the drop down list showed the result.

I carefully examined each and every girl and finally found the correct Ashwini Soni.

Wow! Her profile picture was beautiful. She didn't pout, but smiled naturally, which I loved. I just kept on scrolling her images, enjoying glimpses of her.

Her status was more enterprising.

It said – "Once I met an angel in heaven. She is called Ashwini on earth."

I laughed because she was assuming that she was an angel. However, she looked much prettier than that too!

When I ran my eyes down, I was still able to glance at the number plate – 4651. Why was she so special to me? Because she was the only lady, who communicated with me in a friendly manner after Preksha's departure from my life.

I took out my diary and again wrote everything. Every beautiful moment of my life was captured in it.

I was so engrossed in writing my dairy that I never sensed the importance of time. When I completed writing, I realized that it was now time to go. I again decided to go from the auditorium side. Yes, inside my heart, there was a wish to see her one more time.

"My eyes used to cry when I saw Preksha with other guys. Yes, maybe I am jealous because I never shared myself with any girl, not even in a selfie," I said looking up.

There was no reply.

"I know you will say, it's her life, but still it pains. I have made one decision finally today, and that is to forgive her!" I continued.

Still there was no reply.

"Regardless of your response, I am telling you, rather proclaiming to you, that I forgive Preksha for everything good or bad she did to me. I am here today, giving her forgiveness, by your means," I said, my eyes wet, but still there was no reply.

(*Moods quickly change when you divert your mind from your crush to your ex.)

I was on the way to the arts faculty and again, I looked up as still I had something to say, "I never did anything wrong to her. I stayed loyal to her, loved her, and took care of her. I never let her go away from my arms, never refused her demands, but still if I did anything wrong, I demand forgiveness. Forgive me, forgive her. Please!"

As soon as I said so, I fell on my knees and started crying. Yes, these were the final emotions which were raining out from my eyes. I knew that after today, I wasn't going to cry for her any day, regardless of anything!

I entered the arts faculty campus. As always, it was surrounded by a number of students. It made me feel good as I wiped off my tears and approached the auditorium. I looked left, I looked right, and everywhere, but couldn't find Ashwini. I just wanted a glimpse of her, nothing more.

"I know, everyday you don't give surprises, but this place makes me feel good from inside!" I said, looking up at the skies.

There was no reply.

I proceeded towards the auditorium in hope that I would find her on the way, but I didn't. Finally, when I was entering the auditorium, a speeding vehicle passed parallel to me. Although I was in danger of an accident with that vehicle, I smiled because it was vehicle number 4651, driven by none other than Ashwini. I couldn't see her, but the glimpse of 4651 was more than enough for me.

Her momentary presence again made my day. I forgot that I had ever cried today.

I reached my room safely through the secret passage of the auditorium, which only I knew.

Chapter 4

Location:- Dining hall, Hostel
Time:- 8:00 pm.

"How's your health now, brother?" asked Vrund, as he saw me entering.

"Pretty good," I replied.

"So you are back on Facebook! That's pretty cool. I will send you suggestions of a few beautiful girls. I hope you will enjoy them," he said with a naughty intention.

"No thanks, I can do it on my own, and for your information, I don't add unknown people," I said.

"That is also correct. But dude, Preksha isn't accepting my friend request! I wonder why not?" he asked.

"Maybe she is not interested in being friends with you," I replied.

"That cannot be possible. I look far better than most other boys," he said.

"Now don't talk about looks. Even the ugliest guys are her friends," I said.

"That is also correct. You know her more than me," he said.

Vrund was a guy who was completely attracted to the opposite sex, so I asked him, "Well, do you know each and every girl in our college?"

"Not only our college, any college in Vadodara, and any faculty," he replied.

"But how?" I asked.

"Childhood talent!" he said and this brought a balmy smile on my face.

"So, you can find tidings of any girl? Who she is? Where she is from? Who was her ex? Who is her current?" I asked.

"Yes, I can. So it seems that finally you have found someone for yourself," he said in a loud tone, forcing a few boys to catch a snippet of our talk.

I grabbed his head and pulled his hair in anger, saying, "Go on; tell everyone loudly."

"Okay, okay. Be calm and tell me her name," he said.

"Well, firstly I want to clarify that she isn't my girlfriend, and secondly, I don't have a crush on her. I just want to know who she is!" I said.

He took out his mobile and said, "Tell me her name."

"Idiot, not like this. You have to come with me tomorrow," I said.

"Wow, that's amazing, but where are you going to take me?" he asked.

"It's a good place. You will enjoy it, full of greenery," I said blinking my eyes.

"You mean to say girls?" he said.

(*He was smart enough to understand that greenery stands for girls!)

"Yes, my dear." I replied.

"You are on. I will surely come with you tomorrow and we shall take Dhruvesh also," he said.

"Dhruvesh? But where is he? I haven't seen him after his suspension," I said.

"He realized that he wasn't made for engineering, and after his suspension, no other science college would give him admission. So he has switched to arts," he said.

"Amazing, and which is that lucky unlucky college to bear him?" I asked.

"Our own arts faculty, but don't tell anybody. It's just between us," he said.

"That is the same place which I am going to take you to tomorrow," I said in surprise.

"That's amazing. Why are all the girls who prefer 'arts' so beautiful?" he asked.

"Maybe because they take on less pressure for studies," I said.

"And also because they get good food in their campus," he added

"It is like that only, dear. Now let's enjoy our awful dinner with pure acceptance," I said.

"Do we have any other option?" he asked as we went for dinner.

We took our plates and sat at the dining table.

"How did Dhruvesh manage to get in after his suspension?" I asked Vrund.

"Shhhhh! he has completely changed his identity. Earlier he was called Dhruvesh Patel, and now he has changed his name to Rudresh Patel," said Vrund.

"Amazing, and what about his identity?" I asked.

"Well, you know him. He created fake certificates under different names, gave an entrance exam and entered the college," he replied.

"And what about the looks?" I asked.

"Very simple, dude. He has decided to grow his beard, plus, he has changed his hairstyle. So no one will have any doubt that he is Dhruvesh Patel," he said.

"And what sort of new hair style has he got?" I asked.

"Slinga-Malinga," he replied, and I laughed.

"Why are you laughing?" he asked.

"He looks funny in my imagination. God knows how he looks in reality with that new look," I said, and even Vrund laughed.

After that laughter, Vrund again troubled me by saying, "But I am very serious about Preksha, dude. I want her anyhow. I know she is your ex, but she is single now."

"How come you are so confident about her single status?" I asked doubtingly.

"I mean, yes, but I am not sure! Who cares if she is single or not? She should be mine," said Vrund.

"You mean to say that you will still propose to her, even if she is in a relationship?" I asked.

"Obviously, dude. All guys aren't loyal like you. If you were her boyfriend, I would have never proposed to her, because I know that you are very sensible and the sweetest amongst all the guys. But you have to agree that it was this nature of yours only, which took Preksha away from you, I sense!" he said.

"I don't know. I am what I am. Good she left me, because I couldn't be her type," I said.

"Exactly, mate; this is what I am trying to tell you. You are sweet and sensible, so you deserve a girl who is equally sweet within her heart, and not rude and impatient, like Preksha," said Vrund.

Vrund had a point.

"Then tell me, why do you wish to have her?" I asked Vrund.

"Because she looks beautiful and I am handsome. She is easy going and I am also easy going. She is not narrow minded and I am also open minded; so in every way we match," he said.

"Wow!" I exclaimed. "It seems you know her better than me. How?" I asked.

"It is very simple, dude. The profile picture tells you the whole story," he replied.

He was talking insanely; how could anyone judge a person based on their profile pictures. But it is normal human behavior to do so. If you enter a bar and instead of drinking a beer or alcohol, you drink water, the person opposite will naturally think that you are drinking beer, as you are in a beer bar.

This is a universal law – "*What they see, they assume.*" So the best solution is to ignore it and move on.

"You won't get her any time soon, dude," I said, smiling.

"Why? Am I not handsome?" he asked.

"You are, but try to understand. She needs the perfect guy and you are not that perfect stud for her," I said.

"Perfect guy? In which sense are you talking?" he asked.

"Tell me how many likes you get on your profile picture?" I asked him.

"Between 140–150," he said.

"Forget it; she get over 1750 likes," I said. "How many followers do you have on your Instagram account?" I asked.

"Not more than 300," he replied in a low tone.

"Forget it, she has over 5000 followers," I replied.

"What is your pocket money?" I asked him.

"Not more than 700," he replied.

"Forget it! 700 must be her weekly expense for her fantasies," I said.

"How do you know that?" he asked cunningly.

"Firstly I was her ex; secondly as you said, a profile picture reveals everything," I replied.

He was silent.

To irritate him more, I said, "Take your mobile phone out and open the calculator. I will tell you the exact amount of the expense which you shall bear, if you want to make her your girl friend."

He opened the calculator.

"Your pocket money is 700, and suppose we consider her weekly expense to be 600, then, in one month, your expense will definitely reach up to rupees 2400. So annually you will spend 28,800 rupees on her. Can you afford that?" I asked smiling.

"Fuck, no!" he exclaimed angrily.

"Yes, and you were teaching me about the 21st century. I am telling you the bitter truth. In the 21st century, in order to make a beautiful unknown girl your girlfriend, you should be ready to have a yearly back up of around 30,000 rupees, and practically it is not possible, so you have to take a bank loan for it," I said.

"Loan? What the hell will I tell the bank manager, if he asks me the reason for taking the loan?" he asked.

I laughed and said, "I don't know, but if you say that you want a loan because you want to keep a girl friend, than he will definitely kick you on your backside."

"Horrible!" he exclaimed.

Obviously after my weird but true explanation, there was a TWO MINUTE SILENCE.

When dinner was over, he started shivering, and said, "I have to forget Preksha; she is out of my league. Thank you for making me realize that."

"Anytime, dude, and you are coming tomorrow with me to the arts faculty," I said.

"Of course," he replied and signed off.

I apologized to myself for having given him that weird explanation but what else could I say? Vrund was a kind of guy who could understand things, if we explained them to him in his way but, I could never think the same about any girl.

(*A sweet girl never demands anything from her boyfriend. Sometimes she only needs one hand to hold and a patient heart to listen. If you can be that person, you are her man; otherwise, you are just a guy.)

After a break-up, it is difficult for men to bounce back. Precisely I must say that it is very difficult for *true men* to bounce back. Because once my mother told me that, "Women are indeed strong in that thing. They are Angels and when someone breaks their wings, they simply continue to fly on broomsticks. They are flexible like that."

I went to my room and realized that I had to mug up a few formulas and study till late night, because the final semester exams were approaching.

I had promised myself to study well and not think about Preksha anymore.

After studying for a few hours, I felt sleepy, and so I slept at 1:30 am. After a few minutes, again I felt some pain in my stomach. At first I ignored it because I thought it might be just a twinge, but then, the pain became unbearable; however, I firmly decided not to react to it. Gradually, that pain spread over my whole stomach. Finally I stood up because I felt like vomiting again. I closed my eyes and threw up. I felt somewhat relieved. Something was wrong with my stomach, and I decided that I had to visit a doctor the next day. However, these days, pain killers reduce your pain instantly. I took a painkiller and slept, but this time before sleeping I activated dual alarms, so that I wouldn't miss the morning class, as I had done the day before.

Location:- Class room.

Time:- 8:00 am

First the peon took attendance, than Umar sir started his boring lecture.

"Every student has to look at the book," he said.

Everyone shifted their necks down at same time beneath their books. Mind you, only some had the physics text-book on their desks. Girls were busy reading fiction novels, guys like Vrund were busy reading some magazines, which included the images of beautiful girls, while some had directed their cell phones under the text-books and were busy reading their Whatsapp messages. I was also not less. I also decided to read something. I took out a diary from my bag. It was the diary in which I mostly wrote poems. I opened one random page which read –

'I am distressed in fear,
I am for you here.
PLS open your eyes,
Just see my cries!
I am holding your hand,
Regardless of any trend,
PLS be my friend,
I promise it shall never end.'

(*Actually the above poem was written in the few days after she left me. I wanted her badly; if only as a friend, I missed her like anything at that time. But today after seeing her modern form, I felt that these lines were an insult to her.)

When I turned another page it read –

'Someday Somewhere,

Sometime once again,

With pure heart,

Clean mind,

I am going,

to come once again!'

(*I laughed after reading this, because after six months of our break-up, I was still living in the hope that she would come back to me once again, or that I would go back to her. But fortunately or unfortunately, it never happened.)

And this was my favorite poem which I had written, thinking whether she would ever get the right person in her life or not!

'When my eyes are closed,

I see you as a rose!

From the beauty of the sunshine,

To the everlasting coastline!

The greatest story told,

In the winter nights of cold!

I shall be standing here,

Till you find someone, someone, someone.'

I turned the pages and read every creation which I had written imagining Preksha, and while reading a few poems, tears flowed down my eyes, but I had promised Heenal that I wouldn't waste my time thinking about her anymore. The bell rang, Umar sir went out of the class and all students escaped through the back window.

"Bhavam, what are you doing? Forgot? We have to go there," said Vrund.

His voice reminded me, and I said, "Yes, I am coming."

"I have called Dhruvesh; he will be waiting for us near the gate," said Vrund.

"No, tell him to stand near the auditorium," I said.

"Why auditorium?" he asked.

I then told him about the secret passage which joined the three faculties, and he was shocked to hear that.

"How did you come to know about it?" he asked with anxiety.

"I don't say much, but that doesn't mean, I don't know anything," I replied as we approached that passage.

"I have to agree, people were right; you indeed are a scholar," he said.

"People are wrong. I am not a scholar. But yes, I was a scholar," I said with low energy.

He placed his palm on my shoulder to console me saying, "It happens, dude; sometimes we win and sometimes we lose."

I laughed and said, "Don't repeat those Whatsapp quotes to me. I created them much before they were forwarded."

"Can I ask you something?" he asked.

"Anything, except about Preksha," I said bluntly.

"No, no. I just want to know; were you a ranker when she was your girl friend?" he asked.

"Yes, I was; maybe that's why she was my girlfriend," I said.

"How did you both meet?" he asked.

"I don't want to remember it again and again, please," I said.

"It's fine. I guess, she is becoming your sole fear now," he said.

Everyone was now slowly realizing that Preksha was becoming my fear, so he wasn't new in that list.

I got angry and replied, "She isn't my fear. You want to know the story of our meeting? Than listen, JEE 2010 changed everything. I got my center number at Kendriya Vidhyalay school. I was very nervous because, in order to get admission in a good collage, I had to at least score 150 plus. When I entered to write my examination, only two tensions were running down in my mind. One was about the paper and the other was about my partner, who would be sitting next to me. I was praying that I get someone intelligent. After a long wait, the exam started. All students were in the class except my partner. I was worried whether I would have to write the paper alone!

Finally a beautiful girl with ruddy cheeks and beautiful eyes entered the room and she was my partner. She was so beautiful that each and every boy stopped their paper to have a glimpse of her. I was lucky as she was sitting beside me. I wanted to know her name, so I peeped into her hall ticket and found that her name was Preksha Chahal.

Initially we didn't communicate with each other, but after one hour, she seemed to be somewhat nervous. I looked at her and she also looked at me. I swear, it was such a complex situation for me because I was confused whether I should give her a smile or not. But then without thinking I gave her a very shy smile and in return, she also smiled and tapped her pen on the question paper. She was asking me to show her the correct answers and how could I refuse this opportunity? She ticked all the answers which I had ticked, and it was fixed that we were going to get the same marks. After that she looked relieved, and at the end, when just ten minutes were left, she again tapped her pen in order to divert my attention, and she wrote some ten digits on her question paper. Initially I was confused about what she was trying to tell me. After two minutes, my mind said that she was giving me her mobile number. I noted her mobile number and after that she looked at me and smiled, and I smiled in return.

After we came out of the examination hall, she thanked me. Her voice was as sweet as she was when she said, "Thank you so much for your help." She was in a hurry that day because, maybe, someone had come to pick her up. While going she turned and signed to me, indicating that I should text her soon. I was very happy, because, for the first time in my life, a girl was interested in me, not because of me, but because of my intelligence; but I was ready to take it any way. When I went home, I immediately sent a text message to her and from there, the friendship started, as slowly we became close friends,

One day she told me, "Bhavam, you are more than my best friend." She was not very interested in studies, and I was the opposite. Our ideologies matched because we both loved life. Slowly, we came closer, and one day I just asked her, and thus, the lovely relationship between us started. This was how we met," I said with a catch in my voice, as I was reminded of those days again.

Vrund was silent and then he said, "I am very sorry to disturb you mentally. I apologize for that."

I smiled and said, "No problem, dude, those were such days which still make me happy when I remember them."

"But what was the reason for which she left an innocent guy like you? Did any guy interfere and break your bond?" asked Vrund.

"I am also left with no reason, Vrund. Just prior to our break-up, we used to have many fights, and maybe, she wasn't comfortable with that, so she left, I guess," I said.

"That's not fair, Bhavam. You should have known the proper reason for her leaving you," said Vrund.

I closed my eyes and said, "If she leaves you, it's her decision. Respect it. If she loves you, it's your character. Enrich it. If she hates you, it's her problem. Ignore it. If she cares for you, it's her kindness. Cherish it. If she cries, it's because of emptiness, kill it. If she smiles, it's because of happiness, keep it. So quite simply, dude, I wasn't able to be such a perfect guy for her, so she left me," I replied.

"Your words are as lovely as you. If a guy can respect that, a girl can definitely fall for it," said Vrund as we were now out of the auditorium.

"Call Dhruvesh!" I ordered.

"He told me that he would be here," said Vrund.

"This is the arts faculty, dude. As I told you on, the road is full of greenery, so he must be enjoying that," I said, winking.

"My God, look at this. It seems that we were in jail," said Vrund.

"This is my bunking destination, much better than your Rasalpur and Sind road," I said.

"I agree with you. From tomorrow, it is going to be my bunking destination too," said Vrund.

"Where is that idiot?" I asked, indicating Dhruvesh.

"Hehe, see, he is approaching," said Vrund pointing to him.

Of course, he was looking pathetic with that new look. I wasn't able to control my laughter and laughed aloud.

"I know it looks very bad on me," said Dhruvesh.

"Indeed!" exclaimed Vrund.

"So how is everything going on here?" I asked Dhruvesh.

"Don't ask; it's a hundred times better than our own faculty. Fundamental rights are strictly followed here, I must say," said Dhruvesh.

"And what about girls? Are they beautiful?" asked Vrund.

"Girls are always beautiful, if you see them in the correct way," I commented.

"Here fashion is allowed, so all girls look beautiful," said Dhruvesh.

"Are you in contact with every girl over here?" I asked.

"What do you think? Will any girl talk with me, with my current appearance in place?" said Dhruvesh in an annoyed tone.

We both wanted to laugh again, but controlled ourselves because if Dhruvesh went hyper, he wouldn't help us. I took out my cell phone and showed him a photo of Ashwini. Both were such perverts that they started fighting after seeing her photo.

"My God! She is beautiful!" exclaimed Vrund in delight.

"Yes, she is," said Dhruvesh in a wondering tone.

"Stop looking at her," I said.

"Why? She isn't our 'Bhabhi' yet, so we can look at her," said Vrund giving a hi five to Dhruvesh.

"I will kill you both, if you utter any further nonsense about her," I said fiercely.

"Is she from here?" asked Vrund to Dhruvesh.

"I haven't seen her," said Dhruvesh.

"Are you sure?" I asked.

"Yes, she might be an Architecture student," said Dhruvesh.

"Is it so?" asked Vrund.

"Yes, because in these two days, I have seen every girl of my faculty, but I never saw her," said Dhruvesh.

Vrund interrupted and said to Dhruvesh, "Why don't you become a watchman? The job will suit you."

"You seriously are a girl watcher, man," I said.

"Don't think that I have a bad character, if I do that. I believe in one thing - if you see a beautiful girl, appreciate her beauty, try to impress her, if you can; but if you fail, leave that road respectfully and try impressing another girl. I am sure that one day every guy will get success if he tries so," said Dhruvesh.

"But the approach should be innocent," I said.

"I agree, but not so innocent that she can swindle you," said Vrund.

"It's not about being innocent, I guess. I think both partners should be smart, when it comes to the relationship," said Dhruvesh.

"Smart in what sense?" I asked.

"If you are being cheated, than you should be smart enough to realize that fact," said Dhruvesh.

"And what if we are loved?" I asked.

"I have never been in love throughout my life, so I don't know about it," said Dhruvesh.

"It will be better if we keep smartness in education only, rather than in love," I said.

"Bhavam, don't over react. Everyone has a different perspective," said Vrund.

Dhruvesh took out his cell phone and typed Ashwini's name and then sent her a friend request.

"How can you send a request to a girl whom you don't know?" I asked.

"She doesn't know me, so I will introduce myself. If she is interested, she will talk with me, otherwise not," said Dhruvesh.

(*Dhruvesh was very logical.)

"You are great!" I exclaimed.

"Look, she isn't from Vadodara," said Dhruvesh.

"Then from where?" I asked in excitement.

"She is beautiful, and mostly Punjabi girls are beautiful; so she might be from Punjab," assumed Vrund.

"You are an asshole when it comes to assumption, Vrund. She is from South Gujarat, Valsad," said Dhruvesh.

My heart stopped for a minute when I heard it. She was from South Gujarat and me too. Wow! This was such a coincidence. My native place was Navsari, just a few kilometers away from Valsad. I was very happy when I heard that.

"So has she come here to study?" said Vrund.

"Obviously, dumbo," said Dhruvesh.

"Sometimes you ask very stupid questions, Vrund," I said.

"Ignore him, Bhavam, he is like an empty box. You know once he proposed to a girl…?" said Dhruvesh.

I interrupted and said, "Nothing new in that."

"No, listen! So I was telling you that once he proposed to a girl, but the girl refused. Then also, he kept on proposing to the same girl. Finally in anger, that girl made him a 'rakhi' brother, and till date, he is the brother of more than seven girls, to whom he proposed," said Dhurvesh.

I laughed and said, "Oh now I understood. All girls feel free to communicate with you, Vrund, because they know that if you propose to them, then you turn into their brother."

"Correct!" said Dhruvesh and nodded.

"Enough is enough, guys. I am going to Sind road. Don't follow me," said Vrund angrily and went away.

After a while Dhruvesh also left, and I stood there, in the hope of having at least one glimpse of her, or if not her, then the vehicle number 4651. But I realized that my health was not too good and I had to visit the doctor and take medicines for my recovery.

Chapter 5

The Doctor said that I was fine and advised me to have proper sleep. But I was having proper sleep. Why then was I suffering from such health issues? That too, not throughout the day, but only at midnight! However, he instructed me to have a few medicines, which I purchased from the nearby store.

After visiting the Doctor, I made my way towards my bunking destination, Kamatibaug. That garden was always a source of inspiration for me; plus if Heenal was there, it would be a good time pass for me.

I was at the entrance of Kamatibaug, when I saw a group of girls taking selfies with a lone guy. I looked up at the skies and said, "I know I can never be that lucky guy."

(* Yes, all guys get jealous when they see that.)

I examined that guy carefully and concluded, saying, "Well, he is not that handsome. Maybe I look better than him; then why is he the lucky one?"

Yes, I was jealous. Nevertheless, I entered the green fields and sat at the place where Heenal usually approached me.

15 minutes had passed, but I didn't have a glimpse of Heenal. However, my exams were approaching, and I had to cope with my grades too. It was necessary for me to get at least a B grade in all subjects in order to do well. So I took out my Physics notes, and started mugging up the important points.

(*We live in a country where the answer of the question is more important than the approach of the question to be solved.)

It reminded me of the days when I was very quick in studies. There was no secret behind it. The only mantra was – daily studies, which I didn't do after the break-up.

However, neither could I change my past, nor could I apprehend what the future held for me. The only thing which I had was the present, and I had to make full use of it.

Time:- 5:45pm

"Hey, I have been waiting for a long time; now stop reading," said a soft voice from behind. I knew it was none other than Heenal.

"Where were you?" I asked angrily.

"I will use your lines, Bhavam,

I am rare,

So I am like air.

Feel me every second,

But you can never catch me," she said.

"Nice attempt," I said.

"I like listening to the poetry. I was thinking of composing one, so I tried. How is it?" she asked.

"Amazing, because it contains my words and it is a bad thing to steal somebody's words," I replied.

"Leave it. It's useless to argue with you. You don't have a copyright, okay? So till then, your words are not your own," she said.

"Whatever!" I said in a harsh tone.

"Why so frustrated today?" she asked.

"Too much of tension," I said.

"About what?" she asked.

"Innumerable things," I said. "Firstly, it's about the result, and secondly, it's about the exams," I added.

She laughed and said, "Firstly it should be exams, and secondly, it should be about the results."

"No, no!" I said. "I don't have any tension about the exams, because we people are quite smart, and we can manage anything to fill a supplementary, but I fear the results," I added.

"Pity you, man," she whispered.

"Yes, you should pity me! Look at them!" I said, waving my hand towards those guys who were taking selfies with random girls. "They are so lucky."

"Are you jealous of them?" she asked smiling.

"I am human, and if I don't get what others get, I get jealous," I replied.

"They aren't lucky, Bhavam. Look, this is a simple fact. Girls will never approach you first. You have to make the effort," she said.

"You are wrong. My ex was different, not like these girls. But now she is more than these girls," I said.

"Oh come on, Bhavam, why don't you get out of this thing?" she said angrily.

"Heenal, I am trying my best, and one day I will forget her. That day will come soon because I have already forgiven her," I said.

"Sometimes, we girls are definitely right when we leave you guys alone," she said stiffly.

"That is what you girls can do to satisfy your big egos," I said.

"It's not about ego, babe; it's about love," she said.

"I never cheated on her. I loved her," I said.

"I am not telling about you. I am talking in general. Do you know one other reason why we girls leave you guys?" she asked.

"I am not as philosophical as you, so I don't know," I said.

"Then listen. You guys always love your girl just as a partner. Or you may try to love her as if you are the world's best boyfriend, and yes, she needs that love, but she doesn't deserve such love. Love her just like her father does, and then I bet, she won't ever leave you, because that is the love which she deserves," she replied, and I was stunned.

"If I love her like her father, then she will think that I am boring or narrow minded," I said.

"You are again taking me in the wrong way. Loving her like her father means loving her without any expectation. You guys always love her with some expectation, don't you?" she asked.

"Yes, we do expect love in the place of love," I said.

"In true love, you don't need to expect anything. If your love is true enough, your expectations will turn into reality."

"Tell me one thing; have you experienced everything at such a young age?" I asked her in doubt.

"No, brother, I am only telling you the truth," she said and smiled.

"Your every explanation satisfies me," I said.

She just smiled and asked me, "Many times, I have seen you writing in this diary. What do you write, apart from the poems?"

"There are only two ways for a guy to get out of a break-up. The first option is going and venting all your anger in the gym, while the second is smoking. I started to smoke, but you explained it to me so I left it. This diary is my gym. I vent all my anger as well as happiness in it," I said, sadly.

She mimicked my expression, and then said, "After seeing you, I realized that even a guy suffers a lot due to a break-up."

"I am not joking," I said.

"Yah, I know that, but a girl will come out of a break-up very quickly, because she will always find a friend, who will never make her cry," she said.

"Yes, I could see that on my ex girlfriend's Instagram," I said.

"You know what your problem is?" she asked.

"No," I replied.

"You pay too much of importance to her, while on the other hand, she is going on along on her own way. She is happy, Bhavam. So it's time for you also to be happy. You should be a proud ex-boyfriend," she said.

"Why proud?" I asked.

"You should take pride in that, though you left her or she left you, there is still a smile on her face. So the world won't see you as a bad ex boyfriend. But if you don't smile, if you stay in that darkness, then the world will see her as a bad ex girlfriend. Do you want that?" she explained.

"But I fear talking to other girls!" I exclaimed.

"Fear? I am a girl and look, I am talking to you. Do you like any girl in your college?" she asked.

"I never saw anybody like that after the break-up," I said.

"Well, then look! The world is full of beautiful girls and trust me, you look sweet, and any sweet chick will fall for you," she said in a mesmerizing tone.

"I don't want a sweet chick. I want a sensible chick," I said.

"Don't worry, you will get that sensible chick soon," she said.

"Well, I need to go now. Suddenly exams are scaring me," I said.

"Bhavam, from now you have to smile," she said, holding my hand.

I placed my hand on her hand and said, smiling, "Will this do?"

"Not a fake smile, baby, a sweet innocent smile, which can tantalize any girl," she said.

"I will try my best. You know one thing - I never give up," I said and left.

When I was on the way, I was thinking, "Do I have a crush on any girl?"

My mind said no, but firmly from my heart, I decided that, today, whatsoever happened, I would chat with Ashwini on Facebook. Of course, after having my dinner!

When I went at the dining hall, as always, Vrund approached me. I know he had only one discussion and that was about girls.

"Before you say anything, I am telling you not to discuss anything related to girls," I said to Vrund.

"Why? See, a normal guy can only talk about two things - girls and cricket," he said.

"There are many things other things to do, apart from that," I said.

"You leave that discussion aside. See, today we helped you, so now you will have to help us," he said.

"What do you want?" I asked arrogantly.

"You have to do a setting for someone!" he exclaimed.

"Setting?" I asked.

"Yes," he nodded.

"What is setting?" I asked innocently, even though I knew his intentions.

"Dumbo, setting, means you have to do the role of a match maker," he said.

"For whom?" I asked.

(*WELCOME TO INDIA… If you term 'relationships' as 'settings'.)

He whispered silently, "Dhruvesh!"

"Wow! When did he come into your category?" I asked

"Shut up!" he exclaimed. "I am telling you because you know that girl whom he likes," he added.

"Who is that girl?" I asked, holding my plate.

"Vish Prajapati," he said.

As soon as he said that, I stood up from my place and questioned him, "How do you know her?"

"Relax. We are loafers, dude. We know everything," he said, smiling.

"No, it's incorrect. You are the only loafer," I said.

"That is also correct!" he exclaimed. "I know she stays near your house; she is your childhood friend, and my God, she looks sexier than Preksha," said Vrund.

I clapped my hands and said, "Come out of your sexy world, brother. Vish is a sensible and sweet natured girl. She won't even drop a rupee for Dhruvesh."

"You don't worry about that. He will manage to impress her," said Vrund.

"Then what's my role in all this?" I asked doubtfully.

"You just have to convince Vish to accept Dhruvesh's friend request on Facebook," he said slowly.

I laughed and said, "Now you realize that good girls won't accept your friend requests easily."

"Yes, so you will do this for us," he said.

"But wait, I have never ever chatted with Vish, and plus, I have not been in touch with her for four years," I said.

"So what? She knows you very well, and plus, your impression is good amongst all girls; so that is a positive thing, I guess," said Vrund.

"Okay, I will try my best," I said.

"Thank you!"he replied.

"Have you ever thought that, although you are so famous amongst all these girls, why they don't consider you a good guy?" I asked.

"Reason number one – I am not Bhavam Sharma. Reason number two – I am flirty and reason number three – you are not," he said and left for dinner.

I looked up at the skies and exclaimed, "Wish I was flirty!"

While I was having dinner, sitting on one side, there came a text message from Dhruvesh on my Whatsapp -

"Did Vrund tell you everything?" he asked.

I typed, "I would have been happy, if you had said it to me directly."

He ignored that message and said, "I am now friends with Ashwini."

I got a little shock and asked him, "How?"

'Don't ask me anything now. Tomorrow, the arts faculty is planning a farewell. No students of the science faculty are invited, but I have acquired two extra passes for you and Vrund. So do join me," he said.

"I will see, and inform you soon," I said.

"All right, see you soon!" he said and ended the chat.

Dhruvesh's fortune had suddenly changed since he had shifted to the arts faculty from here. Indeed he was lucky to escape from here.

(*Sometimes college suspensions are a boon.)

The same text message was sent to Vrund, inviting him for the farewell party. So he jumped and approached me saying, "It will be great fun."

I was expressionless and just nodded.

"Don't give that ugly look, Bhavam. Have you renounced your life?" he asked.

"I am thinking of renouncing it. Do you wish to join me?" I asked.

"Never. I have my aims," he said.

"Nothing except impressing girls!" I exclaimed.

"That is also correct!" he said.

"He messaged me that the party location is the auditorium hall," Vrund said.

"Hey, it's great. You know the exact location of it through that secret passage," he whispered slowly.

"Now say that I have renounced the world?" I questioned fitfully.

"Sorry, I was wrong," he said, and laughed.

After completing the awful dinner, we went to our destination.

My life had suddenly accelerated since the last few days. It all started with meeting Heenal, than the surprise meeting with Ashwini. I had trustworthy friends such as Vrund and Dhruvesh. Everything was going on well. Maybe my suffering was slowly ending, and I owed the credit to Heenal and her practical explanations, which were taking me slowly out from my darkness.

I had started to change. I was no longer interested in staying in the darkness, and so I switched on the lights and, as usual, wrote every detail of the day in my diary. I couldn't afford to skip medicines, for otherwise, I would have to suffer for another night. Before sleeping, I had to complete the work which Vrund had told me for Dhruvesh. I had to convince Vish, my childhood friend, to accept Dhruvesh's friend request. I didn't know how to start, because I was going to talk with Vish after four years. I was nervous, but I had seen that she had already accepted my friend request, and luckily she was also online.

I held my breath and wrote – "Hi!"

She saw my message and went offline. I was shocked. Yes, indeed, she had also changed. Why would she ignore to reply me? Just like others, maybe she had also changed. I was dejected, but I didn't think much about it because I had many other things to think about.

(*That is the worst feeling in the world, when they see your message and still don't reply.)

I opened my cupboard wondering what I should wear for the next day's party. Our science faculty also organized several get together parties, but I had never attended them because I was so lost in my own darkness, thinking about why Preksha had left me?

But now, things had changed, and I decided that I would go for the party.

What could I wear? I had innumerable clothes, but was confused about what to choose? I decided to leave the choice for the next day…

Time:- 8:00 am

Location:- Lecture room

"The Farewell party will begin at 7:00 pm, but we have to reach there by 6:30 pm," said Vrund.

"I will be there," I said.

"Not only you. We will go together, because that passage is very strange," he said.

"Strange?" I asked. "I think it is darker than it should be," I added.

"Do you fear the darkness?" I asked him.

"No, I don't." he replied "But I don't like darkness, as it confuses me," he added.

"Don't worry. I am used to the darkness," I said.

"That is also correct!" he said.

"You do one thing. It won't take more than five minutes to cross the passage; so you stand near that passage around 6:20 pm or so, and I will come and we can go together," I said.

He nodded and said, "Done!"

After the lecture was over, as always, we bunked the class and went to our own destinations. Vrund diverted towards Sindh-road, while others started making their own plans. I diverted my steps towards Kamatibaug.

This time I didn't have any trouble finding Heenal, because she was sitting there at the fixed place, where we daily sat.

I approached her and said, "Today I am very happy, sister."

She was wearing white and just smiled. I sat beside her and held her hand because I could sense that she was quite sad.

"What happened, Heenal?" I asked her.

She just hugged me and started crying.

"Hey, please don't cry, Heenal. I don't like it if any girl cries in front of me. As a guy, it hurts me. Please stop crying," I said.

She continued to cry and said, "Crying is better sometimes. It removes all your emotions, and later you feel better. So don't stop me."

"You made me strong and now you are crying," I said.

"Sometimes, the person who tries to keep others happy is the loneliest person in the world, Bhavam," she said.

"I have heard this. You copied it from Google quotes, I know," I said with a shy smile.

This made her calm and she slapped me in a friendly manner on my shoulder and said, "Don't be oversmart. You are right, I got it from Google, but I only gave it to Google."

"Then why are you here, babe? Go and teach Google! These days, it's showing weird things," I said.

"You boys watch such weird things; we girls don't," she said.

"Leave it. I have seen girls also who watch such weird things," I said.

"When did you see a girl ever watching such a thing?" she asked.

"It is a very funny incident which took place just a few days before my break-up. Monica, who was also Preksha's friend, was continuously looking at her mobile for one hour. She was so engrossed that Preksha snatched her mobile and, to her surprise, she found that Monica was enjoying semi nude images of the Hollywood actors. On that day I realized that girls also use Google, just like guys," I said.

"What do you mean by semi nude?" she asked.

"What do you think?" I questioned.

"Whatever!" she exclaimed. "Boys are always perverts for everything," she added.

"Have you done a Ph D in terms of guys?" I asked.

She laughed and said, "Absolutely not, but it is a fact."

"So, according to you, these guys who are taking selfies with these girls are perverts?" I asked.

"Obviously, because all of them are selfish," she said.

"How?" I asked.

"Not only guys, these girls are also selfish. They aren't clicking the selfies for the memories! They click them, just to increase their Instagram status, and to get more followers. Because it is a human tendency that people will only follow you, if you look beautiful or you have beauties around you," she explained.

"So if I ask you to click a selfie with me, will you agree?" I asked.

"Never!" she said bluntly.

"Quite a rude response, Heenal," I said angrily.

"Sorry, but if you can keep me in your heart, I don't deserve to be in that 16 GB memory card, and if you wish to keep me in that memory card, than I will remain as your memory only," she said.

I smiled but said nothing because again she had made me silent by her beautiful response.

"I respect your thinking. Don't worry, I won't ask you for a selfie again," I said.

We both were quiet for a few moments. I remembered and asked her, "But, Heenal, why were you crying?"

"Nothing much," she said. "When I see you as a college guy, I remember myself in the arts faculty. You know, we girls used to have lots of fun. Those days were awesome," she added.

"These four years for me in the college were horrible, because I could never enjoy anything. I took my break-up so seriously that I stopped living my life. There was not a single day, when I didn't cry remembering her. I punished myself. I broke all my social contacts. I left the groups of all those friends, who were even linked with Preksha. I left everything for her, hoping that, on seeing all these, one day she would return to me, but that never happened. Each day after the separation, I was going more close to her, while she was just the opposite. To suppress my depression, I had found an alternative. One day I observed our hostel guard, Vrajen Kaka, smoking a cigarette. While smoking, he used to say that it relieved all his tiredness. On seeing that, I decided to smoke. Initially, my throat was not able to bear that smoke but slowly, I became habituated. This was my college life before I met you," I said.

"It's good now that you have left smoking," she exclaimed in relief.

"That is all because of you. Your explanations solved my grief," I said, thanking her.

"Today you seem to be quite happy; anything special?" she asked.

I told her everything related to the farewell party of the arts faculty and how Dhruvesh and Vrund had managed the tickets. I also decided to tell her about Ashwini. I narrated to her how we met and other incidents.

"Wow, Bhavam. Don't lie, I guess you like her," she said widening her eyes.

"I never said that I like her," I said.

"The way you were describing her, dude, showed all your feelings about her," she replied.

"I am excited to meet her today. Vrund and I will escape the hostel secretly through that secret passage which you showed me that day," I said.

Suddenly she lifted up her eyebrows in anger. Her eyes turned red as she immediately stood up and said, “How dare you tell anyone about that passage?”

“I have not told anyone about it. He is my friend,” I said.

“And what if he speaks about it to everyone?” she asked angrily.

“He won’t tell. He is trustworthy, but why are you getting frustrated?” I asked.

“I showed you the way because I trusted you, assuming that you won’t tell anyone, but you all guys are same,” she said in an enraged tone.

“I am sorry. I never knew that this small thing might hurt you so much,” I said.

“Small thing?” she asked. “It isn’t a small thing. You don’t know anything; leave it,” she said and stood up.

I held her hand and said, “I said I am sorry. Please don’t go anywhere. I need you.”

“Don’t touch me, Bhavam, let me go,” she said.

As soon as I released her hand, she started walking away, ignoring me. How can such a small thing hurt her? I knew she was in anger so I thought that it would be better to let her go.

Overall, it was a special day because, today I was going to meet Ashwini at the farewell party.

Chapter 6

Location:- My hostel room

Time:- 6:00 pm

The time was approaching. I quickly took a shower and was in great confusion about what to wear in order to look attractive. I had never wanted to impress any girl, but was keen to catch Ashwini's attention.

(*Even guys do look at their clothing when they are supposed to go to the same place where their crush is also going to be around them.)

Yes, my heart was admitting the fact that Ashwini had slowly started becoming my crush

All my pains were at an end as I had relinquished my heart to her. This reminded me of one fact which I had written in my diary after the break-up.

"*Someone will surely come into my life. I have to be patient and learn to wait. Because sometimes, a patient person receives the best love story.*"

So would that be the end of my suffering today?

All my questions would be answered today when I finally met Ashwini. Actually meeting wouldn't do anything now; if I had to do anything, it would mean talking with her face to face.

I opened my cupboard and was again confused about what to wear, so I took out my old black shirt, which actually suited me a lot. Preksha had loved that shirt. Whenever I used to wear it, she used to say that I looked adorable in it.

While taking that shirt out, it reminded me that I had worn it last time on her birthday. It was making me nostalgic again. However, I ignored it and got ready. When I looked myself in the mirror, I asked myself, "Wow! Is the old Bhavam back?"

There was something in my shirt pocket. When I checked it, I found a small piece of paper on which it was written –

"Hate me from your heart,
I will love you from my soul.
Love me from your soul,
You won't know what hate is."

This was in Preksha's handwriting and she had written this poem for me. I had kept it in the pocket of her favorite shirt, so that it always touched my heart. When I completed reading it, a teardrop fell from my eyes on that paper, as everything flashbacked in front of my eyes. I sat down on my knees and started crying again over her memories. Every time I wanted to be strong, even her little flashback chagrined me. All the memories were waving in front of my eyes. I was lost; I had to supply a supplement to my body in order to stop my tears. I opened my drawer, and took out the remaining cigarette packet.

"I am sorry, Heenal, I have no choice left," I said with a cry.

I took one cigarette out of that packet and ignited it and started smoking. The smoke of the cigarette brought me relief. Yes, my heart was paining again, thinking about Preksha's image, but the smoke of the cigarette which passed through my heart, took away all that pain. I kept on smoking and ignoring the phone calls on my phone. I knew it was Vrund, asking me why I wasn't ready. But I was lost, and I didn't want to talk with anyone. After giving several missed calls, he stopped calling me. I was still on the floor, lying down, smoking and thinking about Preksha and the poetic lines which she had written. After smoking several cigarettes, I felt restless, and I slept on the floor itself.

That day I slept until my sleep was broken, due to the morning alarm clock.

Next morning when I woke up, I realized that I had missed the farewell party; plus I had ignored Vrund's calls, so today I assumed that he would be very angry with me.

Location:- College Lecture room.

Time:- 8:00 am

As soon as I entered the class, I started searching for Vrund, because I had to apologize to him for my nerdy behavior, the evening before.

I looked at his place but he wasn't there. I took out my mobile phone and decided to message him on WhatsApp, but he was last seen yesterday, that also before 6:30 pm. I got confused, so I messaged him."I am sorry for yesterday. I couldn't be there. But where are you now?"

The message was sent but there was no reply from him.

"This is strange! He is online 24x7; why is he offline now?" I asked myself.

I sat at my place and Dr Umar started delivering his lecture.

"Have you seen Vrund?" I asked Rahul.

He shook his head in negation.

While Dr Umar was teaching, all were busy on WhatsApp, and I sent a message to everyone asking about Vrund.

I received a common reply, "No."

My curiosity was increasing and I was waiting for the class to get over. As soon as Dr Umar left the class, we all escaped, and as I went out of the class, I decided to make a call to Vrund.

I called him. The ring was going through, but there was no response. I again tried, with the same consequence. This worried me, and so I decided to call Dhruvesh and inquire if everything was alright. He answered my call and I asked,

"Is Vrund there?"

"What?" he asked.

"I am asking if Vrund is there with you," I repeated.

"How can he be there with me? No, he isn't here," he said.

"But you both were at the farewell party last night, right?" I asked.

"Don't annoy me. Neither of you came, I actually saved passes for you both," he said.

"What? Yes, I didn't come, but Vrund?" I asked.

"No, he never came," he said.

I was shocked to hear that. Without saying anything further, I cut the call and rushed to his hostel room.

When I reached there, I found that his room was empty.

"Where is he?" I asked looking up at the skies.

I asked his neighboring roommate, and he reported, "It's very surprising but even I have not seen him since last night."

There were only two possibilities now; either he had bunked college since last night, or he had got lost. But he was a big 21 year old fool, so he couldn't be lost. I assumed that he had bunked college, but he had always informed us and bunked the class. But this was the first time that he hadn't informed anyone.

I again called him, but there was no reply. My tension was increasing so I decided to call Dhruvesh again.

"Before you ask me anything, just listen to me, okay. Vrund is missing, brother, since last night," I said.

He laughed and replied, "No, he can never be lost. He might have bunked the class or gone somewhere else."

"I am not a fool that I don't understand such a thing, but he has been missing since last night. You know we both were supposed to come to the farewell party, but due to some reason, I was unable to come. He had called me then, but I couldn't answer his calls, and after that he has been missing. You try to call him, but he won't answer your call. I think there is some problem," I explained.

"You mean that he called you yesterday around 6:30 pm and you couldn't answer his call, after which he is missing?" he asked.

"Exactly, this is what I am telling you!" I said.

"Hmmm…! There seems to be some confusion. You don't get worried. I am coming there," he said.

"But Dhruvesh, you have been suspended from here. You won't be allowed inside the science faculty," I said.

"Don't underestimate the power of my new look. No one has recognized me yet; don't worry, I am coming soon," he said and cut the call.

Meanwhile I again made attempts to call Vrund, but he didn't answer. I waited for Dhruvesh to come and investigate the issue.

I was waiting for him at the college gate, because I feared that Vrajen Kaka would catch him. After a few minutes I saw him entering the college gate. Vrajen Kaka stopped him and asked, "Wait, outsiders are not allowed."

Dhruvesh saw me and indicated that I should tackle Vrajen Kaka. So I interrupted and said, "Kaka, he is my friend. Allow him to come inside."

"Friend?" asked Kaka. "Till now you had no friend and then suddenly what happened?" he asked.

"You know I told you about my one very special friend? This is the guy about whom I was talking," I said.

"Yah, so is he that guy who hacks into everyone's Facebook account?" Kaka asked.

"Excuse me?" said Dhruvesh with excitement.

"Wait a second. I am very familiar with this voice," said Kaka.

I signalled to Dhruvesh indicating that he should stop arguing.

"Leave it, Kaka; it might be hallucinations," I said.

"Which nation?" Kaka asked innocently.

Dhruvesh started laughing silently, as even I laughed at such a question. Then I recovered and said, "Not any nations, Kaka! I said hallucinations."

"Yah, so what is the meaning of that word – ha-lo-cen-ation?" said Kaka.

Dhruvesh was at the verge of bursting into a peal of laughter. He interrupted and said, "It's not 'halo'; we aren't doing *garba* here. It's hallucination."

Vrajen Kaka joined his hands and said, "Get in or get lost."

"We prefer to get in," said Dhruvesh.

Vrajen Kaka glanced at him with a suspicious look and said, "Before going, at least tell me the meaning of that word."

"Actually Kaka, we are in a hurry. You can Google it, and then if you don't understand, my friend will explain it to you with examples. He is very good at explaining," I said, pointing towards Dhruvesh.

Dhruvesh responded in a soft tone, "That's why I was suspended."

Before Kaka could say anything, we escaped.

"Now first of all, take out your fake disguise," I said.

"No, I will be caught," he said.

"There is no one here and even if anyone saw you, they won't tell sir, because all love you here," I said.

Then he saw the hostel building and got nostalgic and said,

"I miss you guys and this place. You know, my new faculty has everything. There is freedom, fashion, good food and most importantly, beautiful girls, but those things were wonderful for only a few days. I miss those daily fights at the canteen. At my place there is no issue to fight over. Though it was torture when I stayed here, still there was a life because we had unity; but at my new place, though there isn't any torture, there isn't any unity either."

"I told you not to argue, but you...," I said, cutting off the matter.

"Well, let me get to the point. Vrund is missing," I said.

"Tell me everything in detail first," he said.

Then I revealed how Vrund and I had made a plan to accompany him for the farewell party. I had to tell him the about that secret passage which joined Science and Arts faculty via auditorium.

"But you never told me about the secret passage and you are such a simple guy. Who told you such a big thing?" he asked.

"All questions are not answerable," I said bluntly.

"Good man. You have developed a sort of attitude, which will surely help you to move on from your ex gf," he said.

"Is it necessary to involve her in every matter?" I asked.

"Take me to the secret passage, because that's the only way left to search for Vrund," he said.

"But before I take you there, you will have to give me an assurance!" I said.

"And what is that?" he asked.

"You won't utter a single word to anyone regarding this passage which joins both the faculties," I said, taking an assurance from him.

"All promises cannot be kept," he replied with an attitude.

"Well, any guy can promise, but only a real man can commit, so decide your category," I said smartly.

"You have become smart after the break-up, I must say. Anyway I won't say it to anyone; don't worry." said Dhruvesh.

Break-up! Break-up! Break-up! Why was I hearing this word everywhere?

We both went to the back of the hostel and moved to that part of the grassland where the secret passage lay. The passage was actually very narrow, but quite clear, so that walking became easy. Obviously it was a very old construction, built during the construction of our college, but surprisingly, no student knew about this passage. Heenal was an ex student of this college and she knew about it, but our generation was totally unaware about such a fact. The reason is simple, because in our generation girls are selfie queens and guys are girl watchers!

"Wow, baby, this is heaven!" exclaimed Dhruvesh.

I said in my mind, "Sorry Heenal, I had no other option left with me; my friend is in trouble."

"We must enter the passage now," I said.

"It's a little dark," said Dhruvesh in a low tone.

"I know you people are nuts. You only show useless bravery in front of girls," I said.

"Well that's not bravery, my dear! It's called flirting," he responded.

"Whatever!" I exclaimed.

"Let us switch on the flashlights of our mobile phones," he said.

I took my cell phone out and put on the flash light. I saw that Dhruvesh was stuck in the middle.

"What happened?" I asked angrily.

"My flashlight isn't working," he said.

"Charge your battery properly," I said.

"It's fully charged, Bhavam, but even then, it's not working," he said in a confused tone.

We moved on in the passage, but Vrund wasn't there. It was a relief to see that nothing bad had happened. Now the passage was ending. We were about to reach the back of the auditorium.

But when my flashlight struck at the door of the auditorium, I was shocked, and my mobile phone fell from my hand. Dhruvesh saw something and he lifted up my cell phone and focused the flashlight on the door. We saw the body of a person, lying flat on the ground. We were frightened.

"Who is it?" I asked.

Without any further questions we rushed there. When Dhruvesh turned the body around, it was none other than Vrund. When we saw his face, we both shouted loudly.

"Check his heart beat," instructed Dhruvesh.

I checked it and replied, "Thank God it's beating."

"Well, don't panic, Bhavam! We have just saved him. Let's take him out of here," he said.

We both lifted him carefully and took him out of the passage. We entered the auditorium but luckily it was empty. When we came out of the auditorium we shouted for help, and the boys, who were sitting leisurely, approached to help. Immediately an ambulance was called and Vrund was shifted to the nearby hospital.

Location:- Maharaja Sayajirao hospital.
Time:- 11:30 am

"Doctor, is he alright now?" I asked.

Doctor looked at us with a doubt and asked, "What relation do you hold with the patient?"

"We are his friends," I replied.

"And what about the family?" asked the Doctor.

Dhruvesh looked at me and replied, "I guess they are on the way."

"Actually the patient is injured due to a minor injury in the brain, but there is no damage at all. He will be well within a few days. Just try to console him and take care of him," said the doctor and left.

When I looked inside the room where Vrund was kept, I felt guilty and said, "This is all because of me. Why did I not receive his calls?"

Dhruvesh consoled me saying, "What has happened has happened; now think about him."

"What shall we do?" I asked.

"I am posting an update on my Facebook wall to pray for Vrund's recovery," said Dhruvesh.

"That's actually a good idea. I too will do that," I said.

We posted his image with a caption –

"Get well soon, brother, you are a fighter. Never give up."

As soon as the post was posted on Dhruvesh's wall, he started receiving calls from common friends, who were friends with Vrund.

Within no time, the hospital was crowded with the well wishers of Vrund. On seeing this, the local nurse became angry and shouted at us saying, "Get lost, you creeps."

I wanted Vrund to see this. He always objected to Instagram and believed that he had fewer number of followers than other people, but he was wrong. I clicked a picture from my camera of those people who were trying to meet Vrund, but were stopped by the nurse.

Suddenly an innocent girl broke the queue and rushed inside the room. Who was she?

To stop her from going inside, I went near her and said, "Excuse me, whom do you want to meet?"

"Tell me where Vrund is?" she asked.

"But who are you?" I asked.

"Please let me go in, I beg you," she said and started crying.

"Hey, please don't cry. He is inside and he is well, but the doctor has said not to disturb him," I said.

Without listening to me further, she went inside the ward where Vrund was lying with a saline drip attached to his body. The girl fell on her knees and started crying, putting her head on the bed.

"Look, look, look," said Dhruvesh.

"Who is she?" I asked.

"Nishu Joshi."

"How do you know her?" I asked.

"Yes, she is one of Vrund's crushes, and apart from that, his very close friend," said Dhruvesh.

"Are you mad? She is crying for him," I said.

"So what?" he asked. "One friend can cry for another friend," he added.

"Look closely. This girl loves Vrund," I said.

"No girl can love him, because he isn't a man," said Dhruvesh.

"Don't say that. If she can shed tears for you, she definitely considers you a man," I said.

"But no! Nishu is very beautiful; she cannot love Vrund," said Dhruvesh.

"My friend, the love which you speak of, is only based on physical attraction but the love which I see is on the basis of the attraction of the soul. Her soul is attracted to Vrund," I said.

"Enough! I have earlier told you that I am a very naked person. I don't understand this theory of yours, so keep it with you. I just know one fact. That beautiful girl deserves the best guy in terms of looks."

"When did I say that I disagree with your thinking? I support you. My own girlfriend left me just because I wasn't the best. I wish I were like you," I said.

"Preksha! She is a real beauty," said Dhruvesh.

I didn't say anything.

Suddenly Dhruvesh said, "But now enough is enough! I want a girlfriend as well."

"What has happened to you suddenly?" I asked.

"Yaar… I feel jealous now. You had Preksha, this Nishu is with Vrund and what about me?" he objected.

"You were interested in Vish, but I tell you she is not your type," I said.

"How can you say so?" he asked.

"The same explanation, which you gave me about attraction a few minutes ago, applies to you also," I said.

"But I like Vish and she is your neighbor; please do something," he pleaded.

"I am trying. Once she answers my message, we will see," I said.

"I will be waiting!" he exclaimed.

"Are you serious?" I asked.

"Yes! Why?" he asked.

"A guy like you will also wait for a girl? Something is surely wrong with me. Are you saying this?" I again asked.

"Don't be so much surprised. I know Vish is exactly opposite to me, but what's wrong in trying," he said.

"You are very good at changing your colors," I said.

He gave me that creepy smile. Meanwhile I saw Nishu coming out from the ward.

Dhruvesh approached her and said, "Don't worry, he will be all right."

She nodded. I was standing beside him and stared at Nishu but said nothing. She felt odd and asked Dhruvesh, "Why is he here?"

I shifted my eyes from her and said, "I am very sorry to have stopped you. I didn't know that you are his very good friend. My name is Bhavam, obviously Vrund's friend."

"Come on, Nishu, Vrund isn't your boyfriend; so don't cry," said Dhruvesh.

"You better improve your thinking, Dhruvesh," said Nishu.

"Ignore him; he is like that only," I said, and she smiled.

"Whatever!" he said. "Well, Bhavam, you accompany Nishu downstairs. I will settle these idiots who are still crowding around and then join you both," said Dhruvesh.

I was shocked. I even glared at Dhruvesh but, in return, he winked at me. Yes, in the past I had had lots of experience talking with girls, but everything was ruined after the break-up. So it was really a tense situation for me.

We both began to walk. Nishu still had tears in her eyes, and looking at her, I asked, "So much of emotion for one single guy?"

"I never show it to him when he is in front of me, because he is very flirty," she replied.

"So what do you do?" I asked.

"Bhavam, you seriously don't know me?" she asked.

"You even know my name, but I have never seen you before," I said.

"You are so innocent. I have been in your class for the last four years, doing textile engineering at KSU," she said.

"Oops… I am sorry," I said with shock and disbelief. How could I tell her that I had seen no other girl since Preksha had left me?

"You don't need to be." she replied.

"So what are your future plans?" I asked.

"I don't know. I just want a graduation certificate from this college. My father has a textile shop, so probably I will join him," she said.

"Good." I replied.

"What are your plans?" she asked.

"Wish I knew my plans. But yes, I too want a degree and a good job through campus selection, but that's not so easy," I said.

She chuckled and said, "Yes, nothing's easy."

In return I smiled.

After a 35 seconds silence, she asked me, "Bhavam, can I ask you something?"

"Yes," I said with excitement because, for the first time ever after my breakup, a girl wanted to ask me something.

"The whole college knows your story," she said.

"Which story?" I asked.

"About you and your ex-girlfriend," she said.

I didn't say anything.

"I am sorry, but you know people just say those things. I have heard them and so I told you," she said.

"It's all right," I said, with a smile on my face. "People want an issue, so they made a story from our separation. Some told me a different story, others told her a different story. That goes on and will always do," I said.

"Can I take the liberty to say one more thing?" she asked.

"Sure, Nishu. Don't be so hesitant," I said.

"When a guy is suffering from a phase of breakup, he is noticed by the girls who belong to his society. Initially the girls think that the suffering guy is a shit, but then, as time passes, slowly and gradually, they check out that guy more suspiciously. Girls do notice if that guy has made another girlfriend after his break-up or not. Girls even notice how that suffering guy looks at other girls, after that particular girl left him and, trust me, we have watched you. You never looked at any of the girls in our class. So loyal you were even after your break-up. The whole class might not talk with you. But there isn't a single girl on the bench, who is not dying to chat with you, because good girls prefer decent guys like you. It is just that you have to make an attempt," she said with encouragement in her eyes.

This brought a big smile on my face.

"Can't you explain this to Dhruvesh and Vrund?" I pleaded.

"Dhruvesh and Vrund are totally different personalities. Don't compare yourself with them. They can only be the crush of some girl and that also, for a limited time during class hours. But a guy with ethics like you is the dream of every girl, a dream she sees when she wakes up early in the morning and late in the night, when she goes to sleep," she said.

"I am not used to so much of praise and appreciation, but thanks," I said with my eyes down.

"You are underestimating yourself. Don't do that. And don't take me in the wrong sense. I only talk with good guys and you are one of them," she said.

"You have asked me a question; now can I also ask you the same? But please don't lie," I said.

"Sure, I will try my best," she said with a smile.

"Tell me the truth, Nishu. Do you like Vrund?" I asked.

"Oh! That's a very tough and personal question; that's cheating!" she exclaimed.

"I won't force you to answer, but I saw that you were crying for him," I said.

"What did you see?" she asked me.

"Nothing but some extra emotions for Vrund," I said.

"Look there's nothing like that," she said.

"You can lie to yourself, but not to me," I said.

"Once he had a chance, but he wasted it, and I don't believe in second chances," she said.

"I don't know all that, but I know that, when you get a second chance to express your feelings, don't take it as an opportunity; take it as a blessing because it's God's message for you saying, "He/She is made only for you," I explained.

"Wow!" she exclaimed.

"This might be his second life, so don't lose hope," I said.

"You speak so nicely, but it's not in our destiny to be one. He is different, though sweet, and it just cannot take place," she said.

"I write a few good things and this is one of them.

When two people are meant to be one, no power can separate them.

When two people want to stay one, no distractions can separate them.

When two people want to get separated, no truth can save them to be one again." I added, "So, Nishu, everything is based on self belief; whatever you think might just happen,"

"Has someone told you that you speak beautifully?" she asked.

I smiled and said, "I only speak the truth."

We reached the parking area, where Dhruvesh was standing, waiting for us.

"I have been standing here for two minutes," he said.

"So what? When you have a girlfriend you might even have to stand for two days; not a great deal," she replied and went away.

"Isn't she beautiful?" asked Dhruvesh.

"She doesn't like you; she likes Vrund," I said.

"Joke of the millennium!" said Dhruvesh and also went away.

On the other hand, I decided that I should stay at the hospital until Vrund's parents arrived. I again went upstairs and sat outside the ward where he was kept, in the hope that he would recover soon. Meanwhile my cell phone vibrated, indicating that there was a message on it. Generally, I ignored looking at messages, but after this incident, I left my rigidity. It was a message from Facebook messenger and it was sent by none other than Ashwini. I suddenly stood up in excitement, and quickly opened her message. She had written -

> You didn't come for the farewell?

Wow! I was so happy to read that. My days had surely changed for good. She was online, and so I decided to reply to her and chat.

> You missed it.

No, I couldn't.

I know, but how was the farewell? Did you enjoy yourself?

It was just awesome.
Maybe the last get together with my friends.

LOL!
You are talking as if we are all never going to meet again.

After a short time she replied.

Very Funny!
But it was our last meeting before the exam.

After that she went offline.

I was very happy. My time had suddenly taken the reverse mood. In no time, I was communicating with girls. I looked up at the sky and said, "This is my move on now."

As if to increase my happiness, the nurse came out of the ward and said to me, "Are you related to the patient?"

"Yes, he is my best friend," I replied nervously. "Why, what happened?"

"Don't worry; now he is all right. He is conscious now. Go talk to him," said the nurse.

I immediately rushed inside the ward. Vrund looked pathetic with a saline drip attached to his body. He had a minor injury on the head, and his nose was injured. I was curious to know what had actually led to all this? On the other hand, I felt guilty, continuously thinking that this had happened because I didn't pick up his call.

When I went near him, he was lying there restlessly. I looked at him and he looked back at me. I didn't know what to do, so I just stared at him. He gave me an odd look. It was a confusing situation for me, so I preferred to sit on the chair which was kept near his bed.

"I am sorry," I said in an apologetic tone.

Though he listened, he didn't reply.

"Yaar…Vrund, please. I know it was my fault. I should have informed you, but I was so lost that… what should I tell you, forgive me, my friend," I repeated.

"I am not talking to you," he replied firmly.

The doctor entered the room and checked Vrund.

"Wow, kid! You are perfectly fine now. Your friends saved you. You were badly injured, but this guy standing here took full care of you when you were unconscious," said the doctor and left.

"You see, I am not that bad," I said.

"Who said you are bad?" he asked.

"So, yes, you have forgiven me?" I asked.

"Do you have any idea what happened to me?" he asked.

"No, I don't," I said. "Do you wish to tell me now?" I asked.

"That horrible thing will trouble me throughout my life," he said with fear.

"Don't fear; just narrate what happened to you," I said.

"Bhavam, all I can say is stop visiting that passage. it's kick ass," he pleaded.

"But nothing happened to me when I visited it. Also, Dhruvesh and I brought you back from there only," I said.

"It's scary, it's dark and most importantly, it's ALIVE!" he said.

"Alive?" I asked. "Tell me everything in detail," I added.

"When I called you around 6:25 pm, you didn't answer my call. You had told me to stay near that passage and that we would go together, but as you didn't reply to my phone calls, I thought that you were not interested in going for the farewell party. I had no option other than to travel by that passage. It was so dark inside, and something was wrong with my flashlight, so there was no light as well. You know that I am quite afraid of darkness, but even so, I made up my mind and decided to travel through the passage," said Vrund.

"And then?" I asked.

"The passage was small, and the road was narrow, so initially I traveled across half the passage comfortably. Then a point came when I felt something strange. I felt as if someone was following me from behind. I felt a little scared but I continued to move on. Than all of a sudden, I could hear the loud sound of crying of a girl. This really scared me, I started running. But unfortunately, my leg was caught in a trap and I fell down. This is all that I remember and I am very scared even now. So don't ask me any further questions," he said.

"This is strange. I have never felt anything like that ever," I said.

"Please, Bhavam, can we stop discussing it? That crying sound is still ringing in my ears," he pleaded again.

"Okay. Relax, but I need to show you something which will please you," I said.

I took out my cell phone and showed him the picture of those people who had gathered around the hospital to wish him. He was very surprised to see that.

"Don't joke. I can't be so popular," he said.

"If you don't trust me, ask the nurse. She sent everyone out from here. People love you, Vrund, and apart from these people, there is one more person who is mad about you. She is a girl," I said.

"No girl can be mad for me," he said sadly.

"How can you talk like me?" I asked. "If she is mad for you, then she is made for you," I added.

"This incident has changed me. I feel as if I am living my second life. You always talked about God, but with my life back, I feel him now," he said, with a tear in his eyes.

"Don't worry; all will be well. You will be back in your colors soon," I said.

"No, brother, the color of my attitude was an artificial one, and now I will not show any color. I am fed up with all these things," he replied.

"Brother, are you seriously okay?" I asked with a doubt.

"Yes, I am. I am tired of flirting with girls. I have realized that flirting won't do anything. It will just afford me a temporary attraction, and nothing more," he said.

"You need a good rest. We will talk later on," I said and decided to leave.

"Wait!" he said, and I stopped.

"By the way, which girl was mad for me?" he asked.

I smiled and said, "Nishu."

He was shocked to hear that.

"How do you know that?" he asked.

"When you were in an unconscious state, we were all worried about you, but she was the only one who broke the line and entered your ward. Sitting at this very same place, she shed tears over you," I said.

"Do you mean that she cried?" he asked with surprise.

"No, she danced," I said in mock anger. "Obviously shedding tears means crying, yaar," I added.

"But it cannot be possible. First of all, all girls know the fact that I am a flirt. So why should she cry for me?" he asked.

"You have ample time. Do think about this, and when you get an answer, just talk with her," I said and left the ward.

Chapter 7

Location:- My hostel room.

Time:- 9:00 pm

After having lunch at the canteen, I was busy checking my Facebook profile. I saw that Preksha was online, and my heart wanted to chat with her, but my mind said, “No!” I had not chatted with her for the last four years, although it was strange that she had accepted my friend request. I clicked on her chat icon and her chat box opened

HEYO

HI

How are you doing?

Enjoying my life.

It rocks. No tension at all.

Yes, being single is good.

Obviously

Nice.

So have you moved on?

Hmmm…

Cool

I gtg….
Ttyl
Bye

Bye. TC

Wow! This was my first chat after our breakup. Preksha was in a mood to ignore me. She said that she had to go. In order to show me that, she went offline for a few minutes, but after that, she again came online. She might have even seen me online but I ignored her, and she was also good at ignoring. This made me sad. Enough was enough; now with Preksha online, I wanted a proper reason for our break-up. I again messaged her.

I know that you don't like to talk with me, but I need to ask you some thing. Can I?

Yah

I need a proper reason for our break-up. I know you left me because I couldn't be like your male friends

As soon as she said so, I felt a deep pain inside my heart. When did I not provide her freedom? I had done everything for her, and even then, she thought so. I really felt very bad at her statement.

It isn't about freedom.
You changed your tastes. And maybe I didn't fit in that list

Fuck! How can she be so rude? Instead of a proper comment, she showed me a thumbs up! It was fucking irritating. I really felt ashamed to talk with her. She said I never provided her freedom. Maybe she was right because I used to call her for nothing and text her all the time. I got jealous when she talked or flirted with some other guy. Yes, I was overprotective, but more important than all that, I loved her more than anyone in this world. I wish I could explain to her that real boyfriends would also not do such things. And if she was blabbering about freedom, apart from all these things, then it was really her problem, not mine.

I was still good at composing poems and short stories, and that 'freedom' comment was still in my head, so I posted on my wall –

One day a man asked God, "What's the difference between your love and my love?"

God replied, "Look up, the bird flying in the sky is my love and the bird in the cage is your love."

To vent my anger out, I wrote everything in my diary.

After a few seconds, I received a message on my cell phone. I thought it was Preksha, but it was Ashwini. She wrote –

Hey, beautiful status.

I had a big smile on my face when I saw that message and I was quick to reply.

Thank you so much

Did you write this on your own?

I was not a fool enough to say no, because I was loyal to my ex.

Yes, I read good things, so I can write. 😊

Yah, I saw that on your wall. You are a great poet too. 😉

Oh Tysm!
Did you like the poems?

I love them. 😘 ♥

Wow! I mean, she just used a kiss smiley! And why did my heart beat when she said the word 'love'. I was confused about what to reply!

I am glad you loved it.
😊 😊 😊

She saw this message but didn't reply further and went offline, but she made me happy. I had been so disturbed regarding Preksha's response, but a few messages from Ashwini made my day. That day was the happiest day of my life. I was jumping. I tried to sleep but my eyes refused to close. I just took my phone and saw her profile picture. She looked so innocent and sweet. From her photo itself, I could guess that she was childlike in behavior. Vrund was changing himself, as he wanted to be more decent and now, even I needed to change. I wanted to be a little flirty after being decent for so long.

My worst day was made wonderful by Ashwini. That night, I forgot the incident with Preksha and I just looked at the profile pictures of Ashwini. I came to the conclusion that she was more beautiful than my ex girlfriend. I also looked up at the skies and said with regret, "You are very bad. Why didn't you bring her earlier into my life?"

As always he didn't reply!

Location:- Class room.
Time:- 8:00 am

This time when I entered the class, I decided that I wouldn't keep my eyes down. So, as soon as I entered the class, I shifted my attention towards the girls sitting on the left hand side. Accidentally my eyes shifted to Nishu. She also looked at me and smiled. Wow! It was heaven. I smiled in return. The boys on the first bench were indeed surprised to see that. One of the mates couldn't control himself, and said, "Is this really Bhavam?"

I looked at him and nodded.

"Finally he is spoiled," commented someone.

"I am also a mango, dude. If not used, then surely I will be spoiled one day," I said.

Hearing this, I could hear the chants of "Bhai bhai… Bhai bhai…"

I had a smile on my face for the first time in front of the whole class and the reason for that smile was none other than Ashwini.

Immediately Dr Umar entered the classroom and saw me laughing.

"Boy, I am here," said Dr Umar from behind.

I looked back and said, "Oops, sorry, sir. I never realized that."

"Hope you realize that you have to get good marks in this semester," he continued.

As usual he was going to give a lecture on how to score good marks. He did that at the end of each and every semester. But the students had a remedy for that. They used to insert cotton plugs in their ears and pretend that they were listening to him. I too wanted to do so, but I was late in inserting the cotton plugs. Therefore, Dr Umar saw me inserting them and I was caught.

"What are you inserting in your ears?" he asked me.

I stood up and said, "Cotton plugs, sir."

"I am suffering from cold, so this is protection, sir," I said, fearfully.

"At 43 degree centigrade, you are suffering from cold?" he asked me.

"Sir, my immune system is weak, so my temperature is not in direct proportion to my health," I said.

Hearing this, the boys in the front benches clapped for four seconds until Dr Umar turned to them. But what was next? The boys from the back benches started clapping, so he turned back. Then the front benchers again started clapping. He looked ahead and the same procedure continued behind. He shouted, "Stop clapping. Are you all transgender people?"

Ujjwal, the scholar student in physics raised his finger and said, "Sir, I have a doubt."

"Sir, what does the term 'transgender' mean? I haven't heard about it anywhere in physics, neither in HC Verma's book," said Ujjwal.

"It's not related to Physics. Please sit down," shouted Dr Umar and Ujjwal got scared.

Rahul from the first bench consoled Ujjwal, saying, "Don't worry, I will tell you everything in detail about it, once the class gets over."

"I am only interested if it has some physics in it," said Ujjwal.

"Fuck off then! *Ghanta physics padhega tu!*" said Rahul in an audible tone.

"Mr Rahul Ravichandran, you are not allowed to use abusive words in class," said Dr Umar.

"But sir, everything has limits. Ujjwal is dying to hear the meaning of the word 'transgender'," smirked Rahul.

After he said that, all the students also shouted, "Explain… explain… explain…!"

It was such an embarrassing situation for Dr Umar. He was left with no option but to explain the meaning of the word.

"See," said Dr. Umar.

"Saw!" commented Rahul from the first bench, and all laughed.

"The characteristic of unusual clapping, which some people like Mr Rahul Ravichandran showed, a few minutes back, proves the behavior of a transgender in his mind. I cannot comment anything about his blood," said Dr. Umar.

The whole class started laughing at Rahul after hearing the hilarious response from Dr Umar.

Chants of "Rahul transgender… Rahul *chakka*," started making waves in the class.

This made Rahul angry, but he maintained his cool and said, "Objection, sir!"

"A few years back, you had created a robot which could walk and do actions; so if I change the 'for loop' of your program, and if that robot starts clapping, will it become a transgender?" asked Rahul.

OMG! What a response from Rahul! The whole class literally whistled at it.

Instead of getting angry, Dr Umar smiled this time, and asked, "Does a dumb boy like you even know how to rotate a 'for loop' in ANSCII C?"

"Sir, we can even rotate the earth; 'for loop' is such a small thing," responded Rahul.

"Bhai bhai...bhai bhai...!" were the chants coming from behind.

"Sit down, you idiot!" said Dr Umar

"So now, we will continue with our semiconductors...!" said Dr Umar, and elaborated the given topic in detail. I had to get good marks, so this time I paid attention to what he was saying. Not only me, but the whole class paid attention to his lecture.

Exams were approaching, and so, this time, no students were operating mobiles in the class. To my surprise, I even found some students mugging up complex equations of Boiler's Theory. My God!

Just a few days before the examinations, all the students had turned serious.

They were trying to do the similar thing which I did when they used mobiles. But this time, I decided to use my mobile phone in class. I did nothing, but looked at the profiles of people.

After a while, even I got worried at the sincerity of people, so I quickly turned off my mobile phone and started doing what all the students were doing.

(* When someone studies in front of your eyes, you realize that if you don't study, you will be left behind, especially in the case of engineers.)

Minutes after the class was over, Nishu approached me and asked, "Is he well now?"

"Yes, he is conscious now," I said.

"Thank God!" she exclaimed in relief.

"I told him that you were crying for him," I said.

"He will never believe that. Instead he will tell you that no girl would cry for him," she said.

I was baffled to hear that. "How could you guess that?" I asked.

"Very simple. Because he is honest enough to agree that he is flirty, but he is also too innocent to accept that someone can care about him," said Nishu.

"What if he stops flirting?" I asked her.

"He is the dark cloud which we see before the rains. There can't be a rain without dark clouds. In the same way, Vrund cannot exist without flirting," she said.

"Are you planning to go and meet him?" I asked.

"Absolutely not. Because he doesn't even have the courtesy to make a phone call, or update the status that he is alright now. Plus exams are also coming, and so I have no time to waste over him," she replied.

"Why do you ignore your feelings, Nishu?" I asked.

"You ask too many questions. If it was someone else in your place, I would have said that I am not answerable to anyone," she replied.

"Listen, before going, at least give me your number, so that we can talk," I said.

"Don't worry, I have your number," she said and left.

What? How did she have my number? Because I remember that I hadn't shared my number with anyone, except a few boys in my class.

I didn't mind sharing my number with a girl; so the source from where she got my number was definitely not important!

Location:- Kamatibaug
Time:- 10:00 am

A few of my classmates went to their bunking destinations, but I preferred Kamatibaug, as always. Happiness had arrived in my life, since the day I had met Ashwini in the rains.

Heenal was upset with me but I really wanted to share my happiness with her. So I just crossed my fingers in the hope that she would be there that day.

I had to change my personality, so I decided to be a bad little boy.

Earlier I had created a group named 'BUDDIES' on my WhatsApp and added my friends to it. It was a group specially created to share only non vegetarian messages. As the days passed, the group became popular and more and more members were added to it.

While I was writing in my diary, I felt Preksha's presence around me. I looked around but she wasn't there. My heart started beating, indicating her arrival, but I couldn't see her.

"Why is it happening again?" I asked, looking up at the skies.

There was no reply. Then again I begin to write, and this time my hands were shivering slightly.

"What the fuck is wrong with me?" I asked to myself.

For a moment when I diverted my attention, I saw Karan.

Karan had been linked with Preksha, before and after our break-up. People used to say that Preksha wanted Karan, and so she left me for him.

So if Karan was here, than surely Preksha would be also there, and, yes, in no time she came into view.

I was seeing her after a long time. She had completely changed her appearance. Earlier she had longer hair, but now she preferred to keep it curly. My Preksha hated to use any makeup, but now she was an expert at it. And to sum up her changed appearance, her plastic earrings had been replaced by a pair in gold.

And me? I was still the same with my hair full of oil.

I decided that enough was enough. I too wanted to change with the flow of time. So after our break-up, I changed my hairstyle to one, which she liked, one that good looking guys sported as well.

Karan looked at me, and indicated to Preksha that I was there in the garden. She looked at me and I looked back at her.

My eyes were full of shame when I glanced at her, but soon after, she ignored me. I don't know why, but it pained my heart.

"That will happen, because you haven't seen her for the last few years. And then when you suddenly see her, such a thing is but natural," said a soft voice from behind.

"I needed you; where were you?" I asked Heenal.

"Leave that. And why are there tears in your eyes?" she asked. "I told you to be strong," she added.

"Look at her. She is ignoring me like hell. What wrong have I done to her? She has such an attitude, one which even enemies don't show to each other," I said.

"Who's that guy with her?" she asked.

I got angry and said, "Go and ask her only."

"Don't get angry, Bhavam. Relax," she said in a low tone.

"How can I relax seeing my ex girlfriend taking selfies with that guy?" I said. "And you don't know that Karan is just…!"

She didn't respond.

"And look, he is holding her waist. Fuck! I can't bear to see it!" I said.

In order to divert my mind, Heenal said, "Well, take out your mobile; we will also take a selfie."

"But you told me that you don't like taking selfies and all," I said.

"I'm doing this for your happiness, idiot!" she said. "Do as I say. You just keep looking at her, and I will take a selfie of us. You should smile like you are the happiest person in the world. Seeing you smile, she will be quite jealous, I bet," she said.

"How can you be so confident that she will be jealous?" I asked.

"Guys get jealous when they see their ex with some other guy. In the same way, a girl gets jealous when she sees her ex smiling and laughing in front of her for no reason," she said.

"But that makes no sense. If she is emotionless about my tears, than how will she be jealous about my smile?" I asked.

"You have the best smile in the world. If I can be jealous of it, then why not her?" she said.

"You are always correct," I said and smiled widely.

"See, she is looking here. Just smile and you take the selfie quickly," she urged.

I clicked the selfie. First ever with any girl, though she was my sister.

Preksha looked at us in a strange manner. Karan was also looked confused.

"Why are they looking at us in that way?" I asked Heenal.

"How do you react when you see an aeroplane swimming under the water? In the same way, we look unique. So they are just jealous. Ignore them," she smiled.

"You are right," I said.

"Always!" she exclaimed.

After Karan and Preksha went, Heenal said, "Listen, don't upload our selfie on Instagram."

"But why?" I asked.

"Because I like to be away from social media. And people will make a joke of you, if you upload this picture. So better don't," she said.

"Why joke? What is so funny in this selfie?" I asked.

"You ask too many questions, dude. Someday a girl will slap you," she said.

"No, she won't slap me. She will just say that she is not answerable to everyone," I said, referring to Nishu.

Heenal laughed on hearing this.

"Tell me something about your personal life," I asked her.

"What do you wish to know?" she asked.

"Tell me the name of the person whom you love the most?" I asked.

She paused for a moment, looked up at the skies and said, "The one whom I love the most is currently not here with me."

"Why? Where is he?" I asked.

"He is not in this cruel world. He is my father," she said, as tears began flowing from her eyes.

"I'm sorry, Heenal, but please stop crying. You are a very kind soul, so your father was surely the best human being. I can tell you one thing. He is seeing you, and he is very happy because you are carrying on the way in which he always wanted," I said.

She said nothing, but just grabbed my right hand, and placed her head on it and closed her eyes.

"Are you okay?" I asked. "Has anyone told you that you look terrible when you cry?" I joked.

"Yes, my boyfriend. I have been waiting for him for a long time. He is committed to me and he will surely come," she said.

"But I don't understand one thing. Why do you prefer to come here to Kamatibaug? I mean, girls of your age do jobs," I asked.

"What are the boys of your age supposed to do during the college hours?" she asked.

"Study, score well, have a girlfriend, and finally, a good job," I said.

"Exactly! And what are you doing currently?" she asked.

"I'm sorry. You've answered my question," I said.

"I tell you one thing. Your life is like a coin; it's in your hands to toss it any way, but be wise to spend it on the correct person, in order to avoid lifelong regret. You shouldn't spend your coin on a wrong person like Preksha," she advised.

"I like a girl, but I cannot forget Preksha. Please help me," I requested her.

"But you won't listen to me," she said.

"I will. I promise!"I said.

"Chatting brought you and Preksha together, now chatting only will take you away from her," she said.

"How?" I asked.

"When you face rudeness from someone continuously, you tend to hate that person or try to cut that person out of your life," she said.

"So what exactly do I need to do?" I asked.

"You have to text her daily on Facebook or whatever and try to communicate with her, even if she ignores you. This is how you will forget her one day," she said.

Meanwhile a text message came on my cell phone. It was Nishu.

Bhavam…
I'm at the hospital.
Vrund is getting discharged today.
Come soon

Wow that's great!
I'm coming soon.

I looked up and said, "Well, Heenal, I need to go now. My friend is getting discharged today from the hospital."

Before I could complete, she had left. Why did she leave me every time without saying goodbye? I think she felt bad because I had diverted my attention to the mobile phone. Nevertheless, I had no option, except to apologize, the next time I met her.

Location:- Sayajirao Hospital
Time:- 2:00 pm

I entered the ward. Vrund was looking perfectly fit.

"There you are, fully recovered," I said in a pleasant tone.

"Nothing can happen to me and I will attend college from tomorrow," responded Vrund.

"But you need rest," said Nishu.

"Exams are coming. If I don't study now, I will surely fail this semester, and my parents will throw me out of the house," said Vrund.

"Looking quite dull, Bhavam?" asked Nishu.

"No, nothing like that!" I said.

"There is something! What happened?" asked Vrund.

"I saw that Karan with her," I said.

"With whom?" asked Vrund.

"Preksha!" I exclaimed.

Nishu came towards me and said, "Why are you still not over her?"

"I will be over her soon," I said.

"No, you won't. Understand, Bhavam, we girls don't look back, once we have left you. So it's useless waiting for her," she said.

"She is correct, Bhavam. Why do you still think about a girl who doesn't even give a fuck to what you say?" said Vrund.

"Look here, Bhavam. You can't waste your time running after her. Four years of waiting for a girl can only be done by a very innocent person. So you deserve the best girl, not a bitch like her," said Nishu.

I felt bad when Nishu referred to her as a bitch.

"Someone suggested that if I try to talk to her, she will ignore me and, in this way, I will forget her," I said.

"You can try that, but you cannot forget her, unless and until you get a new girlfriend," said Vrund.

"Excuse me. What do you mean by the term 'new girlfriend'?" asked Nishu looking towards Vrund.

"New girlfriend means new partner. I mean the perfect girl who can understand him," said Vrund.

"You don't worry, Nishu; he is trying to be a good guy," I smiled.

"Some things can never change," she said. "If he becomes a good guy, it will be an insult to himself only," she added.

"Girls never change," said Vrund.

"What? We never change. Did you even have the courtesy to inform me or anyone that you are all right now?" asked Nishu angrily.

"I'm sorry about that," said Vrund.

"It's useless talking to you, Vrund," snapped Nishu and left

"She needs a break," I commented.

"Break?" asked Vrund as I left the ward.

Chapter 8

Heenal advised me to talk to Preksha. What would I talk with her? I would say HI.

She would reply the same. Than I would ask how she was, and she would reply that she was well. I would then say "Okay!" and after that, she wouldn't reply.

People say that if a guy cannot speak after the work "Okay!" he is boring. So girls generally avoid talking with such guys.

"So maybe I was not her type," I muttered to myself.

"Or maybe she deserves much better than you," replied my conscience.

Finally I decided to make up my mind to chat with Preksha again, to face her rude behavior, of course.

> LOL!
> You are talking as if we are all never going to meet again.

She saw my message, but didn't reply.

That was the first step of ignoring, for which, of course, I was mentally prepared. Although than I was pleased to see that sight which my eyes read – 'Preksha is typing….' on her chat dialogue box.

> Hi

I wanted to avoid formal talk.

Actually I have a doubt.
On Instagram, when I upload my picture, it automatically gets cropped and so I am not able to upload my full picture. So, any solution for it, since I am not adept as you in such things?

Download NO CROP from play store.

Will it do?

Yah

"Please! At least tell her not to do that thumbs up symbol. It irritates me," I said to myself.

"And presently she is irritated by you," replied my conscience from deep inside my mind

I thought that was enough for the time being. I was not used to formal chats with Preksha. Those late night chats had certainly been the best part of our relationship. It brought us close but then, she just went away. How could she?

My mind was very quick in replying to all such questions now, because when you are left with no reason after a break-up, your mind starts to assume anything, randomly.

However, a green colored dot in front of Preksha's name was a sight which I hated, but to replace my sadness, she had come. I became happy, when I saw Ashwini online.

Hey. Are you from South Gujarat side? I am from there too.

Really? Where?

I am from Navsari, just a few kilometers away from your Valsad.

Wow that's great. So we are neighbors. However I am not from proper Valsad. I am from Khargam, which is a village in rural Valsad.

Oh!
So how much time have you spent here?

I will be here till my studies get over and after that I will again go back.

But I tell you. We people from south Gujarat have more understanding in terms of relationship than people over here.

Awww....Thanks
And you are also a good natured person.

Yes. Let me tell you one thing. You have a very beautiful nature. Such an enterprising person you are!

Hehe
I don't think so.
Anyways, thanks

Yah I agree, but people over here also not bad. I love everyone regardless of the place. When people are nice, there's no issue.

No yaar, seriously. You are a very good natured person.

Thanks, Ashwini

After three years, a little self respect appeared when a girl said that I was 'a very good natured person'. Why were my eyes wet after hearing this? Why was my throat indicating a special feeling? That sweet curl of love was slowly beating in my heart again.

My conscience whispered, "Stop Bhavam, stop. Not again."

It was now time to sleep. What a day! Nothing special. First, my heart was hurled down due to that thumbs up symbol smiley by Preksha. But then, the same heart began beating due to a special kisses smiley posted by the most innocent girl on the plant.

I was on my bed, I took my cell phone and opened Ashwini's profile and again randomly started looking at her pictures.

It might look foolish, but I even kissed her photo on my mobile screen. Anyone could make a happy person laugh, but she was the one who produced a smile on the face of a person completely broken from inside, due to the snooty behavior of his ex girlfriend.

"Next time when I chat with her, I will ask for her mobile number," I said to myself.

"She will give it!" replied my conscience.

"And what if she doesn't? Won't she feel awkward?" I asked myself.

"Maybe. But it's the 21st century. Learn from your ex," replied my conscience.

My heart wanted to send Ashwini another message before I went for sleep, so I wrote -

> Anyone can evoke laughter out of a happy person. But you have the art to produce smiles from a broken heart. Thanks!

No sooner was I was preparing to go to sleep, than another message came on my cell phone. However, it was from Nishu this time.

> Still not slept, Bhavam?

> NO.
> I want to sleep but somehow it's not working today.

> Oh go to sleep, otherwise just like the others, you will also feel restless in class tomorrow.

I will sleep soon. Actually I have the habit of sleeping late and getting up early.
But why are you not sleeping?

Same problem, yaar….
Even I want to sleep but somehow can't.

LOL
I guess you are waiting for SOMEONE's goodnight message!

Shut up, Bhavam!
I will kill you if you utter his name.

I know him more than you. He will never ever come to say good night to you on FB.
So go to sleep.

Who told you that I am waiting for him?
You guys are always very unpredictable.

Yes, we are unpredictable but not always, only sometimes.

Whatever.

Now I was sure that she was waiting for Vrund. I wanted to be a genie between them. So I called Vrund.

"Hello…?" he said in a lazy voice.

"BC… come online fast!" I urged him.

"But why?" he asked.

"You see I don't give anyone reasons, so do as I say!" I snapped.

"The last time I followed you without any reason, I woke up in the hospital," he muttered.

I laughed and said, "Don't worry, this isn't that bad; come online fast."

"But Bhavam, I am studying," he said.

"Just for a few minutes. Come online. Please!" I requested.

"When you speak so politely, I have to come," he said.

I knew Nishu would be happy to see Vrund online, and that too only to say good night.

Sometimes, though many people say 'goodnight' in your life, you always wait for that one special person to come and say 'goodnight'. Only after that you are able to get a sound peaceful sleep.

The same goes for the word 'Bye'. Sometimes you don't want to hear the word 'Bye' from a very special person, but destiny creates such a situation when you get separated from each other, and that too without saying the word 'Bye.'

I still remember that day; 24th January it was. The last day of my relationship with Preksha.

After she broke up with me, I decided to leave that tuition which she also attended. As that day was the last one, before going permanently away from her, I approached her and said, "I am going. We won't meet ever again."

She was standing along with that Karan. She looked at me and said with a piteous face, "Don't go, please."

I just looked down and shook my head. I turned and started going down the staircase. I closed my eyes because I thought that she would run down and hug me from behind, and tell me not to go away from her, but she never looked back.

When I turned back to look at her for the final time, she was busy enjoying herself with her friends. My soul cried that day when I came to know that Karan had given Preksha a break-up party. However, it was immaterial that I didn't even drink water that day.

All those things again started rolling in front of my eyes. A packet of cigarettes was now the only choice to stop my agony. I lit a cigarette again, without thinking of anything, and finally I got the deep sleep which only allowed me to get up the following day.

Location:- College class room.
Time:- 8:00 am

The next morning, when I entered the class, my eyes were red. After a long time, I was seeing Vrund in the class. The place next to his was vacant, so I decided to sit beside him.

"So how was your 'goodnight' last night?" I asked.

"I never thought if any girl could be patient enough to wait for a flirty guy," replied Vrund.

"You and Dhruvesh never believe in emotions, but they are very important in one's life," I said.

He said, "I agree with you. Can I ask you something?"

I nodded, looking at him.

"If a guy like me can change, then why not your ex-girlfriend?" he asked.

Ex-girlfriend! Ex-girlfriend! Ex-girlfriend! Was that the only identity left?

"She has already changed, but her change is negative and yours is positive," I said.

"I feel for you because you hardly smile, but now it's good that you share a little laughter with us," he said.

I felt happy because, after a long time, someone cared about my smile, although he wasn't my best friend. But his statement indicated that he was even more than a 'best friend'.

"Let her do whatever she wants. I will be always good to the good, but I will never be bad to the bad," I said.

"Why so?" he asked.

"Because you can produce a fire by rubbing two stones, but you can't wash mud with mud," I concluded.

After the class…

"Hey, Bhavam, stop!" said someone from behind.

It was Nishu. She approached me and remarked, "I need to ask you something!"

Strange! Why were they all taking permission from me to ask me something?

"I know last night you told Vrund to come online," she said.

"So what's wrong in that?" I asked.

"Everything is wrong. He didn't come on his own and I wanted that," she said.

"He cares for you. That's why he came online, despite everything else," I said.

"Care? Don't make me laugh!"she said.

"Google says - Dear girls, if a guy can pause his video game just to reply to your text messages, then he truly loves you!" and

I say, "Dear girls, if a guy can come online for you again, then he truly cares about you," I said and left.

She was stunned by my response. Yes, in the past, I had the talent to make people speechless and I just tried it again today.

Location:- Kamatibaug

Last time when I was here, I saw Preksha with Karan taking selfies together. Preksha had become quite a famous personality on social media. Of course I was not jealous about that. She was beautiful and beauty should be praised.

I wanted to share my happiness with Heenal, so I was looking around for her. We always sat at the same place and the same bench in the garden. I liked that place. Though it was quite deep inside the garden still it was a very pleasant.

One thing was very surprising to me. When I sat alone waiting for her, no one noticed me, but when she came and we started talking and laughing, then suddenly, people would start looking at us. Initially I thought it was because of my dressing sense, but I checked it. It was perfectly all right. On the other hand, Heenal also looked damn beautiful and simple. So there was no question about our looks. So I don't know why everyone looked at us that way.

"What are you thinking?" said Heenal from behind.

"I have one question, actually two," I said.

"Shoot!" she said.

"When every time you come, why don't I sense your presence?" I asked.

"It's because your mind is always lost. So how will you feel my presence?" she said.

I smiled and said, "Yes, these days even my subconscious mind is working."

"Shut up!" she exclaimed. "But you look happy today," she said.

"Of course I am!" I said and narrated the whole chat which I had had with Ashwini.

"And when she said I am "a good natured person", it really felt special, Heenal," I said with a broad smile on my face.

"Finally happiness has arrived in your life," she said.

"After so much pain," I said.

"Everyone wants happiness, nobody wants pain. But there can't be a rainbow without a little rain!" she said.

"Wow!" I exclaimed.

"I am little confused. These days when they post any picture on Instagram or Facebook, they write PC and then someone's name. I can't understand what that is," she said.

I laughed and said, "PC stands for Picture Courtesy. So they write the name of the person who has clicked that particular picture."

"Oh, I see," she said.

"Why? You said that you don't use Instagram and Facebook?" I said.

"But I see others using it and I so asked you," she said.

"All right!" I said.

"But I tell you one thing, Bhavam. It is very tough to know if the Picture Courtesy could really be the real courtesy behind that picture," she said.

I actually didn't understand what she wanted to say, but I nodded.

"So you're talking with Preksha, right?" she asked.

"All the time she is busy ignoring me; wish I could also do the same," I said in a low tone.

"I am very inspired by Gautam Buddha. Do you know who he is?" she asked.

"Of course. The Buddhists worship him as God," I said.

"He says - Show respect to those who don't deserve it. Not as a reflection of their character, but as a reflection of yours," she said. "So don't try to be rude with her, because if you do that, there will be no difference between you and her," she added.

Her knowledge was enlightening me. I asked her, "Why don't you become a motivational speaker?"

She smiled and said with piteous eyes, "What to do? No one else over here listens to me."

Her eyes were slowly becoming watery. I placed my hand on her lap and said, "Hey, don't think so. See, I am talking with you and I will always talk with you. It's a different fact that you don't share your phone number. But whenever I come here, I will talk with you."

"Can you promise that?" she asked.

"I don't promise. I just commit," I said.

"But I can't be here every time. When I shall get my destiny, I will leave this place," she said.

"What is your destiny?" I said.

"Neel and his dream!" she said in a soft voice.

"And who is he?" I asked.

"The person whom I love. I am waiting for him; I told you idiot, but you forgot!" she said.

"Are you sure that he will come?" I asked.

"He has not promised me, like you, but he has committed," she said.

"I will pray that you meet your Neel soon, and once you meet him, we all will meet together, but please, not in this place," I said.

"Why, what's wrong here?" she asked.

"I need a change of location," I said.

"Why are we thinking too much about the future? Just stay in the present," she said bluntly.

"Okay, but say it nicely, not rudely like Preksha," I said.

"I am sorry," she said.

"Actually I have written a poem dedicated to you," I said.

"Oh really? Please I want to listen to that," she said with eagerness.

I took out my diary and read –

"The day you met,
My eyes lit up!
The day you met,
I again had hope!
The day you met,
I again laughed!
The day you met,
My smile, I get!"

She said, "Awww... if you say it to any girl, she will definitely fall for you."

"But this is only for you. I don't know how to thank you. You are the only reason why I am smiling today. I wish that someday, when I have money, I will be able to give you some wonderful gifts," I said.

"I don't want anything. You just remain committed to that commitment which you made in front of me," she said.

I smiled and she did the same.

Location:- Hostel Canteen.
Time:- 7:30 pm

"Finally some good news, folks," said Vrund.

As soon as everyone heard that, they all came running.

"The ban has been removed," said Vrund.

On hearing that, everyone shouted like hell.

"Are you serious? But which ban are you talking about and who told you?" asked Ujjwal Makwana.

"Makwana, will you keep your mouth shut? Let him talk," said Rahul Ravichandran.

"Relax, I will tell you everything. As exams are approaching, a new rule has been made that students will be allowed to go out of the campus, but only to the library. Anyway, we guys are expert enough to manage to escape the campus once the gates are opened," grinned Vrund.

Chats of "Bhai… Bhai…!" started humming over the entire canteen.

Everyone decided to leave the hostel campus without having their dinner. They would enjoy outside food today as a part of the celebration.

"You are coming with me, Bhavam," said Vrund.

"No, I can't. I don't like useless 'rakkhadpatti'," I said.

"What the fuck is rakkhadpatti?" asked Rahul Ravichandran from behind.

"It's a Gujarati word for roaming without an aim." I said.

"Oh! I see!" said Rahul.

Ujjwal laughed at him and said, "He doesn't even know that."

"Vada, what do you call it in south India?" asked Ujjwal to Rahul.

Rahul was from south India and Vada Sambhar is the traditional dish of Tamil Nadu. So these guys mostly addressed Rahul as Vada or Sambhar.

"Why, BC? Are you going to do a PhD on it?" asked Rahul

Everyone started laughing at Ujjwal. It's always fun when a scholar of the class is trolled by someone's witty sense of humor.

It was easy to escape the college campus, by giving a false reason to go to the library.

"Are the girls coming?" I asked.

"Hmm...! This Bal Brahmachari is becoming Emraan Hashmi," said Rahul.

"Yah, all the girls are coming, don't worry. It is going to be an awesome night out, guys. That too after a long time," said Vrund.

"But where are we going?" I asked.

"Yoli!" said Vrund.

"What is that?" Rahul asked.

"It's an ice cream shop, Sambhar. It is the only shop which serves ice cream at this time," answered Vrund.

Vrund came towards me and said in a low tone, "Nishu is also coming."

"Great!" I said.

"And Ashwini too!" he said.

I stopped for a moment and asked, "Are you serious? How did you inform her?"

"Nishu did it. I told her that you like one girl from the architecture faculty and see the luck; some girls from the other faculties are also coming. It's going to be a rocking night," said Vrund.

"But you should have told me earlier that Ashwini is also coming," I said.

"Why?" he asked. "You wanted to gift her something?" he asked.

"Shut up!" I exclaimed. "I am not properly dressed!" I added.

He laughed and pointed towards the other guys, and said, "Look at these animals and then see your clothing. It's far better than that of the others. Rahul, Ujjwal and others, including me, are in our night dress. So you look quite decent."

"Girls like the guys who dress decently and are clean shaven," I said.

"That's not always true, brother," he argued.

"Why?" I asked.

"Some girls really like beards," he said.

"No, never." They like clean shaven guys. I am sure about it!" I said.

"Can you prove it?" he asked.

I nodded as we reached Yoli and said, "Tomorrow morning. Not now."

Wow! For the first time ever I allowed my eyes to have a glimpse of the girls. They were standing in groups outside Yoli.

"Why are they standing in groups and not together?" I asked Vrund.

"You don't know, dude? There is more internal competition among the girls," said Vrund.

"Competition for what?" I asked.

"Who looks prettier and who doesn't!" he said.

"But from here, they all look beautiful," I said, giving a high five to Vrund.

"They are without make up," said Rahul.

"Have you inserted an X ray in your eyes?" commented Ujjwal from behind.

"Vee… Makwana. You won't understand! Studying physics continuously has uprooted your manhood," said Rahul.

"If they can look beautiful without makeup, why do even they apply it?" I asked.

"I will ask Nishu," said Vrund, as we approached the girls. Finally we approached Yoli where, perhaps, the whole of Technology, as well as the other faculties had gathered. Seriously, the owner of Yoli was going to have a good deal tonight.

I looked at every girl there, but I couldn't find Ashwini. Actually I never searched for her. I was just searching for vehicle number 4651. It had a huge impact on my mind.

Vrund called me saying, "Bhavam, come here!"

I went there. He was standing with Nishu as well as the other girls.

"Now ask her what you were asking me," he said.

My God! I was too shy to communicate with them. I was comfortable with Nishu, but the other girls, never!

"Why do you create an embarrassing situation for me?" I asked Vrund.

Nishu interrupted and said with a smile, "Don't trouble him, Vrund. He is here for a different purpose."

And the girls laughed, as I shared a shy smile. Of course they were hinting at my new crush, Ashwini.

"But how did they know about it?" I asked to myself.

"It's a college, Bhavam. Where a rumor spreads faster than Hydrogen gas!" replied my conscience.

I knew that Vrund had spread this thing. I looked at him angrily. He wanted to pull my leg today, so he said, "But please, Bhavam. Let them know your question."

Finally I broke my silence and said, "When we were coming here, all of you looked beautiful from the distance. So I asked him that if girls can look beautiful without makeup, then why do they apply it on their faces?"

All the girls, including Nishu, laughed at my question and said, "Awww…!"

Vrund pulled me aside and said, "You are lucky, bro. You got that Awww expression. Now make a statement."

Nishu stopped laughing and said with a mild smile, "Dear Bhavam. Make up is necessary."

"But that's not the answer to his question," commented Vrund from behind.

"You better talk to our hand, Vrund. Stop interrupting!" said Kajal, another beauty from the group.

"Woo… Woo… Woo… Miss Kajal, show some respect," said Vrund.

"Do you deserve it?" questioned Nishu.

"Whatever!" said Vrund and left the group. Now I was the only guy standing there in front of five girls. It was quite an odd situation now with Rahul, Ujjwal and the others on one side, and on the other side, I stood alone with those girls.

Kajal was one of the prettiest girls in the class. She asked, "Will you boys look at us if we don't apply make up?"

I said, "I don't know about make up, but some guys don't look at girls after a break-up."

All of them started biting their lips after hearing that. Maybe it was due to the chilled ice cream.

"There is no explanation from our side," said Nishu.

I smiled and said, "No issues."

"Wait!" said Kajal.

"You post some amazing and heart touching lines on your Facebook wall. So can you post something related to make up tonight?" she asked.

"Sure," I said.

"Your last status was amazing," said Nishu.

"Which one?" I asked.

"Every girl is beautiful, if you guys are dutiful," said Nishu.

I smiled again.

"But Bhavam, every girl is not beautiful. In order to revive her beauty, she has to put make up," said Kajal.

"Enough, girls! We aren't here for a debate," I smiled.

They all laughed. After having a good conversation with the girls, I merrily approached our boys' group.

"You were having lots of fun there," said Ujjwal.

"Ve… Makwana. He has a good reputation of being a decent guy, not a moron like you!" said Rahul.

"Mind your language, Vada," said Ujjwal with anxiety.

"Earlier people use to approach us for doing settings. Now since you are becoming quite popular amongst the girls, they will approach you," said Vrund.

"I have played enough of the match maker in the past. Not anymore!" I said.

"But man! Kajal is damn sexy. How did you feel talking with her?" asked Ujjwal.

"I am not a scholar like you, so I don't feel anything," I said.

"Hey, I don't like your statement. Why do only scholars and handsome guys deserve a sexy girl?" asked Rahul.

"Exactly. I agree we aren't scholars. I accept that we aren't studs but we can love a girl, care for her, adore her and most importantly, we can respect her. So definitely, we deserve them," said Vrund.

Rahul placed his hand on my shoulder and said, "From now on, don't ever think that if you aren't handsome, you won't get a sexy girl. You will get a girl, though she won't be sexy, but she will still be beautiful," said Rahul.

"Your company has improved us, Bhavam. Earlier we were naked people, now we are trying to be decent like you," said Vrund.

"And you asked about that make up stuff; so tell these girls that all of them are beautiful. Make up can only make them hot, nothing else," said Ujjwal.

"And for an instance, a person is attracted to hot things; otherwise an ideal guy will always prefer a girl who is simple," added Rahul.

I was shocked after hearing them. They had literally changed themselves.

"Now I realized that why people like to take selfies with my ex!" I said.

No one responded.

Tu shayad meri manzil thi hi nahi,
Aur mei tera rasta tha hi nahi!
Mei shayad teri dhadkan mei tha hi nahi,
Par kaise samjau inn saasko,
Jo aaj bhi tera naam lekar kehti hai –
Tu jahan bhi jaye, khush rehna!

Chapter 9

I completed my ice cream and went to the dustbin to throw my cup. A girl from behind dashed into me while I was throwing my cup in.

"I am very sorry," I said.

She turned, and it was none other than Ashwini. My word! What a surprise it was! I looked into her beautiful eyes because they were very expressive. In order to support herself from not falling down, she had grabbed my hand. I wished that touch would remain forever. However, my friends were watching us rather than eating their ice cream. I signed to Vrund with my eyes to get lost from here.

"Bhavam! So nice to see you!" said Ashwini merrily

When she addressed me by my name, I felt as if all my lost self respect was back.

I smiled at her and said, "Nice to see you too. We expected that the whole faculty would come today."

"Actually I come here daily," she said.

"You came alone?" I asked her.

"All of them are busy with so-called studies," she replied.

"Wow! So you are a carefree bird, I guess!" I said.

"Yes, I am. You wish to have some ice cream?" she asked, offering me her cup.

Wow! So generous and lovely her attitude was!

"I just had one," I said.

"But this one is really yummy. You ought to taste it!" she insisted.

"Wait. I will get an empty cup and spoon," I said.

She held my arm with her soft little hands and said, "It will melt if you go and come back again."

After that, all I remember is that I tasted strawberry flavor in my mouth.

She actually took a spoon full of ice cream from her cup and made me eat with her hands. It was just unbelievable! I was completely shocked at experiencing that moment. A spoon of ice cream, that too with her hands, was very special to me.

"How is it?" she asked.

"As sweet as you!" I smiled.

She gave me a shy look.

We decided to accompany each other to our hostels.

"Where is 4651?" I asked Ashwini.

"What is that?" she asked.

"It's your vehicle number," I said with a mild laugh.

She started laughing and said, "Really? I never noticed my vehicle number."

"I will remember it forever," I said in a low tone, audible only to myself.

"You said something?" she asked.

"No, nothing!" I said.

"So tell me something about yourself," she asked.

I smiled and asked her, "What do you want to know?"

"Anything. Okay, what is your dream?" she asked.

I felt special because, for the very first time, someone was asking me about my dream.

"Wish I knew my dream!" I exclaimed.

"What? You don't have any sort of dream?" she asked in shock.

"I love to do many things, but I am confused," I said. "What is your dream?" I countered.

"Buying a Porsche Minicooper!" she responded promptly.

I got stuck! I was a simple guy who had been off from social sites for a long time, and I didn't know what a 'Porsche Minicooper' was.

She continued saying, "That is why I am studying architecture. So that in future, I can design the things which my mind desires. I love to follow my mind, but I do what my heart says."

"I am quite the opposite. I love to follow my heart, but I do what my mind says," I said.

"I miss my mom and dad. I am here in Vadodara, and so they are away from me," she said.

"But Vadodara is a city with so many bunking destinations which won't allow you to miss your near ones," I said.

She laughed and asked, "Bunking destinations?"

"Yes. Like Sindh-road, CCD, Inorbit, Seven Seas, Kamatibaug, and many more. Which destination will you choose?" I asked.

She got confused and said, "None of them."

I was relieved that at least she was different from other people.

Until she said, "Actually I prefer Rasalpur."

"Rasalpur?" I asked in doubt.

"It's a very awesome place. Haven't you been there?" she asked.

"No," I replied.

"Why?" she asked.

"How can you be such an all rounder?" I said.

She gave me a glance and replied, "Because it's me."

There was a two minute silence after that.

"I love moving on in my life, just like this road," she said.

My heart experienced a gentle shock when I heard the word 'move on'. I remembered the words of Preksha suggesting that we should 'move on'.

"All love to move on, except me!" I said.

"Why?" she asked.

"Long story. Will tell you some other day," I said.

"You don't need to tell me. I know everything," she said.

"What do you know?" I asked in surprise.

"I don't know, but I have heard from people that you had a girlfriend whom you loved a lot. But she left you for some other guy, due to which you were badly hurt, and you are still trying to move on," she said.

"Tell me one thing. I never told anyone about my break-up. I never even revealed the name of my ex. How did people come to know about this? And now, even you, from a completely different faculty, know my story," I said in a depressed voice.

"I can suggest something to you," she said. "Don't think about her," she added.

"I have been trying that for ages," I said.

"Look at me. Don't you find me full of cheer and happiness?" she asked.

"Yes, I do," I said.

"I have also faced a break-up in my life, but I thank him instead of blaming him for leaving me. I thank him because whatever I am today is because of the experience he gave me. I believe in one thing, Bhavam, God cannot come personally to teach us heartbreaking lessons, so he sends his messengers in the form of our exes!" she said.

I smiled and asked, "So you mean that my ex was a form of God?"

"Pretty much, yes, and you should accept it," she said.

"But you are so good. Then why did your boyfriend leave you?" I asked.

"When he saw girls taller than me, he said that our chemistry never matched. So that was how it ended," she said.

"What, really?" I asked.

"Yes, but whatever happened was for the best. Later on, I realized that he was a jerk and was double dating," she said.

I didn't say anything.

"If I were like you, I would have hated myself for my short height but I never did that. I never paid a fuck to what he said and moved on. Instead of hating myself, I started to love myself, and trusted in God that someday, He would bring a person into my life, ready to accept me on the basis of who I am, rather than my height," she said.

"I realize that. Thank you!" I said with a shy smile on my face.

"Let's click a selfie!" she said, taking out her Sony Xperia.

We stopped for a moment. She came closer to me. My heart started beating. Her short height was an advantage for, as I was taller, her head touched my heart as she began clicking selfies. I had never been interested in clicking a selfie with her, but I just wanted her to be alongside me. I wished, looking up at the skies, "Can't this moment be frozen?"

As always, there was no response.

"Why are you looking up? Look at the camera," she said.

Instead of looking towards the camera, I looked at her and she pressed the click button. Therefore, a selfie was clicked in which we were both very close to each other. She looked at the camera with a smile, and I looked at her with a shy smile.

"Wow! We both look awesome in this selfie!" she said.

"Because it's us!" I said, blinking my eyes, and she smiled.

"I am in love with this selfie. I will keep it as my Hike DP," she said.

"If you don't mind, can we exchange numbers?" I asked, with a fear of rejection.

"Of course!" she said, and gave me her number. I saved it on my HTC 620 G.

"Wow! HTC is a cool cell!" she smiled.

(POINT #1:- Girls do look at your mobile phones.)

"Gosh, I never realized that we have reached the hostel. Before going, can we take another selfie? This time from my phone. HTC has better selfie quality," I said.

She took my cell from my hand and clicked the selfie again.

"Wow! Amazing click. You are, indeed, a sulfide queen," I said.

"No! No! Queen is too old. I am a princess," she grinned.

"So, goodnight. Your destination has come," I said with a gentle smile.

"I wish the roads were endless," she said.

Wish I could tell her that, from now on, my every road would begin from her. I saw her until she went inside. She was a fun loving, breezy kind of girl, and she never looked back to wave at me. But I had completely fallen for her, so I just wanted to see her always before my eyes.

Now I had to go to the art faculty hostel because I was alone so I didn't want to take the risk of entering through the main door. So the secret passage which Heenal suggested would help me to reach my hostel.

This was the happiest day of my life. Ashwini was on my mind but, indeed, there was one lady who had made me walk again, and she was none other than Heenal! I constantly remembered her.

When I entered the arts faculty, it was completely dark. I had to put my flash light on. I was slowly marching towards the grand auditorium where I would find some light. My friends, who pretend to be smart in front of girls, fear darkness, but I have no fear because I had remained in a dark room for the last four years after Preksha left me.

I entered the auditorium, through the back door. I was heading towards the secret passage. The incident which occurred a few days back with Vrund created goosebumps, but I ignored such feelings. My legs were shivering a bit this time as I entered the passage.

"What's with me?" I asked myself.

"You are in love again," replied my conscience.

I realized that my conscience had become Cupid due to Ashwini's lovable behavior.

The passage was straight, and I closed my eyes and thought about Ashwini and the sweet moments which we had shared tonight. When I opened my eyes, I realized that the passage was over. In relief I said, "If feelings are true, nothing can come in the way."

Location:- My hostel room

Time:- 10:30 pm

I got Ashwini's number now, so immediately I decided to text her.

You always make my day very special. Thanks

No need for thanks and you were quite shy while talking.

Oh really? LOL
I thought I was over expressive

We people from south Gujarat are like that only,

Correct, yaar
Full of feelings.

I hate guys who call me BAE

(For an instance I was confused at what she meant by saying 'BAE'. I had never heard anything like that before. I was sure it was something which I didn't understand because I had been off from the social media for quite some time. But I didn't ask her because it would make me look less intelligent in her mindset and I did not want that.)

Yah…
These idiotic boys in my class have posted idiotic comments on my DP.

BAE?

I immediately opened her DP and saw the comment. It was written –

"Just Amazing, bae."

I laughed at myself when I immediately realized that BAE means BABY. Such a transformation had taken place on social media since I left!

(POINT #2:- When you don't understand what your crush tries to say in a chat, don't be foolish to ask her what it means. If you do so, than you have less than a 100% chance to impress her.)

LOL.
Ignore them.

What is ignoring?
I believe in blocking them.

(POINT #3:- Due to the behavior of 25% of the weird boys, 75% of the innocent guys are blocked on the basis of their being boring.)

That's too much of punishment for them, Ashwini

Why are you defending them?
😠😠

I got a little scared seeing that emoticon, thinking that my impression on her had got a bit tarnished.

LOL...
I am not defending them. If you block them than they will harass some other girl. I have an idea.

I saw that comment and I wish that you should reply to it!

Gone mad?
What shall I reply?

He addressed you as BAE and you didn't like it, so you address him as a BROTHER so he will be shattered.

OMG! ROLF!
I never thought of that, yaar!
I am doing it right now. It will be a good lesson to him.

I said in my mind, "LOL! Do girls ever think?" (POINT #4:- This is the reason now why boys avoid commenting on any unknown girl's DP. Forget about an unknown girl; they even fear to comment on the DPs of the girls whom they know, in fear that they might make them their brothers.)

I saw Ashwini's reply to that comment. She had written -

"Awwwww... ! Thank you so much, my brother."

OMG! The guy was surely going to get the biggest shock of his life when he read it. After that she went offline. She never said formalities like "Hi, Hello, Good night, Good morning, Take care", etc. because she was an easy going girl who loved to keep things simple.

Preksha was completely opposite to her. I realized, at that instance, that all girls are not the same. Some girls like it when you show your caring nature towards them, while some girls love it when you make them laugh. Some girls like the way you speak, while others like the way you remain calm. Then the question arose in my mind that if girls like calm guys, why are most of them mad about Virat Kohli? I left that discussion for the morning with Vrund and others.

Time:- 7:45 am
Location:- My classroom

I reached 15 minutes before time, because now I had a group of people with whom I could laugh and cry.

Vrund saw me and asked, "So early today?"

"Was a bit confused," I replied.

"About what?" asked Nishu.

"Do girls love calm guys or aggressive guys?" I asked, looking at Vrund.

"What? I am not a girl," said Vrund.

"I like aggressive guys!" said Kajal.

"Me too, aggressive," added Aisha.

"But I like calm guys," said Nishu.

"You see they are so smart, that they give justice to everyone; but at the end of the day, they will choose a guy who is neither aggressive, nor calm," said Vrund.

"Then what?" I asked.

"A moderate guy," responded Vrund.

"Shut up! You said that you aren't a girl! Then why do you assume anything?" asked Nishu.

Vrund wanted to explain himself, but I interrupted him.

"Then why are you all mad after Virat Kohli?" I asked.

"Awww… I can do anything for him," said Kajal with a cute expression.

"But why? What is wrong with us?" asked Vrund desperately.

"Are you comparing yourselves with him? If you are doing so, then come out of your little world, because even we girls do fall for the hot guys like VK," said Nishu.

"But what's so hot in him and not others?" asked Vrund.

"Are you jealous of him?" asked Kajal.

I interrupted and said, "Each and every boy is jealous of him because he is the crush of most girls."

"That's what I am telling you. He is our Crush," said Nishu.

"Brother, let's go; otherwise my head will get crushed at listening to the names of their crushes," said Vrund.

Dr Umar came and we all adjusted ourselves on our respective seats.

"What do we need to do to become the crush of any girl?" Vrund asked.

"I don't know, but Google will tell us," I said with a smile.

I typed in that question and the results showed us this;

"To become a crush of any girl: Hit the gym, study hard, get good grades, be good in communication, look into her eyes when she talks to you, listen to her, make her laugh and try to pay her bill when you take her to coffee shops."

"Fuck! Why should I pay her bill?" said Vrund with anxiety.

"That's why; if you can't afford to date a girl, stop dreaming about girlfriends," I said.

"It's just a girlfriend, not girlfriends!" exclaimed Vrund.

"Oh! Sorry, I just forgot that you have decided to be a good guy," I said.

"But I know, these beautiful chicks only prefer handsome hulks as their boyfriends," said Vrund with sadness on his face.

I placed my hand on his shoulder and said, "Any guy can be their boyfriend; it's not a great deal. But only a real man can be her soul mate. So try to be someone's soul mate, regardless of being anyone's boyfriend."

After the lecture was over, we fled away, as always. Nishu and group joined us too. Wow, having girls around suited our status well!

"But you did everything for Preksha, even more than a soul mate would. Still she left you. Why?" asked Vrund.

I got stuck. I didn't reply him for a minute or two.

Nishu showed him an eye and said, looking towards me, "Ignore him, Bhavam. He is a useless piece of shit."

I got stuck. Didn't reply anyone for a minute or two!

Then I immediately looked towards him and said, "She was a different person. I don't know what changed her. Once we visited a local restaurant. As you know, she was damn beautiful; her appearance was enough to attract any guy's attention. On the other hand, I was not too attractive those days. I was a simple guy with ordinary looks. Despite that, she dated me, which used to surprise everyone. That day, her former friends also visited that restaurant. They approached Preksha and greeted her. They took her aside and one of her friends said in an audible tone, 'You still date this piece of shit?'

Another friend said, 'Baby, forget about our status, but do look at your own. You don't deserve this.'

Yet another friend added, 'You are the prettiest girl in this planet. You deserve someone who looks handsome.'

I heard everything, silently got up and decided to leave, very embarrassed. Preksha saw that. When I was leaving, I heard a noise of something falling from the table. I looked back and saw that in her anger, Preksha had thrown the spoons on the floor. She said, 'Just fuck off from here. I am not answerable to you.'

Her male friends laughed at this situation and left. She approached me, held my hand and brought me to the place where we had been sitting.

With my head down, I said, 'They weren't wrong. You are the best, so you deserve the best. I don't match your personality.'

She than placed her hand on my palm and said, 'Don't listen to them. They are jealous of us. You know some of them like me only because I have an attractive body. None of them ever looked into my eyes, but you were the first who really looked into my eyes and said that they are beautiful rather than my body, and so I love you.'

So you see, Preksha was a totally different person at that time."

Each and every girl standing there was stunned after what I had said. Vrund placed his hand on my shoulder and said, "I am sorry, dude. I didn't know that."

"If she was so good, then what she is doing now is equally bad," said Nishu.

My heart was again bleeding for her. I left them immediately and ran towards my hostel room. Locking myself in, I looked in the mirror and said, "I won't cry now." Then also, a tear came out of my eyes. I was completely lost now. So in vain, my hand moved to the deck where the packet of cigarettes was kept. I had made several promises on numerous occasions that I wouldn't smoke further to relieve my pain, but as always, those were just merely words. I smoked until I fell asleep.

Time:- 12:30 pm

I got up soon, but generally after smoking, I never visited anybody because no one knew that I had the bad habit of smoking. I saw myself in the mirror, and my eyes were red, indicating that, this time also, I had cried after smoking.

"I want her. I need to go!" I said to myself

"But whom do you need?" asked my conscience.

"Heenal!" I replied, and ran immediately out of my room. This time I was running at full speed because I desperately wanted her and her beautiful words to create peace in my mind. I soon reached Kamatibaug. I was running quickly, looking all over for her. In my hurry, my leg got twisted and I was about to fall.

Heenal caught me with her hands and said, "This is not the correct time for jogging, and if you want to do, then do it properly."

It brought a huge smile on my face when I saw her. Without thinking of anything, I just hugged her because she was like my sister and it felt good.

"Where were you all these days?" she asked.

I then told her everything that had happened. My meeting with Ashwini and that moment of taking selfies and all!

"So it seems that you have found the correct person to hang out with," she said.

"But still…!" I said, hoping she understood what I meant.

"Come on, Bhavam. Weak people- take Revenge. Strong people-Forgive and Intelligent people-Ignore. You forgot this thing?" she asked.

I smiled and said, "Again you googled it?"

"Shut up! It's not important than where I got it from. The message is important," she said.

"I have enjoyed many happy moments over the last few days, but remembering my ex still hurts me," I said.

"Do you talk to her as I told you?" she asked.

"She won't reply; she has a big ego," I said.

"What if you call her?" she suggested.

"After hearing my voice, she will cut my call, and add me to the black list," I said.

"Black list?" she asked.

"Now don't say that you don't know what the hell a black list is?" I said.

"Exactly. What the hell is a black list?" she asked.

"You know it's just like blocking a particular number from your cell phone. Once you add a contact to the blacklist, you don't get calls or messages from that number," I said.

"Oh, I see!" she said.

"But she isn't your enemy; so she won't add you to her blacklist," said Heenal.

"Is it so? But after our break-up, she immediately added me to her black list," I corrected her.

"Yes, because you were a fool to call her," she said. "Tell me, why were you calling her?" she asked.

"Obviously I wanted a proper reason from her, and more than that, I just wanted to tell her not to go away from me like this. But before I could say anything, she blocked me," I said in a low tone.

"When a girl is upset, she doesn't want to talk with anyone. In that case, calling her would definitely not work. Instead of that, you should have gone to meet her physically," she said.

"She never wanted me to," I said.

"Did she ever say so?" she asked.

"Her actions proved it," I replied.

For a moment, she didn't say anything.

I took my cell phone out and said, "What bad luck. She is always online when I operate my FB."

"Talk to her," she said.

"I have already had enough of her insults. I don't have the capacity to face any more," I said.

"We saw her that day with her current boyfriend. They were talking selfies. I am sure that she also saw you, didn't she?" she asked.

"Yes, she did see me. But just for a moment, and then she ignored me," I said.

"Text her saying that her selfie with Karan is amazing," she suggested.

"Why are you doing this to me? First decide on whose side you are!" I said angrily.

"I am obviously on your side. You have accepted that she is with someone else, so she should also know that you are strong enough to accept that," she said.

I was surprised for a moment, but then I realized that whatever Heenal said was true. Preksha should know that I could happily see her with someone else.

"Okay. But what should I write?" I asked.

"Whatever you wish," she said.

I was again blank.

"You keep thinking; I shall come back after a few minutes," she said.

"Where are you going?" I asked.

She didn't reply and started walking.

On Instagram, Karan uploaded a picture with Preksha and wrote -

'After meeting you, I wonder how I lived my life so long without you. 😘

I JUST LOVE YOU BAE ❤️.'

Wow! Karan had surely copied it from Google, because he lacked the capability to create something original. I was really good at composing romantic and poetic lines for Preksha when we were in a relationship, but I guess girls these days don't like original creations. If a person has taken engineering and if he is in love with some girl, and by chance, if he is intelligent, then his mind starts working like a flowchart, assuming innumerable assumptions. However, if a guy has faced a break-up, he will start accepting that his assumptions were true. Just like the situation as described here in the form of flowcharts:

CASE 1

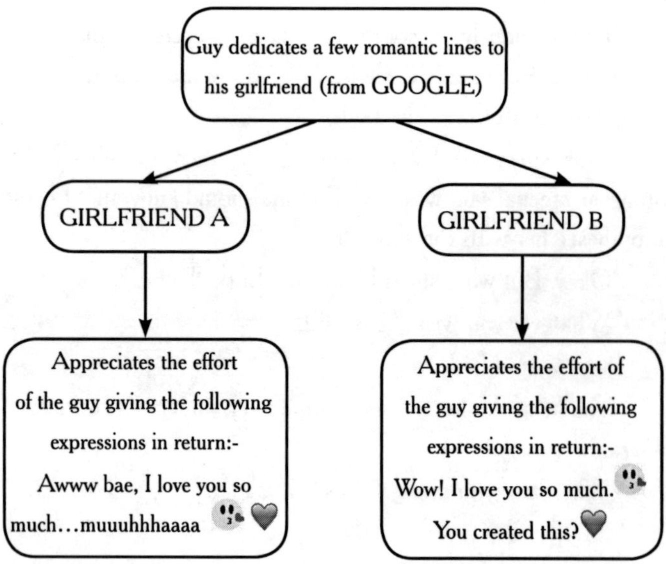

Observations (For Girlfriend A)

1. If Girlfriend A is a bit smart, she won't ask her guy if he copied those romantic lines from Google or not, because she knows the limitations of her guy to create such beautiful things. But despite that she will love him because she feels that she is something special to her boyfriend, who cares enough to make her feel so. So she won't give a shit if those lines are from Google or from his mind.
2. If Girlfriend A is not smart enough, she will never even wonder if her boyfriend copied such lines from Google or not. Instead she will be only interested to give on his every message, whether it is simple text or romantic lines.
3. If Girlfriend A is also the Girlfriend C of some other guy, then such lines are immaterial to her. However, she won't be partial enough to compliment this guy.

Conclusion (For Girlfriend A)

If Observation (1) is applicable to you, then your relationship is safe.

If Observation (2) is applicable to you, then your relationship is sweet.

If Observation (3) is applicable to you, then this is a relationship leading to a break-up. There will be a two minute silence from my side.

Observation (For Girlfriend B)

1. If he is an unpredictable guy, then only Girlfriend B will ask if he really created such lines. However, this doesn't mean that she doubts her boyfriend's ability. She is surprised and further, excited to see such creativity from her guy in future.

2. Sometimes a girl might test a guy's ability to speak the truth. So in such a case, it totally depends upon the guy to speak the truth. If he willingly accepts that he copied those lines from Google, then the girl's trust in the guy increases, and if he says that he created them himself, then the girl will check. Ultimately that will result in future conflicts related to trust issues.

3. If she knows that this guy is smart enough to compose such lines, then in order to confirm, she will ask him if he created those romantic lines by himself. If the guy is sincere enough, he will not hesitate to agree that he copied them from Google. She will be pleased to hear that and will give a , while an insecure guy will lie that he created those lines on his own because he is afraid that his girlfriend will consider him dumb. However, he too will receive a .

Conclusion (For Girlfriend B)

If Observation (1) is applicable to you, your girlfriend won't leave you because she will expect a lot from a short surprise package like you. Of course, her expectations are nothing more than an exciting love. In this case, your relationship has the chance to last longer. Maybe not forever, but it also depends upon the type of person.

If Observation (2) is applicable to you, and if you come out as an honest guy in her thoughts, I guarantee that Girlfriend B won't ever leave you. Girls do test their guy and if he passes that test, they trust him forever. However, if a girl finds that her boyfriend is not honest enough, she won't leave him. But whenever in future, a dispute between the two arises, she will take this reason to prove that her guy was dishonest. So guys, please be honest.

If Observation (3) is applicable to you, then don't worry. Your relationship is quite safe and Girlfriend B will respect this guy because despite having been smart enough, this guy is sincere enough to accept the truth. In the practical world, such guys are rare to find.

P.S. "GIRLS, IF YOU HAVE SUCH A GUY, ADORE HIM."

But all this is applicable to you if, and only if, you are in a relationship. The situation for folks who are facing a break-up is also prescribed in the form of flowcharts, as given below:

(Definitely after a breakup, only a fool can send a romantic message suggesting 'I LOVE YOU' to his ex, but some guys like me tried to send formal messages to their ex, and here are the results)

CASE 2

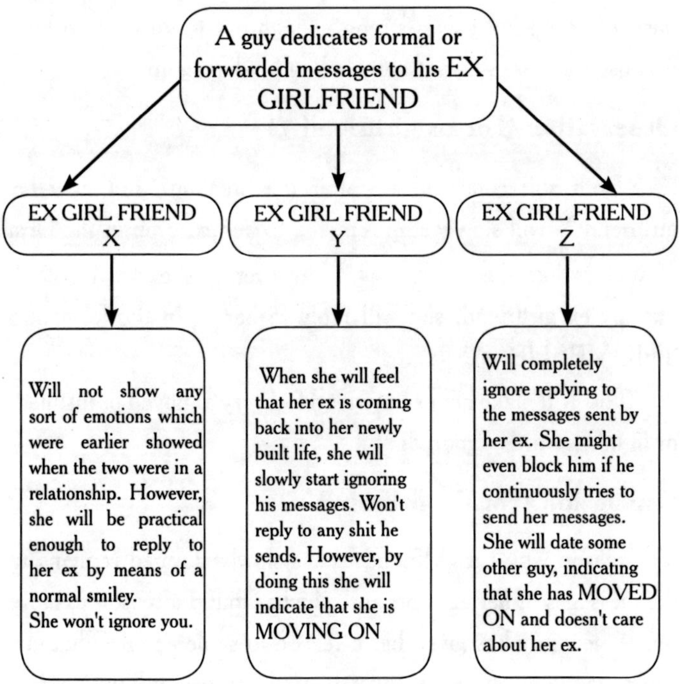

Observation (For Ex girlfriend X)

We live in a modern age where the 'break-up' couple still talks to each other by means of WhatsApp and Facebook. So consider a situation where the two still communicate with each other. She will see her ex's forwarded jokes or messages on WhatsApp and reply in form of smileys, such as 😊, 😃 etc.

Both of them may be desperate to send 😘 ❤, but both know that such a thing is now not possible, and they will try to stop themselves.

Conclusion (For Ex girlfriend X)

Such behavior from Ex girlfriend X after the separation proves that she is single after the break-up. She is a little depressed and misses her ex, but she is strong enough not to go back to him, because she doesn't want him back in her life again.

Observation (For Ex girlfriend Y)

👍 Both still communicate after the break-up, but now Ex girlfriend Y will slowly stop replying to her ex, even in the form of smileys like these - 😊, 😃.However, if she is a bit kind. like my ex girlfriend, she will reply to her ex in the form of a THUMBSUP.

This will make her ex boyfriend feel very annoyed or insulted, or in other words, ignored!

Conclusion (For Ex girlfriend Y)

The reason why Ex girlfriend Y has slowly stopped replying to the messages of her ex is because she has found a reason to move on. A new guy has given her a reason to smile again. That guy evokes laughter on the face which cried because of him. So dear boys, if you think that you belong to this category, then START TO MOVE ON.

Observation (For Ex girlfriend Z)

Ex girlfriend Z, despite seeing the messages of her ex, won't reply him. If her ex keeps on messaging her, one day she will be forced to block him so that ultimately, her ex will not message her ever.

Conclusion (For Ex girlfriend Z)

It proves that she has completely moved on. She is in a relationship with some other guy, or she has decided to stay single for the time being. But she has completely erased all memories of her previous relationship. Ex girlfriend Z indicates that she is completely independent to decide her life and her choice of guy. If any third person tries to negotiate between her and her ex boyfriend, she is so strong that she can show her middle finger to that person and say, 'My life, my rules, so fuck off!'

Thus, when you summarize CASE 1 and CASE 2, you can say,

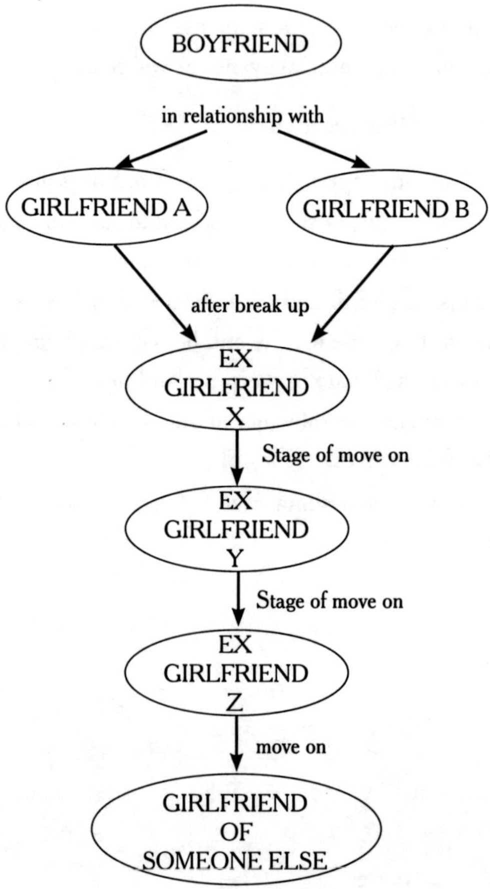
BOYFRIEND
in relationship with
GIRLFRIEND A
GIRLFRIEND B
after break up
EX GIRLFRIEND X
Stage of move on
EX GIRLFRIEND Y
Stage of move on
EX GIRLFRIEND Z
move on
GIRLFRIEND OF SOMEONE ELSE

Chapter 10

While writing stages of a break-up in my diary, I never realized how quickly time passed. I was still sitting at the same place in Kamatibagh. After creating those flowcharts in my diary, I realized what actually an engineering guy can do!

Heenal said to communicate with Preksha. So in confusion, I decided to text her on FB.

> You and Karan are looking awesome in this DP.

(She was online, so, as soon as I texted her, she saw my message. I waited for a bit but she didn't reply.)

I looked up and asked God, "Is she becoming Ex Girlfriend Z?"

As always, there was no answer.

> I guess it is the click of Kamatibaug, right?

(Again she saw my message, but didn't reply.)

> Everything all right?

(Wow! This time she had replied with a Thumbs up. Fucking irritating it was!)

> You both really look awesome. I think I was there that day at Kamatibaug.

> If you know all this, then why are you asking me?

> My wish

> Than keep your wish to yourself only.

(Tears started rolling from my eyes when I heard such a response from her. I expected that she would be rude, but I never ever expected this third grade torture. I didn't know how to reply her after such conversation. When we were in a relationship, she took a promise from me that whenever she was sad, I would give her a big smile and that her sadness would go away. Though now we weren't in a relationship. I decided to do that, expecting a positive outcome.)

> 😊 😊

She saw that last message with smileys, but didn't care to reply. I took out my diary again and wrote about this whole conversation with Preksha stating,

"Sorry, I couldn't be her world's best boyfriend,

I even tried to be her world's best ex boyfriend,

But today I failed."

I stood up from the place where I was sitting, and silently started walked off like a defeated loser towards my hostel.

Location:- Hostel Canteen

Time:- 8:00 pm

"Everything alright, brother?" asked Vrund, on seeing my depressed face.

I nodded in affirmation.

Rahul held my shoulder, and asked, "What happened, Bhavam?"

I smiled and said, "Don't talk with a loser like me; please go away."

"Loser?" expressed Vrund in surprise. "You aren't a loser. Who said so?"

"Bhavam, just tell us what happened!" asked Rahul politely.

I showed them my chat with Preksha. They were stunned to see that!

"You still talk to her?" asked Vrund in complete shock.

"This is horrible. Stop talking with her, yaar. Block her," said Rahul.

"I can't," I said.

"But you don't deserve this. In fact, a person like you doesn't even deserve to share a word with crap like her," said Vrund. "I know. She is doing everything under the influence of that Karan, her current boyfriend," he added.

"Enough is enough, BC. Will have to teach that Karan a good lesson which he will remember forever," averred Rahul.

"What will you do?" I asked.

"Where words don't work, hands do!" said Rahul with attitude.

"Exactly. Now it is time for '*babal*'," said Vrund in support.

"Don't be mad, guys. You cannot beat up someone like that. And avoid doing *babals!*" I said.

"And he has the full right to destroy your life by means of your ex girlfriend?" asked Vrund.

"Relax, guys! I know you both are right, but still we can't beat up someone like that. I have never raised my hand against anyone. Besides, he is the reason for the smile on Preksha's face, so how can I beat someone who makes her smile?" I remarked.

"How is he making her smile?" asked Rahul. "He just has more money and he is dancing on the basis of that," he added.

I took out my mobile and said, "See her Instagram post. Karan has posted a selfie with Preksha. As the caption he has written –

"It was a million tiny little things that, when you added them all up, meant we were supposed to be together and I knew it. I knew it that very first time I touched her. It was like coming home."

She loved it, and she wrote and said – "Awwww 😘 😘 I just loved it. You don't know how quickly you can make me smile."

So this proves that Karan can make Preksha smile. So I can neither beat up the person who is the reason of her smile, nor allow anyone to do so."

Rahul immediately took out his mobile and started typing something.

"What are you doing?" we both asked.

He signed to us to wait, and then he handed me his mobile and said, "See this. That Karan has copied that caption from here."

I took his mobile and saw that. Indeed he was right. It was a dialogue of a Hollywood movie of 1993 named 'Sleepless in Seattle'.

"So what?" I asked. "I thought that he had copied it from Google, but that's immaterial. What is important is that Preksha smiled because of this," I added.

"Are you supporting Karan?" asked Vrund in a melodramatic tone.

"I don't know, but I have respect for that guy. He can make her smile and I am happy that my ex girlfriend will now smile on a daily basis," I said.

"If you are happy, then why do you look depressed?" asked Rahul.

"Because I could never copy a caption for her from Google. I wasted my time to create an original one," I said with an innocent smile.

Both Rahul and Vrund looked at each other in surprise. I am sure they thought that I had gone mad.

Rahul placed his hand on my shoulder and said, "She is fake, so she will like only copied captions. Naturally she can never ever respect your original captions, but don't worry; one day you will find a girl who isn't fake like her. She will respect you and your original creations."

Hearing this at least gave me some positive hope.

"By the way, under which name was that caption copied from Google?" I asked Rahul.

"10 most romantic movie dialogues," he replied and signed off.

I laughed.

Location:- My hostel room.

Time:- 9:00 pm

I only remembered about studies when I entered my room. The books looked innocently at me, indicating – "Read us, son, otherwise you know we won't go away from you." Study books are the only exceptional thing which we engineering students think should go away from our life as soon as possible, but as it is said, what comes around, goes around.

I looked my study table and realized that if I worked a bit hard, then maybe, IIT Delhi would be not just a dream. I was a smart and intelligent student. IIT was definitely within my reach, but then all other distractions came my way and I suffered a tremendous setback, forcing me to study textile Engineering at KSU. But I stayed positive, thinking that in four years time, I would crack GATE and do my masters from IIT. But the break-up put a brake on my dream.

Yes, my dream was not strong enough, but it was real, and I just hadn't put in the required efforts.

"I spoiled my career through my own actions as well as because of her," I said to myself.

"Wow! How selfish you have become! For everything you blame her!" replied my conscience.

"Now you also support her. Great!" I said.

"Even IITians have girlfriends, so it's not a great deal," said my conscience.

The thought of Preksha was again forcing me to smoke.

"No, I won't smoke. I won't. I won't!"I said, holding a cigarette in my hand.

I threw the cigarette down and crushed it with my feet. I was down on my knees.

However, that thought again troubled me as I took a second cigarette in my hand. With a firm heart I ignited it, and smoked until my heart got relief from that undesirable pain.

Location:- My class room

Time:- 8:00 am

"Dear students, here's the schedule for your final semester exam," said Dr Umar.

As soon as he said that, all the students banged the desks with their hands and expressed their grief.

Dr Umar laughed and said, "This won't work now. You have to give exams and mind you, this time, the Physics paper is really tough."

Rahul Ravichandran raised his hand and said, "One question, sir."

Dr Umar looked at him and said, "Yes, Mister Ravichandran, go on."

"There has not been a single semester when the physics paper was easy, sir," said Rahul.

Chants of, "Correct, Vada...Correct, Vada...Correct, Vada...!"' came from behind.

"Before I answer that, why are they all addressing you as Vada?" asked Dr Umar with an enquiring look on his face. It seemed that today, he was in a good mood.

"Because it is something related to me, sir. In future, whenever they hear the word Vada-Sambhar, they will remember that there was a guy named Rahul Ravichandran in their class," said Rahul.

Whistles started blowing from behind.

"Terrific answer, Mister Ravichandran!" said Dr Umar.

"Sir, it is Master Rahul, not Mister Ravichandran," corrected Rahul.

"Oh, sorry. I thought that Ravichandran is your surname," said Dr Umar.

"No sir, in South India we have the tradition of writing the name of our father just after our name. So, in that sense, Rahul is my name, while Ravichandran is my father's name," explained Rahul.

"Alright, good you told me. I never knew that," said Dr Umar.

"Happens, sir! We also don't know physics, as you do," said Rahul.

"Oh dear, first of all, sit down, Rahul! I need to say something to the class," said Dr Umar politely for the first time ever.

"His wife must have reminded him of the old days," commented Vrund, and the girls laughed

"But what about my question, sir?" asked Rahul.

"It will be answered in my explanation; so please be seated," said Dr Umar.

Rahul was a smart guy, so without any further arguments like Dhruvesh, he sat down.

Dr Umar held his breath and said, "I know that you guys hate me and I also know the reason why you do so. I know that you guys don't even respect me. Forget about respect, you guys don't even consider me as a professor, right?"

All students in the class were stunned on hearing this. We all looked at each other. For the first ever there was pin drop silence in the class.

"I agree that I do set the toughest of the question papers, but where is your hard work to reply to my toughness? The real courage of an engineering student is not looking eye to eye in their partner's eyes, but in looking eye to eye in a mirror at yourself before an exam," said Dr Umar as though he was a motivational speaker.

For the first time ever, we found some respect for Dr Umar.

He then went near Rahul and asked, "So yes, Rahul, what did you want to say?"

"I am sorry sir. I am answered!" said Rahul politely.

Dr Umar smiled and said, "Giving reasons for your failure won't always help you. It's not always about the process, but about the results. You have still got some time to recover and I am sure you can all crack it, because you all have that 'Never give up' spirit, I guess!"

We all stood up and started applauding at what Dr Umar had said. This time we weren't making fun of him for we were damn serious!

He interrupted and said, "No need of that applause, students. I just need to ask you one thing. Is there any student who can compose a few poetic lines for me?"

The whole class diverted its attention towards me.

"Oh, I see!" exclaimed Dr Umar. "So Bhavam Sharma, is that your hidden talent?" he asked.

"Sorry to interrupt, sir, but he is a born poet," said Vrund.

"Okay, then can you compose few inspirational lines in front of me within 30 seconds?" asked Dr Umar.

For the first 10 seconds, I closed my eyes and took a deep breath and then said -

Let them throw stones,
You convert them into milestones.
Let them laugh,
At your decreasing graph.
One day you shall again rise,
Paying the biggest price.
Your life will be made,
Dark memories won't easily fade!

As soon as I said that, all including Dr Umar, gave me a standing ovation. My ears had been thirsty to hear such an applause for a long time.

"That was amazing, kid!" said Dr Umar. "But can you explain what they mean because a layman can't understand poetic lines."

For a moment I was like, "Then why did he ask?"

But I nodded my head and said, "Sir, zero (0) was discovered. From it came binary (0–1) language, and computers were invented. Later on, mobile phones were invented, followed by laptops, smart phones, tablets and innumerable useful gadgets. All these were possible because of ZERO, so at present we are ZERO, but that doesn't mean that we are losers. It's just a path to major success."

"Simply awesome, Bhavam Sharma. My dear, you have chosen the wrong field. You could have done very well if you were associated with literature," said Dr Umar, looking at me.

Finally Dr Umar concluded, saying, "So give respect to each and every question paper in your life. If it is easy, it will make your life. If it is tough, it will surely inspire you to be better, and ultimately that effort to be better, will make you THE BEST."

After the class was over, all of a sudden, my mobile started receiving lots of random notifications and friend requests.

I handed over my mobile to Vrund and said, "Why am I suddenly receiving so many requests?"

Vrund looked at me and said, "What you did inside was nothing less than magic. You are lucky, mate, that you have received someone's request from the opposite side, and that too from the girls."

Rahul approached me, joining his hands in salutation, and said, "Please teach me this art."

"Relax, guys. Keep it simple!" I said.

"Anyway this time, we are seriously planning to study. So we have decided to do group study in the library. Are you interested in joining us?" asked Vrund.

"Of course, yaar… after that motivational speech from sir, even I wish to study," I said.

"Alright, then let's go to the Arts faculty library and study," said Vrund.

"Hey, wait… wait… wait… wait… wait!" I said. "Why so? Our faculty also has a library. Then why do you want to visit the Arts facility's library specifically?" I asked.

"That is correct, but our library doesn't have many books, while the library in the Arts faculty fulfills all the requirements," he replied.

"Are we going there just to read books only?" I asked with a doubt.

"Of course," he said with a big smile, and ran away.

While running, he said, "I will be waiting for you."

I laughed because I was sure that he was not interested in studying there. He was just going there to see the girls.

When I was in the first year, the seniors made this usual statement.

"It is the nature of a Science faculty guy that he finds the girls of Arts faculty sexier than others."

I wonder if that trend is still applicable to most colleges. On the other hand, the girls of the Science faculty in our college were no less.

They used to follow this motto,

"Guys in our faculty are boring, while guys in other faculties are hot."

Rewind your memory and think of an incident when your father told you,

"Your mom cannot be understood."

And then when you were growing up, one day, suddenly, a girl gave you a smile when you were in 1st standard. Your little mind must have surely asked,

"Was that for me?"

Slowly come back to the present situation where your girlfriend left you without giving a proper reason, and you continuously ask yourself,

"Why is she doing that?"

All these situations prove that girls cannot be understood.

No matter how many flowcharts you prepare! At the end of the day, she will only do the thing which she wants.

What is the definition of a *modern girl?*

If a guy is soft and sincere, he has no other option, than to accept it. If he is dominant, then she knows how to treat him; this is a modern girl.

But is this the thing which she deserves?

Yes, she is definitely demanding, but never dominating.

She wants you to spend most of your time with her, but when she knows the fact that you are really a busy guy, than she will respectfully accept your absence with a smile on her face.

Yes, if she is beautiful, it is definitely her dream to become a popular selfie girl on Instagram, but with ONE guy only. If you can be that guy, you are a man.

Therefore, relationships these days are like an earthen pot. If you don't handle them with care, they will shatter into pieces.

Location:- Arts Faculty Library
Time:- 11:24 am

"My Gosh! The temperature is really hot," said Vrund looking towards the girls who were reading silently in the library.

"They are quite serious about reading; don't mess with them," I said.

He laughed and said, "Come; let's sit nearer to them."

"I thought you were really serious when you meant that you will stop all this," I said.

"That was just for a few days as a part of regret," he said.

We sat at the table which was at the adjacent side of those girls.

"Gosh! I have never ever been in such a situation. They look very serious plus hot, and if they realize that you are flirting, then I bet that this library will become your graveyard too," I said, looking anxiously towards Vrund.

"Don't worry. They are open minded girls," he said.

"How do you know that?" I asked.

"If she had any problem, she would have definitely given us one look. But instead of doing that, she is reading her stuff indicating that she doesn't have any objection," replied Vrund.

"Dumb! She isn't looking at us because she is totally engrossed in reading," I said.

"That is also correct. You can take it that way too," said Vrund.

"What are we going to read?" I asked.

"Well, do you think that you will pass in every subject?" he asked.

"I don't know but this is an exceptional semester for which I have worked," I said.

"Don't make me nervous, yaar. I don't know anything. What will I do?" he asked with a bit of tension on his face.

"Great, and I guess watching girls here will help you!" I said sarcastically.

"Please, Bhavam, help me. It's necessary for me to pass this semester, otherwise I am gone!" he pleaded.

"But how can I help you when I am also in the same dilemma?" I said.

"I was never ever intelligent, but you were intelligent. Tell me how you studied during your prime days?" he asked.

I smiled as I heard the word 'intelligent' being associated with me.

"I was very hardworking. I used to only study, nothing else," I said.

"But how? Especially when the exams were approaching?" he asked.

"This is a process, my dear. When we are school students, we always had the tension to finish our course just one month before the exams, so that we could have enough time for revision. Later on, when we got into higher standards, our priority was to finish the course one week before the exams. While in higher secondary, we finished our course just one day before the examination, so we always gave exams under pressure, and then the situation completely changed when we entered college. Here we are so careless that we inquire about the course, just a few days before the examination," I said.

"Whatever you said was true, but now what to do?" he asked.

"We have only one option left," I said.

"What?" he asked pleasantly.

"But for that we have to go to our own Science faculty library," I said.

"But why? What's wrong here?" he asked.

"Firstly, from there we will collect the question papers of the last ten years. From that, we will study only two sets of questions. First, those which are repeatedly asked, and second, which have not been asked till date. That is the only way to crack something during the last days," I said.

"Are you sure about it?" he asked doubtfully.

"I know that I am not that genius anymore, but when I was a genius, I figured out how to study. These days, even paper setters don't take pains to set new questions. So don't worry. Let's leave something to God," I said.

He smiled and said, "You are still a genius."

"Feels good to hear that!" I smiled.

So now again, we had to go to our own library.

"I know that we have to go, but the greenery over here just fascinates me!" he said.

I placed my hand on his shoulder and said, "The choice is yours."

He shook his head and said, "Let's go."

When we reached the exit doors of the Arts faculty, my eyes shifted to a vehicle, which was entering at full speed. It was 4651.

I jumped, and said with delight, "Hey, 4651."

Vrund was shocked and asked, "Are you okay, brother? What happened?"

"You go to the library. I am just coming in a few minutes," I said.

He was puzzled, wondering why I was saying that. Then he realized that Ashwini was there, and he said, "Choice is yours. Okay, I will be waiting."

While going, he said, "It's your time now, Bhavam. Girls do bring the end of suffering in life. She is the one made to end your suffering."

For the first time ever, he had said something which touched my heart. I immediately rushed to where Ashwini was parking her vehicle. I stood behind her, with a big smile on my face, in the hope that when she turned around, she would also do the same.

She did turn around, and on seeing me, she returned my smile and said, "Oh! Why are you here?"

I still remember, her eyes were damn attractive that day because she had applied dark black eyeliner.

"Actually I came here to the library with my friend," I said.

"To study?" she asked.

Why was she asking me that? I could definitely not tell her that Vrund had brought me there to see girls, though I never wanted to lie to her, because I had promised myself that this new friendship with Ashwini would not sustain on lies.

"I… I… Actually we came here for to study, but then my friend and I realized that we can't study in the library of your faculty," I said.

"Why so? It isn't that bad," she said.

(*God only knew that the library wasn't bad, but we were!)

"The exams are approaching and we can't study with girls inside," I said clearly so that she could understand what I meant.

"Why? Did the girls disturb you?" she asked.

"Oh, Ashwini, don't you understand such a simple thing? Guys cannot study with girls around!" I explained.

She was blank for a moment, and when she realized what I was saying, she started laughing and said, "You are amazing."

(POINT #6:- Don't hide anything from your girl. If she isn't smart, then also she will love you; but if she is smart, she will definitely love you more.)

"So where are you going now?" she asked.

"The exams are approaching, and so we going to our faculty's library to study," I said.

"Oh! Then you are also not free today! Leave it!" she said with a depressed face.

I thought there was something exciting, and therefore, said, "I won't study 24 hours; so I am not busy."

"Actually I want to go bowling once. I need someone to accompany me. Will you?" she asked.

For the first time ever, I felt as if happiness was at my doors, and so, without any hesitation, I said, "Of course I would love to accompany you."

"So that's done. I will text you the details. Got to go now as the classes are there! See you soon. Bye!" she said and left.

I just smiled without saying goodbye because I was feeling on top of the world.

I hurried to reach our own library in the Science faculty where Vrund was waiting for me.

This was my MOVE ON now. I posted on my Facebook wall –

Left is your road, right is mine!
We both met for a few moments, that's totally fine!
Friendship is your road, Love is mine!
We both shall follow it, that's totally fine!
Aggression is your road, Calmness is mine!
I shall accept it, that's totally fine!
Goodbye is your road, waiting is mine!
We both shall meet again someday, that's totally fine!

Chapter 11

Location:- Science Faculty Library.
Time:- 1:25 pm

"What a status!" exclaimed Vrund.

"Come on, let's study quickly, I don't have much time," I said.

"Woo… woo… woo… you were talking with Ashwini, right?" he asked.

"Yes," I replied.

"Every time you speak to her, you become happy," said Vrund.

"That's right!" said Nishu from behind.

"Oh! When did you come?" I asked Nishu.

"That's not important, but what is important for you is Ashwini," said Nishu.

"Correct!" said Vrund, supporting her.

"But guys, she is just my friend, nothing else," I said.

"What were you both discussing? Because you took so much of time to come here?" asked Vrund.

"Actually she wants to go bowling, so she asked me if I could accompany her or not!" I said.

"Wow!" exclaimed Nishu.

"You don't even know how lucky you are!" said Vrund.

"I don't know about luck, but yes, it felt like happiness when she asked me to join her," I said.

"So are you guys going alone?" asked Nishu.

"I don't know; her message will come. But guys, will you do me a favor?" I requested.

"Always ready!" answered Vrund.

"According to me, she will come with her friends, and in that case, it will be a very awkward position for me. So will you guys please accompany me?" I asked.

They both looked at each other, and replied, "But there is one problem, Bhavam."

"What?" I asked.

"We both don't know how to bowl! Do you?" she asked.

"Oh! So what? Even I don't know how to play. We are just going there to enjoy ourselves, not to compete," I said.

"But Bhavam, it's not only about enjoyment. People will make fun of us, if we don't play well," said Vrund

"Don't worry! Nothing like that is going to happen," I assured him.

Meanwhile my cell phone vibrated.

"It must be her message!" I said joyfully.

"How excited you are to read a girl's message, huh?" said Vrund.

"He isn't like you," said Nishu, taunting him.

Today 6 pm. Inorbit mall. Time zone.

"Time zone?" I asked Vrund.

"It's a gaming arena, idiot, where you can go bowling," said Vrund.

"Oh! I see!" I said.

"Oye, but first ask her with whom she is coming," said Nishu.

"Point!" I said.

Surely I will be there.
But are you coming there with your friends?

Yes. Why?

(POINT #7:- It's in the blood of every girl to bother a guy asking WHY????)

I handed over my cell phone to Nishu and asked, "Yaar, Nishu, what to say now?"

"Hehe…you are badly stuck," commented Vrund, looking at my face.

"Don't worry. Let me chat with her under your name," said Nishu.

(POINT #8:- That's why it is very necessary to have a lady friend, who is always ready to help you.)

They are nice guys, my very best friends, Nishu and Vrund. If you don't mind, can they join us?

Sure! Why not!
Your friends must be equally nice, just like you

Vrund was silently peeping at what Nishu was writing. When Ashwini used that smiley, I felt a little shy and embarrassed.

"Ahaa, Bhavam, kisses and all, haan?" asked Vrund suspiciously.

I diverted my attention to the book kept in front of me.

Nishu said, "Chill, Bhavam, don't be embarrassed. I am a girl and I know everything."

"But why do you guys not believe me? She is just my friend. I am damn single after my break-up," I said.

"And your ex was in a damn relationship straight after the break-up," said Vrund.

I looked at him angrily and said, "At least don't remind me of her today. It's a happy day for me."

"You know one thing, Bhavam, God has gifted you this tiny ANGEL in your life whose name is Ashwini. Don't lose her. Forget Preksha; she never deserved you. But this girl here definitely deserves you," said Nishu.

"Yes, I like her, but I don't have the strength to love someone again after what Preksha did with me!" I said.

"We boys always fear to love after a break-up," said Vrund.

"Oh, when did you have a break-up, dear Vrund?" asked Nishu angrily.

"Break-up is nothing new for me. I have it every day. I like many girls and they make me their brother. So now, I have stopped proposing," said Vrund.

"It's not like that! We girls are quite unpredictable," said Nishu.

"Very unpredictable!" added Vrund.

Nishu closed her book and said, "When our eyes are closed, we wish to have a guy who is popular and handsome. When our eyes are open, we wish to have a guy who can hold our hand in every situation. But in reality, such guys exist only in fairy tales."

I closed my book, and said, "I disagree, Nishu, there are guys who are ready to support a girl in every situation. But they won't come when your eyes are closed. It is also not necessary that they will come when your eyes are open. But true guys will surely come during the momentary blink of your eyes and they will say just one thing."

"And what is that?" asked Vrund respectfully.

"Your every blink is mine now," I answered.

Nishu was speechless after what I said.

"Don't worry, Nishu; he has that ability to make people speechless!" said Vrund.

"I don't know about you, Vrund, but I am surely going to accompany Bhavam this evening for bowling," she said, and packed her books, getting ready to leave.

"Where are you going?" asked Vrund.

"We all are going in the evening; so at present I have to study. You both do whatever you want," she said and left.

"That's the reason why every girl is a topper these days," I said to Vrund.

"It's not always about the girls. Some of them literally work very hard to crack IIT, but they still fail," said Vrund.

"You know, even I wanted to go to IIT-Delhi, but now here I am!" I said.

"You can still go there and do your masters by cracking GATE," said Vrund.

"Fucking JEE was out of my reach and you are blabbering about GATE. It's not possible now, so leave it," I said.

"But why is everyone so mad for IIT?" asked Vrund.

"It's as simple as that. Your annual salary package is equivalent to their monthly package, and there isn't a single person who doesn't want to become rich. So people dream to go to IIT, rub their ass continuously on one single bench or table daily, and study sincerely for four years," I replied.

"Oh! I see, but I am sure we are still happy," said Vrund.

"After years of graduation, we will see them earning in crores, while we will still be dealing with thousands or lakhs. It won't be difficult for them to get married because they continuously receive marriage invitations due to their graduate degree from IIT. On the other hand, people like us will have to give an advertisement in the paper for our marriage. Forget about marriage, their first car will be a BMW or a Porsche, and that too without a loan, and we will be striving to purchase even a Nano. They will see movies in expensive multiplexes, while we will watch the same movie in a single screen cinema hall. They will have VIP status, and people like me will still hang around only with Facebook status. So a degree from IIT is more than a heaven," I proclaimed.

"I agree with what you say, but still we will be happy. I know we won't have money, so definitely we won't have honey. The way I have worked in these four years, I know that my future house will be small. But I really don't care about it because I have decided to accept what I get. Though I am flirty, I will become a one woman man after marriage, because that girl will be the one in the universe who will live with me, without looking at my house. I don't want VIP status because I will stand in a queue and make more friends over there. BMW or Porsche will never be within my reach, but still I will happily play NFS in my Xbox with any car of the world, imagining that they are all mine. Let the rich ones see the movies silently in the big multiplexes, but they won't be able to whistle like us when we see a beautiful heroine in a single screen cheap cinema hall!" said Vrund.

When he said this, there was a tear in my eyes. I stood up and sat near him and said, "You are mature now."

"But now, please let us sort the questions from these papers, otherwise we will fail," he requested.

We both began the work of sorting out the common questions from the previous years' question papers. While studying seriously for the first time, we never realized that we had skipped our lunch. For the first time, I felt satisfaction that I wasn't in IIT, because I was sure that happiness lay here, in these surroundings…

(POINT #9 :- No matter in which college you study, it is totally up to you and your friends to decide the kind of life you wish to live.)

Location:- Inorbit mall
Time:- 5:45 pm

"Where is she?" asked Vrund.

"Still 15 minutes are left," I said.

"These girls never come on time," said Vrund angrily.

From far, we saw a beautiful girl approaching us.

"My God! Who is that beauty and why is she coming towards us?" he asked.

Even I was stunned, looking at the beauty of that girl. She was some distance away, so we were not able to see her clearly.

"Oh. It is Nishu," I said, stunned.

Vrund asked, "What did you say?"

"It's Nishu! That girl who is approaching us," I said.

"Nah! I see her daily in the college. She does not look that beautiful," he said.

After a while the girl came near us, and said, "Shall we go now?"

Our eyes could not accept the fact that the lady standing beside us was Nishu.

"My word, Nishu! I bet that, at present, you are the prettiest girl in the entire city. You look awesome today!" I said.

"Awww! Thanks, Bhavam," she said shyly.

"Wait… wait… wait… this is a trap, Bhavam. This girl looks like Nishu, but she isn't Nishu," said Vrund.

"What do you mean?" she asked.

"Don't mind me asking you one question. Are you Nishu's sister?" he asked.

"Just Shut up!" said Nishu, in a very loud tone and everyone turned around.

"Yes, confirmed! Only Nishu can show such anger. So you are Nishu. But why don't you dress up like this every day?" he asked.

"Bhavam, tell your friend that he doesn't deserve an explanation from me," she ordered.

"I am sorry. I was just joking, Nishu. Don't take it seriously," said Vrund.

"Why shall I take you seriously, dude, when you have never taken me seriously?" she questioned.

"Yaar, Nishu, stop this please! You also know that whatever I say is just shit," said Vrund.

"Because you are a shit itself. A loser, a defeated person, perverted, flirty, self centered and most importantly, a dumb guy! Whatever adjectives I use for you are less!" said Nishu angrily, in very loud tone.

"Nishu, please!" I said, holding her wrist.

"Today don't stop me, Bhavam, from speaking. I have had enough of him!" she said.

For the first time ever, Vrund was feeling bad and insulted in his life. Many people looked him and he felt more embarrassed.

"You people go and enjoy your bowling. I am going. Bhavam, you were right. We have happiness, but no respect," said Vrund as he turned away. We both saw him rubbing his hands over his eyes. He wanted to cry but he was strong enough not to do so in front of us. Nishu was strong as she didn't show any emotions.

"Nishu, we all know that he is nuts. Then why did you do this?" I asked her.

"Our last semester is ending. I have waited for him for four years. Now this is only the way that I can forget him!" she said.

"But, Nishu, that is not the way to forget him, by insulting him in front of this vulgar public. Forget about erasing him from your mind. This incident will trouble you even more," I said.

"I am sorry, Bhavam. I can't accompany you. You please enjoy yourself with Ashwini and don't get involved in this," she said and left.

What happened was a brutal verbal exchange of words between Nishu and Vrund. Both had left the Inorbit mall and so I was alone now.

The crowd, which had gathered due to that verbal scene slowly started scattering.

"Bhavam," said a soft little voice from behind. I knew it was Ashwini. Despite all that tension, I was able to give her a warm smile.

"Were they your friends?" Ashwini asked.

"Yes! You saw that right?" I asked.

"But why was the girl insulting that guy?" Ashwini asked.

"What shall I tell you; it's a very long story." I said.

"No story is long! It's either boring or interesting," she said.

"They were Vrund and Nishu, my only true friends. Vrund is very easy going and a flirt from day one of college. However, his tactics impressed Nishu. Many times she has tried to convince Vrund that she loves him, but Vrund is so dumb that he thinks that as he is a flirt, no girl can love him. So today, Nishu created this drama, in order to erase Vrund permanently from her mind," I explained.

"Oh! Poor girl!" she exclaimed.

"And you were supposed to come with your friends, right? Where are they? They also fought?" I asked.

She laughed and said, "No…no…! They can never fight and they are here only."

"I can't see them. Where are they?" I asked.

She took out her keychain on which two cute baby dolls were hanging. She lifted it and said, "These are my best friends."

I smiled at her innocence. She was still a child in her heart and I was also like her.

"So what are their names?" I asked.

"The name of the first doll is Roho and the name of the second doll is Pruru," she said.

"Wow! That's amazing. Can we have a selfie with Roho and Pruru, please?" I requested.

She immediately took out her Sony Xepria and took a selfie. I loved it when she took a selfie because, every time she did so, she came close to me.

"Don't they look cute?" she asked.

"Yes, Roho and Pruru look cute with us," I agreed.

We reached Time Zone, the ultimate gaming arena.

"You know I love this place?" she said.

"Have you ever been here before?" I asked.

"Many times, but I always missed bowling because my card balance gets over very soon," she said.

"So it means that today we will only bowl?" I asked her.

"Yes," she said.

She took out the gaming card from her purse, and also a 500 rupee note and started going towards the gaming cash counter.

I hold her hand and said, "What are you doing?"

"To recharge this card," she said.

"You won't ask for my share?" I asked. "I am not like that!" I added.

"No, yaar, it's nothing like that. You were the only one who was ready to come with me, despite the pressure of your approaching exams. You just give me your company and that is worth more than the money," she explained.

Taking out my wallet, I said, "It's not fair, Ashwini. I know I can never be your best friend, like Roho and Pruru, but you will have to take my share of bowling."

"Who told you that you cannot be my best friend?" she queried.

"Everyone till now made fun of me when I told them that these non living key chains are my best friends. You were the first person to understand me and my childlike behavior when you asked me to take a selfie including them," she said with an emotional smile on her cute little face.

I looked into her eyes and asked, "Don't you have any friends who are human?"

She laughed at this and said, "Yes, I have a few friends, but they all are selfish and busy with their boyfriends."

This was the best opportunity to ask her the question which I had always wanted to ask, "Never had a boy friend after the break-up?"

"No. Why?" she said.

"Not like that, but girls move on more quickly than guys," I said.

"Moving on for a girl is not always making a new boyfriend, but realizing the value of the friends who support her after the exit of that guy from her life," she explained.

(POINT #10:- For a girl, her friends are everything after a break-up.)

"But you have to take my share," I insisted.

"If you want our friendship to be built upon money, than go on," she said.

This was a very odd situation for me. I made a compromise, saying, "Okay, if the bowling treat is from your side, then tonight's dinner is from my side!" I said.

She smiled and immediately agreed.

(POINT #11:- To your crush, always try to repay your share of money in the form of a dinner. I bet she will love it!)

We went inside the bowling arena. Many guys were there along with their so-called BAEs. Nishu was right. It was a competitive game.

I immediately asked Ashwini, "You know how to play it?"

"Yes, daily I bowl on my cell phone," she said.

"But reality is different. You see how they are taking the stance. The way they are throwing the ball. We have never tried this," I said.

"Why are you so worried, yaar? We have come here to enjoy the game. So get the gaming card scratched, so that we can start playing," she urged me.

When I was going there, I saw a stranger approaching Ashwini saying, "Will you compete with us?"

She was friendly with everyone, and she replied humbly, "No, dude, we aren't professional like you. We are here just to enjoy ourselves, not to compete. Please find someone else to be your competing partner."

When I returned to her, I saw that the guy who was communicating with her was none other than Karan, the current boyfriend of my ex girlfriend Preksha. He was surprised when he saw me coming. I stared fiercely into his eyes. "Come, let's go, Ashwini and play," I said in a rough tone.

Karan commented from behind, "Oh, girl, wait! That's why you aren't competing with us. You already have one loser with you who doesn't even know how to protect his own girl."

My eyes were down when I heard that nonsensical comment from Karan. Ashwini stopped immediately, turned around and said in a loud tone, "What do you mean, haan?"

I touched her soft hands and said in a low tone, "Leave him, Ashwini. Let's go."

She looked at my face and asked me, "You know him? Who is he?"

"He is Karan. The current boyfriend of my ex," I said.

Although I tried to stop Ashwini, she again approached Karan and said, "Don't you dare call him a loser. He is a winner. You want a match? Guess what? You got it."

"Leave it, girl. We don't play with kids," mocked Karan.

I took Ashwini aside and said, "What are you doing? Why are you challenging him? He is perfect at bowling, and we are here for the first time. Everyone will laugh at us. I don't mind people insulting me because I am now used to it, but I will not be able to bear people laughing at you."

She placed her palm on my cheeks and said, "You still fear. That time you were alone, but now you aren't alone to face them. Let's show them what we can do as a team."

She then went to where Karan was standing, and said, "Hello, Mister, let's play the game."

Karan and his friends looked at us and said, "But where is your team? We are five in number."

"We two are enough for you," said Ashwini boldly.

Karan approached me and whispered in my ears, "You weren't a man and that's why your ex is with me today. Think it over twice before competing with us. I hope this girl won't leave you after you lose to me today, because you are a born loser."

I had never felt so angry in my life, but I looked at Ashwini, who was quite excited to take this challenge. I replied to Karan, "You are right, I wasn't a man at that time. But the times have changed. Now you are a daddy and I am a man."

The stage was fully prepared for a one on one bowling match between me and Ashwini against Karan and his team. It was the culture here in the bowling arena to name your team before playing the match.

The guy who was managing the bowling arena approached us, and asked, "What is the name of your team?"

Ashwini got confused by that question as she could not think of a name immediately.

I closed my eyes and said, "ANGELS."

She looked at me as I said, "The name of our team will be ANGELS!"

The guy noted the name and approached Karan to ask for their team name.

"Wow! That's a pretty good name. How quickly you invented it!" she said.

The big LED screen which was placed at the high epicenter of the bowling track showed 'ANGELS VS DEVILS'.

The music, which was humming in the time zone, suddenly stopped, and a host came and started announcing, "Ladies and

Gentlemen, boys and girls, have you even heard ANGELS competing against DEVILS?"

The crowd responded, "No."

The announcer responded, "Then your wait is over. Today we have an interesting match between ANGELS and DEVILS, and whosoever wins today, will receive a gift voucher from Time Zone arena. Before the game starts, it's my humble duty to tell you that it is Ten-pin bowling game. The ball is really heavy with three finger holes in it. Five chances will be given to each team and at the end of play, whichever team is more successful in knocking the pins out, will be the winners. So here we go!"

The crowd surrounded us, as we began to play.

"All of them are going to laugh at us today," I said, looking at Ashwini.

The first set began. From their team, Sarthak was the first person to start the resending.

He grabbed the heavy ball in his three fingers, took the measurement and immediately threw the ball. The ball rolled over the entire lane and hit the pins. His target was so perfect that, at his first attempt, he was successfully able to knock over seven pins.

The crowd erupted when the pins were knocked down.

From our team, Ashwini was the first one to go. She took the ball in her hands. I knew that she was feeling the weight of the ball. She looked uncomfortable. She took a little bit of time to release the ball. When she rolled the heavy ball on the wooden lane, the ball immediately changed its direction and escaped the wooden lane, causing it to be a foul as no pins were knocked down. Karan and team laughed at this. The crowd showed a negative reaction by booing us.

Ashwini kicked the floor and looked quite depressed as she came back.

"There is something wrong in this wooden surface. I threw the ball in a straight trajectory, but it changed its direction on its own," she said.

"Relax. We are new and this was bound to happen," I said to her in consolation.

As I was a science stream student, I understood the reason why the ball changed its trajectory. But it was impossible to make her understand.

So at the end of first trail, the scores which were readable on the LED screens were ANGELS (0) and DEVILS (7).

Mehul was the second person to come and knock the pins off from the opposite team. He perfectly pinned nine out of ten pins down. Only one pin was left to fall down. It is called 'strike' when all ten pins get knocked down at once, and luckily that didn't happen. From our team, I was the next person to go.

"All the best!" said Ashwini.

I saw that if I throw the ball in a straight direction, it will definitely turn. So I decided to throw it from a bit of a reverse angle so that it would exactly strike at the middle. I closed my eyes as I fingered the ball in my hand. Before throwing the ball, I looked at Ashwini. Her fingers were crossed. I took the normal stance, but by mistake, I overstepped the wooden surface. It was oily and smooth, and I lost my balance and slipped down horizontally as the ball fell on my face.

I knew I had created a scene. All the people who had gathered around started laughing at me. Some of them even clapped. Although I was in deep pain, it was a horrible scene for me to witness.

However, Ashwini immediately came to console me. She got down and placed her hand on my head and asked, "Are you alright?"

Tears were in her ears as she said, "You were right. This game needs a bit of practice, but I didn't listen to you. Because of me, you are in deep pain now. I am so sorry."

I wiped off her tears and said, "No, Ashwini, we still have three trials and we will play. Now when I am inspired, don't be negative."

After the end of second trial, the huge LED screen showed - ANGELS (0+0=0) and DEVILS (7+9=16).

In the third set, Jalesh from their group was able to knock down eight pins. It seemed like the crowd was only cheering for the DEVILS. No one was supporting us.

For the third trial, Ashwini again took the chance.

"Hey, listen!" I said.

She turned back.

"Don't throw the ball heavily in the straight line. Just make a little change in your projection. All the best!" I said.

This time I crossed my fingers, because if we were unable to score this time, then we were surely out of the game.

I looked up at the skies and said, "Please, this time don't disappoint us."

Ashwini released the ball. It started spinning this time, instead of rolling. The ball just managed to hit the pin which was on the right hand side of the main pain.

As a result, for the first time, the pins were down. When I looked up, I saw that Ashwini was successful in knocking six pins down.

There was a shy smile on her face when those six pins were knocked out. There were only a few who clapped after our first little breakthrough.

Therefore, at the end of third trial, the scores were ANGELS (0+0+6=6) and DEVILS (7+9+8=24)

Karan said to Sarthak in an audible tone, “That’s good to see. But I bet that Bhavam won’t be able to knock a single pin down tonight.”

“How can he? He is a born loser,” commented Mehul from their team.

Ashwini united her fingers in my empty hand and held my palm, saying, “Don’t listen to them. You aren’t a loser. Prove to them today, what you can do when you are angry.”

When the fourth round began, we were depending more on luck. I closed my eyes again in the hope that something would happen in our favor, so that we could at least reach closer to their score. Dhruv was the next person to come from their team and deliver.

Dhruv was an old friend of mine too. He had been my classmate till the tenth standard. We were good friends but then suddenly, when we got separated having taken different streams, he changed his group and got in contact with guys like Karan. He knew everything about me and Preksha. Till the tenth, he was an honest guy, who favored me. But today he was playing for Karan, despite being my friend.

Dhruv fingered the ball and looked at me and gave me the shy smile which he used to give when we were in school. I was so tense that I didn’t smile in return. He then took a stance and threw the ball on the wooden surface. Surprisingly the ball escaped the wooden lane and didn't hit any of the pins. All were surprised to see that. After that Dhruv again looked at me with the same smile and signed with his eyes that he was on my side.

I realized that he had deliberately done that. I was happy to know that he still cared and respected our friendship.

It was my turn now. I was a little charged up this time, and hoped to do something because I had no option left except to deliver.

I fingered the ball and concentrated on the pins which were kept at the end of the lane. I was distracted for a moment when I saw one known face in the crowd. I looked up and found that it was someone like Heenal. However, this time, when I threw the ball, it rolled and touched the centered pin first. To my surprise, this time, nine pins were knocked down by me. Now the crowd became quite interested in the game and cheered a bit more than the last time for us.

After the fourth trial the scores were:- ANGELS (0+0+6+9=15) and DEVILS (7+9+8+0=24)

Now the fifth and the penultimate round arrived.

Karan was the only one left to deliver.

In order to win this game, we needed to strike all the ten pins down. If we were successful in doing that, we had to score one more time in order to win the game.

A known face again came into my vision. I carefully tried to examine who she was. But the crowd was so excited that I was not able to see her properly.

Karan took the stance. When he was going to deliver, Ashwini hugged my arm and muttered, "Please no, please no."

Karan rolled the ball and it did hit the pins but not perfectly. Only five out of ten pins were knocked down by him, but he seemed to be happy because that was enough for his team to win.

"Bhavam, I am very nervous. We need a clean strike, knocking all the ten pins down in this final trial," she said, holding my hand.

"You will do this for us!" I said.

"I am shivering. I can't even hold the ball now," she said.

I motivated Ashwini, saying, "Look, we are not defeated yet. We still have a chance and if you do a clean strike, we will have a golden chance to win. Come on, you can do it!"

Her face looked even more innocent when she was nervous.

She said, "Will you forgive me if I am unable to deliver?"

I smiled and said, "We have already won. Because ANGELS never lose. You know why the word ANGELS came out of my mind when that person asked me to name our team? Because you are an ANGEL. You don't have any idea about the happiness and smiles you have brought in my life. You can make a dead person smile, and hence, this is such a small thing for you. I trust you, go on!"

She hugged me emotionally. I hugged her too.

Karan, who was standing there, might have been jealous seeing this.

While she was hugging me, Karan clicked our photos from his cell phone. I knew that he was going to show this to Preksha and make a story out of it, but I never cared as I had a real woman in my arms.

She looked determined as she grabbed the ball in her fingers. She took the stance and was ready to deliver. This time she looked at me and I showed her a thumbs up, indicating 'All the best!' In the fraction of a second, she released the ball. The ball started rolling. It hit the pins with maximum force. The force was so much that all the pins internally touched each other, and of them only eight were knocked down.

We had lost!

I thought that was it! But one of those two pins was vibrating, and after a few seconds, it fell down, giving a mild touch to the other pin as well, due to which those other two pins also fell down. It was a clean strike.

The crowd erupted into a huge cheer, as for the first time there was a clean strike in the game. Even Ashwini was not able to believe it. Karan and his group looked stunned after seeing this. However, Dhruv was the exception who smiled innocently from their side. Ashwini came and hugged me tightly and said, "I can't believe this."

I controlled her, saying, "We aren't done yet."

After that strike the scores were ANGELS (0+0+6+9+10=25) and DEVILS (7+9+8+0+5=29).

It is the rule in bowling that, when you do a clean strike by knocking all ten pins down, you get one more opportunity to score. So we had that golden opportunity.

"Bhavam, now it's your turn to score," she said.

"No, dear, you deserve it, since you made this happen," I said.

"My heart is telling me that you should knock the winning hit!" she insisted.

(* But my heart was telling me one thing and that was to adore her. I was completely bowled over by her.)

"Even my heart has something to say…!" I said.

"And what is that?" she asked.

I thought that I was crossing my limits, so I controlled myself. For the last time I fingered that ball in my hands. When I took my stance, I was clearly able to see Heenal in front of my eyes, standing there in the crowd. She signaled to me to concentrate on my game, indicating that she was with me. I wondered how she was here. She even showed me a thumbs up and I touched the ground, indicating that I was taking her blessings.

Looking at this, she smiled and gave me a flying kiss.

I released the ball. It started spinning this time, instead of rolling.

"No…!" came a shout from Ashwini because the ball was on the verge of escaping the wooden surface again before hitting the pins at the end of the lane.

I thought that I had made a mess.

Karan and his group started celebrating.

But somehow, the ball managed to hit the very last pin in the lane, and then it escaped the surface. The last pin started vibrating and it caused four more pins to get knocked out.

Five pins were down and we roared in happiness because now, after that blow, the scores were ANGELS [0+0+6+9+10(+5) =30] and DEVILS [7+9+8+0+5=29]

We had won the game with a difference of one pin.

Ashwini was in tears when she realized that we had just won the match. After that strike, everyone in the crowd started applauding us and chanted, 'Angels…Angels…Angels…!' I was so happy and so was Ashwini.

She again gave me a tight hug and I happily accepted it.

"We won. Really?" she asked.

"Not only we," I said.

I indicated her key chain which had two dolls named Roho and Pruru and said, "They are also part of our victory, so they are the winners too. People thought that we were two and they were five, but in reality, we were also five. You, me, Roho, Pruru and Heenal," I said.

"Who is Heenal?" she asked.

"She is like my sister. She is here. I saw her when I was making that final hit," I said.

Karan and his losing group were preparing to leave. I went there and placed my packet of cigarettes in Karan's hand and said, "This defeat will hurt you, but don't worry; this will help you to accept the fact that I am not the loser anymore."

In anger he threw that packet of cigarettes down and left angrily. However, Dhruv was still standing there. As soon as Karan left, I gave Dhruv a very big hug.

"Thanks, dost! I don't know why you did this," I said.

He again flashed that innocent smile and said, "I know everything, Bhavam. I have been with this Karan since college and now I have realized that he is a damn cheat. I can't leave his group because if I do, than he will torture me daily, as we are in the same college. But the day I realized that he had come between you and Preksha and created a spat, I started hating him. When he created a spat between you both, I wasn't there. But today I was here, and I knew that if I scored, you would lose. So I intentionally did that and I have no regrets that I have cheated him, because of you and your loyalty, firstly towards Preksha, and now to this girl."

Ashwini came, looked at Dhruv and said, "Thank you."

Dhruv replied, "He is the nicest of the guys you will ever find, dear. Don't lose him. You go and get your gift hamper from them. I need to go now."

Usually you find a massive change in the attitude of your tenth standard friend, but Dhruv was still the same.

(POINT #12:- There are still some people who don't change with the times. If you ever realize that you have that one person who has never changed his attitude towards you, no matter what the situations are, than give him a big hug because he deserves it.)

After Dhruv left, Ashwini merrily went to the bowling counter and asked, "Where's our gift?"

The in-charge over there handed her one envelope, saying, "Congratulations! You both are getting free passes of Ablas Imagica for one whole day, which includes lunch and dinner."

When she heard this, she jumped in the air! However the smile faded away from my face, because I was petrified of roller coaster rides.

"So when are we going there?" she asked.

"I can accompany you to the bowling alley, but roller coaster rides are not in my range," I said.

She laughed and assured me, "Don't worry! Nothing will happen to you."

How did she realize that I was scared? I never told her that. Girls are so intuitive sometimes. (Only sometimes!)

"I mean I can't accompany you because my exams are approaching. It's a big roller coaster which I have to pass, and after that I will have the courage to sit on the real roller coaster," I said.

"Don't worry. My exams are approaching too. We will go in the vacation because these passes are valid up to one month," she smiled.

I could not deny her anything because she was my crush.

Not Crush! Even more than that!

Chapter 12

Location:- Inorbit mall
Time:- 7:45 pm

"Where is she?" I asked myself, as we were eating our meal at KFC.

"Who?" asked Ashwini.

"Oh! I told you about Heenal? I am looking for her. We both saw each other," I said.

"It's such a big mall. You cannot find someone again after you see them once," she said.

I said in confusion, "But if she saw me, then she would definitely have approached me. I wonder why she didn't!"

"Why do you think so much?" she asked. "She might have gone. Life is like that only. Today you see someone and tomorrow you won't," she added.

"You mean to say that you will go away from me?" I said.

"No. I didn't mean that. But someday I have to go," she said.

"Although you may go away, you will still be there with me always," I said.

"How?" she asked.

"Generally people store lovely memories in their brain, but the moments spent with you are stored in my heart. So whenever you are not there, I will close my eyes and enjoy our memories," I said.

"And what if they bring tears in your eyes?" she asked.

"They won't bring tears; they will only bring smiles because you are only made to make others smile," I said.

"But I don't trust people. That's why only Roho and Pruru are my best friends," she said, the dilemma showing on her face.

"All guys are not the same," I said.

"It's not always about the opposite sex. I mean there are always internal conflicts with close friends, and some conflicts are such that can never be resolved," she expressed.

(I was getting hints that she had no real life friends.)

"You can share everything with me. I know I am not your best friend, but still I am trustworthy," I said.

"Again that same thing you said!" she exclaimed. "You are more than a friend for me. Isn't that enough for you?" she asked.

"It's more than enough for me," I replied, as she looked in my eyes.

I was confused. Why was she staring at me suddenly? I interrupted and asked her, "What happened, Ashwini?"

She said nothing. I was nervous, wondering why she was showing zero reaction.

I placed my fingers on her palm and suddenly understood what she meant. I said, "Life would have been completely different, if you had met me before."

I knew what she was emphasizing. She meant friendship, although I assumed love, and replied, "Better late than never."

On hearing this, she smiled.

(POINT #13:- Those beautiful moments when you are having the time of your life with your crush, and you imagine that your story would have been totally different, if your current crush had come into your life before your ex.)

Whenever Ashwini used to smile, I felt as if that smile was only made for me.

I wanted to tell her that her smile meant a lot to me, but rather than saying anything, I just looked at her, enjoying that smile.

She suddenly remarked, "Every boy is a thief."

I was surprised, and wondered why thought so.

"But I didn't steal anything from you," I said.

"Not you. I am talking about other guys," she explained.

(POINT #14:- When she continuously addresses you by the term 'other guys', you definitely doubt if she considers you a GUY or not.)

"But what do other guys do?" I asked desperately.

"They impress a girl. Give her fake promises of oneness. By cheating, they win her trust, and after trusting him, she allows him to kiss her and be intimate with her. Then, one day, that guy goes away and she regrets everything, thinking that it was her fault. Isn't this correct?" she questioned me with determination in her eyes.

I looked into her beautiful eyes and replied, "Maybe that's why you call them guys, and not men, because a real man won't ever do this."

She seemed to be convinced by my answer.

After we completed our dinner, she said, "Let's go to Akota bridge."

Akota bridge is the longest and the only bunking destination in terms of bridges in our city, Vadodara.

I suddenly realized that I had come along with Vrund in the same vehicle, and since he had left, because of the dispute with Nishu, I had turned vehicle-less.

"I'm sorry, Ashwini, I can't come," I said sadly.

On hearing this, she too made a sad face and asked, "Why not?"

(POINT #14:- When you a reject a girl's proposal for a casual hangout, she expresses her agony by making a sad face.)

"You know that I came with Vrund, and we shared the same vehicle. Now since he is not there, I don't possess my own vehicle and so…!" I said, hoping that she would understand my point of view.

She laughed at this. I felt strange and said, "I am not joking. Seriously, I have no vehicle."

At this, she laughed loudly and said, "Then why are you making your own joke? It's simple; you will have to ride behind me."

(*Any other person in my place would have taken this as a golden opportunity because it is the dream of everyone to be on a ride with their crush.)

However, for an assurance I asked her, "Don't you mind sitting behind me?"

(POINT #16:- A girl may like an opportunistic guy, but she will definitely love the guy who takes an assurance before even kissing her.)

Blinking her eyes, she said, "Of course I don't mind. But you have misunderstood me."

"About what?" I asked.

"I am not sitting behind you. It is you who will be sitting behind me," she said and started walking.

It was a very uncomfortable situation for me.

"Walk fast, Bhavam!" shouted Ashwini from ahead.

She looked back and asked, "What happened?"

Then directing her face towards me, she brought her lips near my face. I thought she would kiss me, but instead, she whispered in my ears, "I was joking to test you. You will drive; now come fast. We are already late."

This brought relief to my heart.

"I would love to drive 4651," I said, indicating her vehicle.

"Hehe…very funny!" she smiled. "You are talking as if my little vehicle is an aircraft."

"But you are no less than a pilot," I said, and smiled, looking at her innocent face.

She held my hand, and subjected her little finger in my empty seedless palm and said, "I needed a friend like you."

(*I wanted to tell her that I too needed a girlfriend just like her, but sometimes, if some things are said at the proper time, only then are they fruitful.)

We reached the parking lot where she had placed her 4651.

"You know I don't need to search for your vehicle, because it is so close to my heart that I can even find it in my dreams," I said, giving her another sign that I liked her.

(POINT #17:- Each and every relationship in any form is a step by step process. Guys always express their feelings by giving minor signs and girls are smart enough to understand this. While for a girl, the job is so easy. She just has to give a beautiful smile by mistake and the guy will do the rest.)

"How can you be so sure about guessing my vehicle even in your dreams?" she asked.

I laughed and said, "It is so simple! Your vehicle would collide with someone in every rainy season."

Hearing this, she said, "Shut up, Bhavam! That was just an accident. I usually don't collide with anyone like that."

"But that is the reason we are here together," I smiled.

(*Wish I could tell Ashwini that, it was not only her vehicle but she herself, who collided with me, even in my day dreams.)

I sat on her 4651. She placed her right hand over my shoulder for support in order to sit. I focused my mirror, so that I could see her beautiful face. Then she lifted her pretty legs. My focus was on the mirror as I was attracted by the beauty of her legs, yes, they were sexy.

(POINT #18:- Each and every girl is sexy for a guy when she wears one piece.)

I accelerated 4651 and headed towards the Akota bridge.

"Drive fast, Bhavam!" she urged.

"Ashwini, I am not a biker," I protested.

"But I love bikers! They are so passionate about speed. When they drive at 80 plus speed, it feels as if the wind is kissing our faces," she said.

Initially I felt jealous about that imaginary biker, but I replied, "Every one has different passions. Bikers can make you feel the winds, and unknown poets, like me, can touch your heart by composing a few lines."

"I can see that by your posts on FB," she said. "I wish to hear those short cute lines in your own voice," she demanded.

For a moment I got lost in my thoughts, and then said,

"Bae...
Every morning from now is a bliss,
Waiting for you was a gift!
Bae...
The stars are in its horizon,
Love isn't cheap like things on Amazon!

Bae…

I'm alone, though I pretend to be happy,

The day you see me, you'll agree!"

As soon as I completed my poetry, I felt her touch on my back. Yes, indeed, it was true. After hearing my poem, she had placed her head on my back and her sweet hands were near my waist. If I were God I would have frozen that moment for ever.

Location:- Akota Bridge

We both felt as if we were on the top of the city, because the whole of Vadodara looked beautiful from there. Railway lines created a crackling sound from below and aeroplanes flew above our heads, as we were standing there on the pedestrian lane, especially provided for the bridge walk.

"Every day I wish to be here, but today it feels special. I have never felt so, even though I have come here frequently," she said softly.

"It's very tough to stay alone. A person can live without love, but he can't live without friendship, and our friendship is true. That's why you are feeling special," I replied.

"You always fascinate me by your responses." she said.

"I am fascinated by you, Ashwini!" I said.

She listened but didn't reply, as she was lost in her own world.

The moment was perfect for the proposal. I wanted her to be with me for my whole life. I wanted to tell her that she had taken that empty place which had once belonged to Preksha. I made up my mind that, anyhow, I would propose to her. But I was afraid of rejection.

"What is this so tight around your neck, Bhavam?" she asked.

My heart stopped for a moment when I touched my neck. I smiled mildly and said, "Preksha gave me this locket when we were in a relationship."

She seemed tense after hearing that, and asked, "And you are still wearing it? Come on, yaar, why?"

I broke the eye contact and whispered, "I don't know."

"Enough, Bhavam, remove this locket from your neck. You don't have any idea. It's so tight that it can damage your neck in the near future," she said.

(POINT #19:- Guys love when their crush shows such caring behavior)

"I can't separate it from my body, Ashwini. It was given by 'that Preksha' who loved me. So this locket is very close to my heart," I said.

"She must have thrown all your similar gifts and memories in the junk and you are still bearing a piece of shit around your neck," she said angrily.

I didn't respond.

"You said that our friendship is true, and so I am only telling you the truth. Keeping her things with you won't help you to move on. Before being Preksha's boyfriend, Karan was just her friend. He interfered and broke your relationship. And today as your friend, I'm requesting you to throw this locket because you have lost your smile since she left you," she explained.

Again I listened to her, looking at her face, but didn't say anything.

"Don't be silent; say something. Okay, tell me, do I have any right over you?" she asked.

I nodded and said, "Yes."

(*Wish I could tell that she had started ruling my heart too!)

"All right!" she exclaimed, and placed her palm before my neck in order to remove that locket.

I stopped her, holding her hand as I said in a loud voice, "Ashwini, it's enough. Tell me one thing! Will you ever forgive me if I throw out your Roho and Pruru?"

She felt insulted by my words and I noticed her eyes getting wet.

I immediately apologized by saying, "Hey, I'm sorry. I shouldn't have insulted you like that."

"I'm going. You stay with your ex and her memory only. The day when you realize that it's high time to give up such things, you talk to me," she said.

She turned and started walking. I held her wrist from behind, and she turned and said, "Oh Bhavam! Please, I am sorry. Don't cry, yaar, please. Stop! You never insulted me. Please calm down, dear," she pleaded.

Tears were still falling from my eyes when I took her right hand near my face. I got hold of her other hand and said, "Please don't leave me. She has already left and now if you leave then…! Please don't go. I'm sorry. I… I…!"

She than wiped away my tears and said, "Now don't cry. I'm not going anywhere. I'm here, forever with you. What did you think? That I will leave you? Never, Bhavam. Our friendship isn't that weak."

She came much closer to me. My eyes were still wet. She closed her eyes and fell into my arms. Without thinking about anything, I wrapped her in my arms. I felt as if her body was touching my soul.

After a deep long hug, she moved away. My eyes were still closed. She placed her beautiful fingers on them and said, "Does it feel good?"

I gently opened my eyes and said, "What do you think?"

"I see my image in your eye balls," she said, with a smile on her face.

I smiled back and said, "It's you, and not your image."

"Bhavam, at least now trust me! Throw away this locket," she requested.

I placed my right hand on that locket, and said, "You are right. I almost lost you because of this thing. I can't afford to lose you even in my thoughts."

I tried to open the knot which I had tied tightly over the last few years. It was so tight that I asked Ashwini, "Will you help me to untie it?"

She placed her hands over my neck in order to remove that locket. She applied a bit of pressure, and it was hurting me. That pain seemed to lessen with her touch.

"See it has created a mark over your neck due to the continuous friction between the locket and your skin," she pointed out.

"God created you to free me from this," I said.

"Bhavam, we have to cut it. Otherwise it won't get separated from your neck," she said.

"Do you have scissors in 4651?" I asked.

"Ehh…? It's my vehicle, not a saloon," she joked.

"Okay, don't worry. When I will go to the hostel, I will cut it myself," I said.

"No. I don't trust you in this matter. You have to do it right now in front of my eyes," she said.

"But how?" I asked.

She came close to me. Again she closed her eyes, and I did the same. I thought it would be a kiss, but she detached a thread of the locket with her teeth. The locket was now off from my neck. She took that locket in her hands and said, "Here is that thing. Now it won't trouble you anymore."

The shape of that locket was imprinted on my neck.

"But the mark of the locket won't leave me," I said.

"It will make you realize that she was the biggest mistake in your life and hence, you won't repeat that mistake ever again," she explained.

I just looked into her expressive eyes. They were full of love.

Ashwini handed over the locket to me, and said, "Come, Bhavam, now throw this locket from the top of this bridge, imagining that you are getting rid of all the pains which she gave you!"

The locket was in my hands. My heart still hesitated to throw it. She was staring at me.

"I need your hand to support me to throw this away," I said.

She encircled her tiny fingers in my palm and said, "I am with you."

What was next? With maximum velocity, I threw that locket from the top of the bridge.

"See, Bhavam, all the pains which she gave you have gone very far away from you," she said.

I looked until the locket vanished in the night skies.

"We should leave now, Ashwini," I said.

We got seated on 4651 and departed for our respective hostels.

When we were on the way, she asked, "So now, will you make a new girlfriend?"

Was she providing me another opportunity to propose?

I applied the brakes to 4651.

"What happened? Why did you stop?" she asked.

I took a coin from my pocket and took a firm decision that I would toss the coin. If it was heads, I would propose to Ashwini on the spot. If it was tails, I would propose to her later on.

I handed over that coin in her hand and said, "Toss this coin, Ashwini! Everything is in your hands."

She got confused and asked, "Why?"

"Don't ask questions. Just toss the coin and let me know the result," I said.

She placed that coin between the index of her thumb and first finger and tossed it.

When the coin was in the air, I crossed my fingers because I was confident today, and I was expecting heads.

The coin rolled down and it was tails. I cursed my bad luck because I wanted it to happen today.

"Tails it is!" said Ashwini and lifted up the coin.

I shrugged my head and said, "Let's go now."

"But what was that?" she asked.

"A big decision in my life which you just made!" I said.

She held my hand and again came close to me and asked, "And what was that decision?"

"I can't tell you that right now," I said.

"Then when?" she asked.

"I don't know. May be tomorrow or maybe some other day, but not now," I said.

"Okay, I will be waiting," she promised.

What a situation it was! She was waiting and I was controlling.

(POINT #20:- Sometimes a girl is just waiting for a guy to express his feelings about her, and the guy controls those feelings in fear of losing the friendship.)

After that, she again got seated and placed her hands over my shoulders for support.

"WTF!" she exclaimed suddenly, as we were smoothly approaching our destination.

"What happened?" I asked in surprise.

"Look at the time, Bhavam. My hostel won't allow me to enter after ten," she said, with tears in her eyes.

"Chill, what is the need to cry over such a small matter?" I said.

"Small matter?" she asked. "You are saying this as if you are going to shelter me in your hostel," she added.

"Don't worry, Ashwini, you put your trust in me and gave me the most beautiful evening of my life. So now it is my duty to make you reach in your hostel safely," I said.

"But how?" she asked desperately.

"Trust me, dear. At least have this much of faith in me," I said, looking into her eyes.

She was relieved when I assured her.

(POINT #21:- No matter what the situation is, once you assure her that you are with her, she will feel relieved, even if it is temporary.)

"But where are you taking me?" she asked.

"The Arts Faculty," I replied.

"But that's the boys' hostel and I want to go to my hostel," she protested.

"Shhhhh! Once I have said that I will take you safely to your hostel, then trust me," I assured.

She didn't reply this time.

We reached the Arts faculty. There was no one outside because the gates were officially closed.

"See, it's closed now. I told you, but you…!" she said angrily.

"It's just closed, not locked," I said, indicating the main gate.

This time she felt embarrassed as she realized that she had panicked for nothing.

(POINT #22:- When she is panicked, she will never accept that she is wrong. However, when the situation becomes normal, she will change her attitude.)

I opened the main gate as we stepped in. I explained to her everything about the secret passage.

After a few moments we were in front of that dark secret passage.

"No, Bhavam, I will sleep better on the footpath, rather than walk through this dangerous place," she said with a shiver in her voice.

"I am there with you, so don't fear," I said, reassuring her.

"I fear darkness and it's so scary here. It gives me goosebumps," she said.

She started walking away. As soon as she turned, I grabbed her hand and encircled my fingers with her soft little fingers and asked, "Are you still afraid?"

"I'm still a little frightened," she said.

"But what's there to fear in the dark?" I asked.

"Some things don't have answers," she said.

"But Ashwini…!"

She interrupted me and said, "Shhhhh…! I don't want to listen to anything, Bhavam. It's final that I'm not placing my leg in this scary place."

What to do now? I was confused but determined to make her reach safely.

"Okay, I promise you that you won't have to place your feet down. Just put both your hands around my neck and don't worry. I'm not going to do anything wrong," I said, in the hope that she would agree.

Without thinking further, she placed both her hands around my neck.

"I know that you won't do anything wrong!" she said.

(POINT #23:- That is the most beautiful moment when she says that you won't do anything wrong, despite the opportunity.)

As she encircled both her hands around me, I got hold of her back with my hands and lifted her up in my arms.

My God! She looked stunned when I did that!

"Before you ask me anything, I will tell you the reason why I lifted you in my arms," I said.

She again interrupted and said, in a more convinced tone this time, "I don't want to hear any reasons. Just get me out of this darkness."

I started walking into the passage. It was total darkness inside the passage but as she was so close to me in my arms, I was able to see her face. I avoided looking into her eyes this time because I was feeling very shy. But when I finally stole a look at her innocent face, I found that her eyes were closed.

Looking at this innocent act of hers, I said, "Arre, Ashwini, you are so cute. It's already dark, and still, you have your eyes closed."

"If I open my eyes, I will scream aloud," she said.

"Who is telling you to look at the darkness; you can look into my eyes," I said.

"Why only eyes?" she asked.

"Firstly, because my eyes don't fear the darkness, and secondly, because my face is not that handsome," I said.

She smiled and said, "Oh gosh! You can even make me smile in such a situation."

(POINT #24:- A girl will never leave the guy who can make her smile in any situation, but she can definitely leave a guy who took her tears when she just needed someone to share her grief.)

In a short time, we came out of that passage. I wished that the passage would never end because I wanted to keep her close to me forever, but sometimes some things are just not possible. After that, I placed her on the ground. She was still looking into my eyes.

"You said that you didn't want to place your feet in this passage, so I lifted you in my arms in order to overcome your fear," I said.

She gave me an innocent look and immediately fell into my arms. This hug was a damn tight one. I made it even tighter by placing my arms all around her again.

"Thank you, Bhavam," she said in a soft tone, as her head was on my shoulder.

A thrill passed through my heart when I sensed her hug.

That was such an awesome feeling for me. It made me recount those long hugs which Preksha gave me. When we were ONE.

The last hug which Preksha gave me is imprinted in my memory. That was probably a day, just a few months prior to our break-up. We were in our mathematics class and it was an evening session. The teacher was teaching his stuff but barely anyone was interested in that. Suddenly the lights went off and every one shouted like hell because every student in the class was bored. We all ignited the flash lights of our cell phones. I saw Preksha, and she was looking at me, focusing her dimmed flash light. Taking an opportunity, I went near her and placed myself beside her. Our feet were naked because, in those days, footwear was not allowed inside the classroom. I gave a gentle touch on her toes with my right foot. This might have created a thrill of sensation in her heart that day. Her toes were soft like butter, and I felt like eating them. She was wearing blue tight jeans that day, I placed my palms all over her size zero waist, and at this, she felt shy and pushed me away. I smiled and whispered in her ears, "Shona, I want to hug you, please."

It was dark and all were flashing their flash lights on us. So she was feeling shy.

I still remember, she said, "Sonu, I am feeling very odd as all these people are here."

When I heard that my face became dull. However, those days Preksha could never see me sad. So without thinking about anyone, she just fell into my arms, kissing my chest. It was not that long a hug because everyone teased us by focusing their flash lights on us.

Alas! That was the last hug which she gave me. After that, she searched for peace in Karan's arms.

God has given us five senses, even though we aren't able to predict what can happen at the next step. Even for a moment, if I had any clue that the hug which Preksha gave me would be the last one, I would have never allowed her to move away from my arms.

The same feeling was running through my heart at the present moment when Ashwini hugged me tightly. I was not sure about the future, so I considered that hug from her as the last one and just enjoyed it.

(POINT #25:- Assume that each and every hug from your partner is the last one because you never know if you will be able to see those arms opened again, ONLY FOR YOU.)

That hug was, indeed, the longest hug I ever had.

When we got separated from that awesome hug, she said, "You have taken away my fear of the darkness."

At this I smiled and replied, "Then can you run through that passage again for me?"

She pinched my cheeks and said, "If you accompany, then why not?"

"I don't possess the energy to lift you again," I smiled.

"Huh!" she expressed mock anger. "I'm not that heavy," she added.

"Ehh… I wasn't talking about your weight. If I lift you again, I will lose my entire energy looking into your eyes. They are beautiful," I said.

"Awww… but they aren't beautiful," she protested.

"You aren't the person to conclude that," I said.

She giggled and replied, "They are my eyes; so I can be the judge."

"You can judge and I can conclude. And the conclusion is that they are beautiful," I insisted.

"But why are they beautiful?" she asked.

I thought and replied, "Because they are innocent."

When I said the word 'innocent', an image of Preksha's eyes came into my vision. Yes, they too were beautiful. More than beautiful, and once upon a time, they were innocent too.

Our tutors were quite strict and they hardly allowed the opposite sexes to communicate. So Preksha and I always used to communicate through our eyes. When I entered the class, she used to shift her attention towards me. When I said something in class, she used to look straight so that her ears faced me and she could hear everything I said. Then after the class, she used to text me saying that the particular shirt/t-shirt looked amazing on me. Those days WhatsApp was not that popular, so we used to recharge our SMS packs, instead of DATA PLANS. We both belonged to middle class families; so we weren't rich. Hence, sometimes we lacked money to recharge our SMS packs. Whenever she needed money, I used to skip my breakfast and save that money in order to recharge her account. Sometimes she used to recharge my account. However, we never told each other from where the money came. Such was the beauty of our small and sweet relationship. But then Karan came and everything just changed. Maybe our love was not strong enough to be sustained forever, but whatever we did for each other was special.

(POINT #26:- Happiness is recharging your SMS PLANS rather than your DATA PLANS.)

When I look back at those days, I realize one thing that some things are just not within our reach. If the creator had written someone else's name in Preksha's life, then it was in our destiny to get separated. But the way in which she left was not proper. I am not a bad guy. If she wanted to hold someone else's hand, she could have told me about it.

But no, she followed the modern trend and broke up with me. Thank God there are no legal procedures like divorce in our country for a break-up. If there were any procedures, I bet no lawyer in our country would stay unemployed.

(POINT #27:- Looking at the average Indian population, we can conclude that, at every third second, a relationship starts and at every second second, a break-up happens. So the average time period of any relationship is just one second, and 90% of the people are included in this category. Therefore, I guess they say that life is moving fast.)

Chapter 13

Location:- Class room

Time:- 8:00 am

"You had the time of your life yesterday, I guess?" asked Vrund.

"You can't imagine that how awesome it was," I said.

He looked upset, of course, owing to the fight with Nishu at Inorbit yesterday.

"Yah… so it seems that you both are still not talking to each other. Come on, guys, don't act like kids!" I admonished him

"I am acting like a kid? Really? Really?" he said angrily. I'm not going to talk with her. She insulted me in front of everyone yesterday and this has changed my perspective towards her. It's over, Bhavam. Forget about liking each other, we can't even be friends," he concluded.

(POINT #28:- 90% of guys don't want the same girl in their life, even as their friend, after heart breaks. However, there is a great regret in that decision too.)

I saw Nishu entering the class. Earlier both of them used to exchange smiles and laughter when they saw each other, but now the situation was completely different. Vrund saw Nishu, and gave her a look, but she didn't give a damn response to Vrund. She pointedly ignored him.

"This girl has so much of attitude," he said.

"All girls have attitude and they show it in different ways," I said.

"But ignoring someone is such a bad thing!" he expressed with a shadow on his face.

"This happened to me too," I said.

It again brought the image of Preksha in front of my eyes as I told him, "That was the first day after our break-up. She entered the class. Obviously I wanted to talk to her and convince her to forget whatever happened, but she didn't even give me a damn look in response to my continuous staring. Finally I assumed that she was totally not interested in talking with me and therefore, she was not even looking at me."

"Nishu is also following her footsteps," he said.

"No, Nishu isn't your girlfriend. And you don't make the mistake which I made," I said.

"Which mistake?" he asked in doubt.

"Just like you, even I was broken. She ignored me and, in return, I too ignored her, without knowing the fact that, just like me, she was upset regarding our break-up. At that time, if I had tried to communicate with her in a pleasing manner, then who knows? The story of our relationship might have been different. So you don't repay what Nishu is doing. Be that original Vrund whom she loves."

He showed zero reaction as Dr Umar entered the class and started delivering his normal lecture.

During the lecture, I saw that Vrund was writing something in the book. This surprised me because Vrund never gave friction to his pen other than during exams.

I asked him, "What the fuck are you writing?"

He smiled and said, "Don't worry, I am not writing the fuck."

I smiled and said, "That's my dialogue."

The class got over. Dr Umar left. Vrund folded one paper and said, "Give this to Nishu and don't open it."

I took that paper and immediately went to Nishu and said, "This is for you."

"What's this?" she asked. My God, she was not in a good mood. I indicated Vrund and said, "He…!"

She took the paper hurriedly from my hands and looked at Vrund angrily. What she did next was totally unexpected, even in my dreams. She tore that piece of paper and said, "Tell your friend that I don't want to talk to him ever."

There was no reaction on Vrund's face. He had seen everything. He approached us and handed over one more piece of paper in her hand and said, "Now don't tear this…! This includes the actual message."

I was like a little baby, not able to understand what the hell was happening.

"But she tore your first letter! Is that what you were writing throughout the class?" I asked.

"Yes, but the piece of paper which I gave you was blank, because I knew that she would shower all her anger on it," he said.

No sooner had Vrund completed his say, than Nishu tore the second piece of paper and threw it on his face. My God! I hadn't ever witnessed such a thing ever.

I threw a pitying look at Vrund's face.

"Don't worry, Bhavam. This was too a blank paper," said Vrund merrily.

He converted my seriousness to a mild smile as I said, "Now that's the original Vrund."

I looked at Nishu and said, "Forget everything. You have been the best of the friends for a long time. Don't break your bond."

Before Nishu could say anything, Vrund interrupted, "No, Bhavam, if she wants to break this bond let her break it, but only after reading my letter."

"Where the hell is your idiotic letter?" she asked.

"This time, finally, I am giving it to you, but don't tear it again," warned Vrund.

"Depends!" she responded.

Vrund turned towards me and asked, "Is every girl like this?"

"Why are you asking him?" she asked him. "He isn't a girl," she added.

"But you are not talking to me, so how can I ask you?" he replied, with an innocent look at her face.

"Okay, I'm going. I want to go away from you and your idiotic talk. It always distracts me," she said.

I was about to stop Nishu but Vrund signaled me not to say anything.

He gave his Physics classwork book in Nishu's hand and said, "Don't tear the whole book. Of course it doesn't include any study related work. If you still wish to tear the pages in order to flush out more anger, than tear it from the first page because it's blank," he suggested.

Nishu took the book, opened it, but found nothing. This even made her even angrier. She again started tearing the pages.

We all know the symmetricity of the note book. If we tear the first page than automatically the last page gets separated from the notebook. So as soon as Nishu tore the first page, the last page of the notebook fell down. Now this was not a blank page. There was something written on it. Nishu picked that page and glanced at Vrund.

He gave us a tense look and decided to leave. I was standing on Nishu's side, so I was able to read that letter –

Dear Nishu,

Surprised? For the first time ever in my life, I have addressed you as 'dear' but trust me, I have always considered you as 'dearest' from my heart, but I never dared to express it. Though you might say that I don't care about you and our friendship, but that is wrong. I do care about you. I know that I don't look at you often, like at other sexy girls in the class. But today, when you ignored me, I realized the pain which you always faced when I ignored you for the other girls.

I don't have the strength to say sorry while looking in your eyes, but indeed, I am really sorry. I know that we like each other but there is a reason why I don't express my feelings. You are a very sweet, decent and innocent girl while, on the other hand, I am a bad, ill-mannered and flirty guy. You deserve the best, and I am not the best. I can make you laugh, but I can't keep you smiling, which is the reason why I never expressed my feelings for you. Though trust me, despite whatever happens, you will stay in my heart forever, because my heart wants you, but my mind says no. Every day I convince my heart that it has to control its feelings towards you, but today I expressed it because I am going far away from you and your life. I will miss you and our friendship too. I didn't tell anyone about this, but immediately after graduation, I will fly to Indonesia to handle my relative's textile factory. All I want to say is that I LOVE YOU…!

But Bhavam is right. Some things are just not made for us, and likewise, this is not made for us.

(I lack the words to express my feelings, so please ignore this.)

After reading this, Nishu's angry eyes were now moist. The letter fell from her hands as she began searching for Vrund.

"Where is that idiot?" she said, as tears streamed down from her eyes.

Our heads were down as he had left the class.

"I am asking you something!" she exclaimed.

"He left from here as soon as he handed you this book," replied Rahul.

The intensity of her tears increased. She took hurried steps and started searching for Vrund. I made a call to him, but he didn't answer.

I looked up at the skies and said, "Please unite them."

Tears too fell from my eyes while I saw Nishu so desperate for Vrund. This reminded me of my memories with Preksha. I still remember how desperate she would get when she didn't see me in front of her eyes.

(POINT #29:- If she is truly in love, she gets desperate, when she doesn't see her bae in front of her eyes. When there are no text message replies from her bae, she generally feels insecure.)

Such was the feeling running through Nishu's heart right now.

I went near her and said, "I told him the same and I tell you the same. Give him some time."

With an innocent look, she replied, "But he's going away from me. Not for love, but he is going far away from our bond of friendship. There wasn't a single day for the last four years, I have spent without him. He can't go away like that."

"I'm surprised too. He never told me that he's going," I said.

Nishu went away in search of Vrund, but I knew that she wouldn't be able to find him because when guys are generally sad, they find a lonely place to hide in.

Yesterday was the best day of my life with Ashwini, and so I was very happy about it. I wanted to carry the fragrance of that happiness for a long time, but when your best friends are desperate and sad, you also tend to feel sad, regardless of the eternal happiness gifted to you by the saws of the time.

Sometimes some situations are not within our reach. Nishu and Vrund had become an important part of my life. I wanted to share this with Ashwini. She was the alignment source of all my problems now. I messaged her about the whole issue and she immediately saw my message and I was able to see her reply.

(Ashwini was typing…)

Okay, Bhavam.
Let's meet today!

See you at Kamatibaugh soon, sweetness!

(POINT #30:- That feeling is the most wonderful feeling in the world, when you send your message to your crush, and she immediately reads and replies.)

Wow! Again God was kind on me because, within 24 hours, this was my second meeting with Ashwini

Location:- Kamatibaugh

Time:- 12:30 pm

Things were totally changed now. This time I was happily standing in the intolerable heat, just waiting for her. I recounted how I had spent my bad days standing under this heat, in the hopeless hope that Preksha would come, and we would be one again.

I called Ashwini and she said that it would take her a bit of time to come. I had no option except to sit and wait for her.

I went and got seated at the same place where I used to meet Heenal. But this time she wasn't there. I had written everything in my diary about the events which had occurred during the last few days with me. Ashwini had totally erased the tinge of sadness from my soul.

"Bhavam, great, you have also forgotten me!" said Heenal from behind, placing her soft hands over my shoulders.

I suddenly got up, sensing her touch, and looked at her with moist eyes because all happiness in my life had arrived because of her advice and affection. I was not able to control myself and I hugged her.

"I missed you and I really mean it. Ashwini has changed my life," I said.

"I can sense that by your expression and I am happy for you," she said.

"Any girl would have made me smile, but you taught me how to smile again. You don't know how much I owe to you," I said.

"Have you proposed to her?" she asked.

I told her everything about the Akota bridge incident.

She gave me a serious look and said, "Love is not a cricket match where you decide a stipulation by tossing a coin. Why are you waiting, and for what are you waiting? Don't you feel insecure now?"

"Why insecure?" I asked.

"Even if you are late by a fraction of second, then someone will come into her life, and you will just stay her friend," she said.

I was puzzled and asked her, "But I don't know even if she likes me or not!"

"Leave that decision to her. You do what you have to do." she said.

"We are going to meet here today!" I said.

"Where? Here, in this desert?" she asked with a blink of her eyes.

I nodded.

"You guys seriously don't have any courtesy to treat your crush," she said.

I got confused.

She gently slapped me on my face in a loving manner and said, "Take her to some restaurant or coffee shop; that will impress her."

"Why do coffee shops fascinate you girls so much?" I asked angrily

"How will you feel if she accompanies you for a live cricket match in a stadium?" she questioned.

At this, I laughed and replied, "I lack the money to buy a movie ticket, and you are talking about match tickets!"

(POINT #31:- 90% of pocket money goes away for hostel parties, 3% for mobile recharges and at last, we have only 7% of the money left with which we have to manage. No management issues at all.)

She got tense and replied, "Oh come on! It's just a fantasy. Tell me really, how would you feel if she really accompanied you to a place which you love?" she asked.

"Without doubt, I'll feel great," I suggested.

"Similarly, she will feel great if you accompanied her to the coffee shop," she said.

"But why only coffee shops?" I repeated."Because we girls love coffee," she said.

(POINT #32:- I still wonder why Coffee shops are the best hang out places for your bae?

P.S. – Only she can answer this in a better way.)

"I won't go to CCD, so you suggest some cool coffee shops!" I asked Heenal.

"Take her to Chocolate room. She will love it."

I called Ashwini and told her that instead of Kamatibaugh, we would go to Chocolate room.

Instead she said, "I'm bored with coffee shops. Let's go at Maji Sainik."

I was confused. Now what in the world was 'Maji Sainik'?

I put my left palm over the speaker and asked Heenal, "What is Maji Sainik?"

She shrugged my head and said, "Dumbo! It's a restaurant."

I nodded to her and told Ashwini that I would be there in a few minutes.

"Are you non vegetarian?" asked Heenal.

"Why this sudden question?" I asked.

"Because the place you are going to is famous for all egg items!" she said.

That increased the jangling in my nerves as I said, "But I gave up eating non-vegetarian food long back."

She just smiled and said, "That girl is giving you back everything which you lost to someone else."

I said nothing.

"But were you non-vegetarian?" she asked.

"I eat everything, but since Preksha was pure vegetarian, I gave up my desire to eat non vegetarian food."

(POINT #33:- Never leave a guy who can change his food habits for you. Remember if he can do that, he can do anything for you.)

"That's bad; you shouldn't give up your food habits for someone. Instead you should convince the opposite person to agree with your habits," she said.

"I'm not smart like you," I admitted.

I had to now go to Maji Sainik as I didn't want to make Ashwini wait for me.

"I need to go now. She might be waiting for me," I said.

She laughed and replied, "When I used to tell someone to come at a particular time, I always reached there 10 minutes late."

"Oh! Why so?" I asked.

"Because I know that most of the guys are not serious regarding time issues. So we girls know that you guys will come late by five minutes. Therefore, we reach ten minutes after the decided time, so that you guys also have to wait for five minutes," she said with mild affection on her face.

"Hats off to you and your logic!" I said.

(POINT #34:- That's why girls are smarter than guys.)

"But don't they like punctual guys?" I asked.

"Like is a wrong word, Bhavam. Girls adore punctual guys. Go! Don't make her wait," she said with a lilt in her voice.

Her eyes were suddenly moist.

I placed my fingers on her black expressive eyes and said, "Why there is H_2O in your eyes?"

She said nothing, and instead she just tightly hugged me.

"What happened? Just a few moments back, you were happy and now suddenly you are crying! What happened?" I asked.

With innocence all over her face, she replied, "You know that I'm with you, right?"

I held her hand and said, "I'm also with you!"

"Whatever happens, I'm going to be with you, right?" she assured

"Yes, I know that. But why are you saying all this suddenly?" I asked.

"Because very soon, you will get your gf and after that, you naturally won't come here," she said.

"Who said so?" I asked. "Today you have to accompany me to Maji Sainik!" I added.

She desperately said, "Never! I won't."

"This is my wish and you have to complete it," I said.

"If I come with you, then people will make fun of you," she said.

"Why will they make fun?" I asked. "Whatever! I don't care!" I added.

Before she could say anything, I caught her hand so that she was forced to come with me.

We reached Maji Sainik. Ashwini was standing there. My God! She looked even more beautiful in formals.

(POINT #35:- For true guys,

Girls in traditional dress>Girls in formal dress>Girls in one piece.)

"She looks pretty, but not more than me!" smiled Heenal.

"Maybe. But her soul is as beautiful as yours!" I said

We approached Ashwini. I introduced her to Heenal. Both greeted each other in a typical girlish manner. When Ashwini greeted Heenal, all the people who were outside Maji Sainik gave them a strange look.

Now I realized that Maji Sainik was a special place where you only get the egg preparations.

"I've never been here. So whatever you find great, order it," I said generously.

Heenal interrupted and said, "You know, Ashu, my brother is more than nice. Because he has never visited such places."

(POINT #36:- You might feel annoyed when your sister teases you in front of your crush, but you definitely feel great when she praises you in front of her.)

The expression on Ashwini's face suddenly changed.

I placed my palm on her shoulder and assured, "All well, Ashwini?"

Instead of looking at me, she looked at Heenal and asked very politely, "Did you address me as Ashu?"

Heenal smiled and said, "Sorry, if you felt it was wrong, but it just came out naturally from inside."

Ashwini stood up and hugged Heenal.

I was also surprised by Ashwini's action until she explained, "Roho and Pruru also call me Ashu. You are the only person, after them, to address me by that name. Thank you! It felt good."

Heenal also embraced Ashwini in her arms and said, "You're like my cute little sister."

Wow! I was fascinated to see such affection between them in their first ever meeting.

At that instant I started believing that there might be some connection between us in our past life.

Everything was pleasant. Only one fact was pinching me.

"Hey guys, there is something wrong with us," I said.

"Why are you saying that?" Ashwini asked.

"Why the hell are people staring at us?" I asked.

Before anyone could say anything, Heenal interrupted, and said, "Ignore them. We are all extra attractive, that's why."

At this Ashwini laughed and I enjoyed the sight.

I looked at Heenal and said, "Ashwini is a selfie-queen."

Ashwini giggled and said, "Correct. Let have a group-fie."

Heenal was always reluctant when it came to clicking selfies. I was able to sense that by her desperate face.

"Ashu, instead of a selfie, let's click a proper front view photo," she said.

Ashwini had no objections.

I called a waiter and requested him to click a photo of us.

"Will you please click a photo of us?" I said to the waiter.

The waiter merrily took my HTC and adjusted the focus.

"Are all three of us in the frame?" asked Ashwini.

The waiter looked a little astonished as he said, "You and sir are perfectly seated in the frame."

"We are three. So we all should come in the frame," I said.

He looked very confused. Heenal was sitting between us. Both Ashwini and I placed our hands on her shoulders to create a photogenic effect. The waiter clicked the photo and handed over my phone to me.

"That is very strange! Everyone is giving us odd looks today," I said.

"Forget that!" said Ashwini. "Let's order something. I'm hungry," she added.

I was not a regular visitor of that place but Heenal and Ashwini were. Ashwini ordered something.

After a few minutes, the same waiter brought our order and again gave us a strange look.

I was frustrated this time. I just wanted to ask him what the hell was wrong!

However, my first priority was to satisfy my hungry belly.

"This is called rock and roll," said Ashwini indicating the ordered items.

"It looks similar to a Frankie!" I said.

"Shut up, Bhavam! You don't know anything!" said Heenal.

(POINT #37:- It is definitely the nature of Indian society to give extraordinary names to simple things.)

But rock and roll was brilliant. What came next was even more delicious! The name of the dish was 'Gaadbad Gotala'. From the name itself, I thought that stuff might include the mixture of all the leftovers and guess what? I was right!

Gaadbad Gotala was a recipe made by the combination of several vegetables with egg curry!

"This is the same stuff which we daily eat in the canteen," I said.

"Wow! So do they serve eggs in your canteen?" asked Ashwini.

Before I could say anything, she said, "So lucky you are!"

I was tantalized by her innocence. I gave a look at Heenal, but she was enjoying the food. Ashwini was a food loving girl and I was also a food lover.

(POINT #38:- It is a wrong assumption of any girl that she can impress a guy with a size zero figure. The road towards a zero figure is not easy. Apart from exercising, you have to stay hungry. It is to be noted by the girls that zero figure can only make her earn adjectives like HOT, SEXY, GORGEOUS, BAE etc.

but it is her small cute habits which make her BEAUTIFUL for her bae.)

Lunch for food loving people is not complete until they have something sweet as their dessert.

"I don't understand one thing," said Ashwini, as we proceeded towards Havmor ice cream parlor

"And what is that?" I asked.

"When we go to eat unlimited pizza, they serve us as much as we want, but limitations appear when they serve dessert," she said.

On hearing this, Heenal laughed and said, "These things are just like relationships. You get unlimited love, but you go through a break-up only once, and it is limited."

I wanted to make the atmosphere livelier, and so I said, "My college friends are no less. Once they went to enjoy an unlimited Gujarati *thali* near the Railway station. They were as hungry as tigers because, in order to enjoy the unlimited offer, they had not eaten anything since morning. But when they went, the hotel was full. So they were forced to wait outside. Finally when they got in, they themselves knew what was going to happen. The poor guy started serving the courses. Initially he served papad and on the very first round, these guys ate 20 papads amongst the group. In the second round they took 20 more papads. Seeing this, the restaurant owner got worried. They were not interested in eating anything, except papad, because that was the thing which was available instantly."

"So? What was so funny in that?" asked Heenal.

"After a few minutes, the restaurant owner had to hang a board outside stating that papad is limited," I said.

Heenal and Ashwini were not able to control their laughter after hearing this.

(POINT #39:- There is no greater pleasure for a guy if he can make any girl laugh.)

While we were having ice cream, Heenal approached me, and said in a low tone, "This is the perfect opportunity, Bhavam. Go tell her your feelings."

"Shhh! Don't say anything about that right now. I'm planning to propose to her, but not now," I said.

"Then when?" she asked desperately.

"After our final exams," I said.

"I again tell you, don't take the risk of waiting!" she warned me.

"I'll take the risk!" I exclaimed. "Risks are taken by strong people and I'm strong enough to wait for the correct time," I added.

"But you don't know what can happen to a person in the very next second. Than how you be so sure that the fact you have assumed is true?" she asked bluntly.

I looked in her eyes and asked, "Tell me, do you see any girl other than her?"

"Preksha!" she said softly, as Ashwini approached us, and our conversation was left incomplete.

"So, Ashu, do you have a boyfriend?" asked Heenal, placing her hand over her delicate shoulders.

She blushed and replied, "No!"

"Have a crush on anyone?" asked Heenal.

At this Ashwini replied, "We girls daily have crush on someone, but that doesn't mean it's a permanent crush!"

(* A dreadful thought suddenly started running in my mind after she said that. What if she had a secret crush on any guy?)

"So what kind of guy do you wish to have?" asked Heenal, giving a side look to me.

What the hell was she up to? She was definitely pulling my leg.

Ashwini was blank for a moment, but what she said next definitely fascinated my heart, "I don't want a guy who is able to hold my hand in public. I want a guy who can hold my soul. I want a guy who will readily accept me as his child, not as his bae!"

(POINT #40:- Any guy can hold your hand and promise not leave it ever, but only a true guy can hold your soul and ensure that it's forever.)

"You don't like the coffee shop-type of guy?" I asked fearlessly.

"Coffee shops?" she asked. "Not really!" she added.

It brought relief to my heart. Was she my type? I was engulfed in my thoughts.

"You guys will never ever understand us," said Heenal proudly.

"Correct!" said Ashwini in her support.

"It's not like that!" I exclaimed. "I know that, to be a good boyfriend, all you need to do is take your girlfriend regularly to the coffee shops. I have seen that, and that's why I am telling you so."

Heenal looked at me as she understood that I was talking about Preksha.

"Yes, she definitely needs a boyfriend who can hang out with her at the coffee shops, but hell, yeah, she definitely deserves a soul mate who could just listen to her endless blabbing, patiently," replied Heenal.

I was stunned because she had again proved me wrong. My eyes were filled with pity, not because of the fact that I wasn't the best boyfriend, but because I had tried my best to be Preksha's soul mate.

"And what if you try your best to be her soul mate, and still she doesn't give any encouragement to you?" I asked.

"You never have to be one. Soul mates are not created on earth. They are prepared by God much earlier, even before your birth," responded Heenal.

Wow! She seemed to be echoing God's words.

Ashwini, who was quietly listening to all this, finally had a say, "I will miss you guys a lot!"

"Hey! Why?" I asked in fright. "You aren't going anywhere, right?"

She placed her milky hand on my chest and said, "I'm sorry but I didn't tell you. After the exams I will have to go to my home in Valsad. So it may be good bye to this beautiful city. I won't be able to come here again."

Emotions ran through my nervous system when I heard that she would be going away from me.

My expression suddenly changed. Heenal could sense that by my face.

"You can't go like that, Ashu," said Heenal.

Ashwini looked helpless and said, "Wish I had an option to stay in this beautiful city forever. Four years spent here were just splendid but…!"

Wish I could tell her that my four years were nothing more than hell, and that I had felt a little heaven when she came into my life. She taught me to laugh again, smile again, have fun and now, she was going away from me.

I made my heart strong and asked her, "When are you going?"

"Maybe next week, after my exams!" she responded dully.

I wanted to smoke, but unluckily, there were no cigarettes in my pocket.

We walked silently for a few more minutes without saying anything.

"I have to go somewhere from here, so see you guys," said Heenal.

Ashwini went ahead and hugged Heenal and said, "It was so awesome to meet you! I will miss you."

"Take care, Ashu," said Heenal.

"Wait a minute, Heenal. I got something for you," said Ashwini, holding her hand.

She than crossed the road and entered a flower shop.

Meanwhile, Heenal told me, "Bhavam, time waits for none. Don't postpone your feelings for her. She's going away from you."

Tears ran down my eyes as I said, "Everyone is going away from me. Initially Preksha and now she!"

"Tell her that you love her and leave the rest to nature," said Heenal, assuring me.

I saw Ashwini coming, and so I quickly wiped off my tears, and brought an unwilling smile on my face.

She had two yellow roses in her hand.

She gave one of the roses to Heenal and said, "That's the beauty of our bond, just like this rose. Do accept this as a farewell gift from my side."

How can any girl be so sweet?

Heenal happily took the rose and again hugged Ashwini.

"Will we meet again?" Ashwini asked Heenal.

"The day this rose turns red, we shall meet again," responded Heenal and left.

After walking a little distance, she stopped and waved to us again. Yes, Ashwini was emotional as she was seeing her, maybe for the last time, but why did I feel that even I was seeing Heenal for the final time?

However I ignored such negative feelings that buzzed in my mind.

Chapter 13

She gave me the remaining yellow rose and said, "Thank you, Bhavam, for giving me life long memories to live by."

"You are telling this?"I asked. "You are a fool," I said, as tears fell from my eyes.

She saw that and placed her thumb to wipe it off, but I shoved her away.

"What's wrong with you?" she asked.

"None of your business. You are going away from me, naa...?" I said.

She wanted to embrace me but ended up saying, "Bhavam...!"

I said, "I never gave you memories. It is you who has given me life long memories to live by. I was dead, but after meeting you, I realized what it is to live for a second time. And after teaching me how to live, you are going away from me."

Her lips were shivering, and she wanted to say something, but I didn't know what was stopping her.

We both kept our feet moving with the blistering evening making its way!

I stopped at the 'Crossword' shop and told Ashwini to wait outside as I wanted to gift something to her.

I entered the shop and asked the lady attendant to suggest me a few novels based on friendship.

I randomly picked a book by the well-known writer, Sudeep Nagarkar, titled - 'YOU'RE TRENDING IN MY DREAMS.'

I realized that this novel would be a perfect gift of friendship to Ashwini.

However, I made my mind firm that whatsoever happened, I would express my feelings for her.

I opened the book and wrote on its first page -

These days are happy it seems,
You're trending in my dreams!
Your smile creates all beautiful themes,
You're trending in my dreams!
Your touch is a rainbow beam,
You're trending in my dreams!
Your memories are like a golden rim,
You're trending in my dreams!
I know,
I can never be a guy of your dream,
Though still,
You're trending in my dreams!
My love for you has reached all extremes,
You're trending in my dreams!
I love you, Ashwini!

After writing that short sweet poem, I closed the book and went outside where

Ashwini was waiting for me. I placed that novel in her hand and said, "My farewell gift."

She smiled, but before she could open the book, I grabbed her hands and said, "Not now. I want you to open the first page of the novel when you are alone."

This time without questioning, she agreed to what I said.

(POINT #41:- You love girls when they don't question you. But trust me; she will only question you when she truly loves you.)

My heart was beating fast because I was in fear, thinking about a negative reaction to my proposal. If it happened so, than I bet our friendship was also in trouble. However, I pulled myself together and enjoyed the walk with her.

We both started to reminisce of the moments we spent together. I hardly spoke anything because she was continuously speaking.

"So what was your most loveable moment?" I asked.

"Our first attempt victory in bowling at Time Zone," she replied.

"And which is the most touching memory, the one where you will miss me the most?" she asked.

"While eating ice cream," I said

"Is it so? Wait, we shall revive it again!" she exclaimed.

She held my hand and directed me towards Yoli ice cream shop again.

We both went inside. This time she told me to wait and bought a single scoop of strawberry ice cream.

She plunged the spoon inside the cup and offered it to me with her own hands. Maybe this was for the last time now. I took that spoon from her hand and made her eat the same with my hands and said, "That was the reason why it was special."

She looked into my eyes but said nothing. She wanted to say something, but she didn't.

(POINT #42:- When she looks in your eyes, she has definitely a word or two to say.)

After that we again continued our walk.

"You know, you were the first girl with whom I chatted after my break-up," I said.

She laughed at this and asked, "Why? Did your ex give you a punishment not to talk to other girls?"

"No, I was just afraid," I said.

"Afraid of what?" she asked.

"I don't know. Maybe each and every nice guy suffers from that fear after a break-up," I said.

"But do you know what I did after my break-up?" she asked.

"How would I know that? I wasn't there with you at that time," I said.

"Arre…I mean after my ex cheated me? I started communicating with more guys on FB and that was how I moved on," she replied.

In dejection I said, "Wish even I had done the same!"

"No, no, no yaar…! You aren't gay!" she said with a smile.

I stopped for a moment and asked, "What did you say?"

She laughed again and proclaimed, "I mean you don't need to chat with guys. Girls are better for you."

"I will kill you, Ashwini." I said, as we approached our respective hostels.

(POINT #43:- Golden rule for moving on – 'Talk to any girl.')

"But you know, we girls only chat with selected guys. Others are just to pass time!" she said.

"So I am in which category?" I asked.

"Selected, of course," she muttered.

"I still don't understand this theory! What is a time pass guy, according to girls?" I asked.

"FB is full of time pass guys. They are guys who frequently message girls just in the hope of chatting with us, and we show them attitude by not replying to them. However, when we don't have any selected guy to talk to, we show some kindness to time-pass guys," she said.

"Two slaps to your thinking!" I said a little roughly.

"Don't take it seriously. You can never belong to that category. We girls chat on the basis of how you guys talk!" she said.

(*Now I realized that Vrund was a time-pass guy for most of the girls.)

Her hostel was approaching.

"Bhavam, I have my exams from next week," she said.

"Great, good luck for that!" I said.

"No yaar…I still have to start my syllabus," she said sadly.

"Don't worry! Do selective questions; the rest are just time-pass," I said taunting her.

"Shut up! That's not funny. I have to score passing marks anyhow," she said.

"Don't take too much of load! You will do it," I said.

"Architectural drawings are the toughest thing to do," she said.

"Not more than our Engineering Graphics. Only I know how I cleared it," I said.

"Why did you fail in that subject?" she asked.

"I was always at the Oxygen line," I replied.

Finally her hostel approached. She stood in front of me and said, "Thank you for another awesome day."

I smiled and said, "I hope there are many such days in the coming future."

"But I am going, Bhavam, after the exams," she said.

This again reminded me of the fact that she was going away from me. My proposal was in her hands. But I didn't remind her to read it.

Suddenly she just hugged me tightly and said, "You are the best person I have ever seen."

I crushed her in an embrace and said, "I will miss you."

After that all I remember is that she left for her hostel. I never knew if I was seeing her for the last time, so I just looked at her, until she vanished from my sight.

When I closed my eyes, I was able to see the scenario of the day 24 hours before my break-up with Preksha, four years back.

I was riding my Rodeo and she was on her Active. I sensed that something was cooking between her and Karan, so I refused to talk to her. I had started suspecting that she was flirting with Karan. I still remember that she said, 'Believe me, Bhavam, Karan and I are just friends!'

Although I was angry I didn't care to reply to her. Then the turning came and she went towards her home.

That was it! That was my last ride and perhaps, the last face to face communication with her. That day, I cried a lot. Slapped myself for not protecting my babe. I punished myself as I suffered slashes of my own belt with my very own hands. I was so mad that I even scratched my white hands with a blade till they were full of blood. I was very sensitive at heart, and so the next day, when she told me about our break-up, I was at the hospital because my pulse rate had suddenly dropped down and I was suffering from a breathing problem. The doctor believed that it was some ache, but I knew that it was nothing but the pain of the separation.

However, as days passed, I felt that I was wrong in thinking that there was something between Preksha and Karan. So again, I lived for a few years in regret, thinking about my decisions. But no! I was correct, as they were not only friends, but they were FRIENDS WITH BENEFITS.

I was so dumb that I didn't even know that what 'friends with benefits' meant. But Google these days has all the solutions.

(*POINT #44:- Remember, friends with benefits provide a few moments of satisfaction, but leave behind lifelong regrets.)

Location:- Dining hall, Canteen, hostel
Time:- 8:00 pm

I constantly checked my cell phone in the hope of Ashwini's response. I was curious, wondering if she had opened the first page of the novel or not!

Vrund came and sat beside me. Even his stars were not going well!

"Did Nishu respond?" I asked.

"She called me several time, but I didn't receive her call," he said.

"Why are you doing this, Vrund? What do you get by playing with the heart of that innocent girl?" I asked.

For the first time he had tears in his eyes as he said, "She is innocent, and that's why I am not bonding closely with her."

"You know you love her. You know that she too loves you. Everything is set, and you even expressed your feelings. Then why are you doing this?" I asked stiffly.

"Bhavam, I am not like you. Please spare me from all this!" he exclaimed as a teardrop fell from his eyes onto the dining table.

"I don't know anything, but if the reason of these tears is Nishu, then you are committing a big mistake by ignoring her!" I suggested.

He exploded this time. On seeing this, Ujjwal and Rahul also approached us.

Rahul consoled Vrund, but he was still full of agony.

That day I realized that even flirty guys could have hearts with feelings.

"Give her a call, Vrund," I said.

"I can't. She will hate me," he said.

"She also might be thinking that you hate her. Come on, Vrund, give her a call," I repeated.

I placed my own cell phone in his hand and said, "Go, talk with Nishu. I am sure all will be well!"

Finally he took the cell phone and went outside the dining hall to have the talk of his life.

(POINT #45:- Why don't we give our feelings one more opportunity? Why do we refrain from accepting the fact that we love someone? Sometimes we make assumptions that the opposite person might hate us due to our acts, and at the same time, that person might also think the same. There is no place for the word 'hate' in this big world which is full of love. Life moves on and it doesn't stop for anyone. In the same way, feelings also move on and they change, as per the time.)

"Why is he taking so much of time to talk to her?" asked Ujjwal anxiously.

"Makwana, it seems that you are more desperate than Vrund!" said Rahul.

"Vada, don't make me more angry; otherwise I will pour this sambhar on you," said Ujjwal angrily.

"Do it! Then see what I do," said Rahul threateningly.

"Vada, are you provoking me?" asked Ujjwal.

"Fuck off, Makwana! Lega mera?" abused Rahul.

Their conversations were always funny, but not this time because I was anxiously waiting for Vrund to come and tell us what happened.

Finally after a long wait, we saw him entering the room. We rushed to him and asked him one common question, "What happened?"

He was expressionless for a moment. Then he shoved us and sat at the table to eat his remaining dinner.

Rahul went near him and asked, "What the hell are you up to?"

Vrund looked at us and said, "Arre...Why are you guys so serious? I have to learn now how to tolerate awful food."

"Why so?" asked Ujjwal in doubt.

"Because Nishu doesn't like fast food!" he responded.

Vrund's eyes were still wet. He looked at me and gave me a shy smile, indicating that Nishu was his girlfriend now.

For the first time in my life, I shouted loudly. Yes indeed, that indicated my happiness.

Ujjwal and Rahul also realized the fact and they roared with joy. Vrund was a popular guy in the college, and the whole hostel became lively on hearing this news.

After everything was cleared, he approached me and said, "Thanks, yaar...I realize what a big mistake I was going to commit by ignoring her calls."

"What did she say?" I asked.

"When I said that I will try to change myself for her, she said that she would accept me the way I am!" he exclaimed.

I smiled and said, "You are an idiot...!"

"That is also correct," he said. "Do me a favor. I want you to type my first ever love message for her!" he added.

"Me? But I cannot do that!" I said.

However, he forced me to do so, so I typed for him...

Nishu,
Early morning is a bliss,
Waiting for you
Was a gift…I LOVE YOU.

Awww….
I love you too!!!!♥
Please send me a few more poems.

I tapped Vrund's shoulder and said, "Wah, Beta! That went so fast!"

"I hope that she doesn't realize that you are composing those lines," he said.

"Of course she knows that! But she won't say anything because she respects your efforts," I said.

The day I saw you,
Channels changed!
The day I saw you,
Voices ranged!

The day I saw you,
Onsets arrived!
The day I saw you,
Sadness departed!

The day I saw you,
Future envisioned!
The day I saw you,
Past flickered!

"Damn! She will love it!" expressed Vrund.

I am turning the pages of your story,
Trying to live each moment you went through,
Seeing the world through your eyes,
I never want to stop turning those pages!

(*These particular lines are composed by LITTLE MISS POET)

However, this time, Vrund didn't take my help to compose the reply, but what he wrote next touched my heart.–

Life is a beautiful stage,
The day you turned my page!
I felt I got everything,
Desire now for nothing!
Emptiness is now on other way,
Coz…
Your way is now our way!

I left Vrund to have the time of his life! Indeed, happiness had stepped into his life. The entrance of a girl in your life is very important thing. Either she can make you or else she can destroy you. Preksha destroyed me; Ashwini revived me. That's the power of a girl.

I don't know why some societies think that girls can't do anything. Close your eyes for a moment and see that one person who sleeps late at night and still wakes up early in the morning. She is your mother, the infinite source of energy.

If you are in a serious relationship with a sensible girl, just see how many efforts she makes just to save your relationship!

Remember if she can go to space, if she can perform better than a male and win gold medals in boxing; if she can give birth to you, then she can do anything. Therefore respect her, love her and don't worry if you don't have your bae, because I know she is there, away from this cruelty, waiting only for you. I bet she will come, breaking all trends, only for you. I am sure if you are not fake, she will accept you, regardless of who you are and what you possess. Because your every heartbeat waited for the piece of your heart to come and fill your heart!

When life is full of LIGHT, the guy has money, fame and social status and

therefore, he can afford to take his bae to expensive restaurants and coffee shops.

But,

When the life is full of DARKNESS, the guy has no money, no fame and no social status, and he cannot afford to take his bae to expensive restaurants and coffee shops...

Then what does he do?

He introduces his bae to his parents.

Since he has DARKNESS in his life, he will ignite a candle of love, and prepare Maggie for his bae, and together, they will enjoy it without any complaints!

Sometimes small things provide more happiness.

(POINT #46:- Dear girls, if you have ever left the guy who introduced you to his parents, you have committed a big mistake.)

Preksha was full of attitude because she believed that she was the one who was correct. She now believes that her social status is her success, but I am sure that, one day, nature will teach her what failure is, and her failure will definitely make her humble, but by then, it will be too late.

Dr Kalam once said, "Life is a difficult game. You can win it only by retaining your birthright to be a person."

It still hurts me because Preksha has forgotten her birthright as a person!

But now, my heartbeat was waiting for Ashwini's response. Still there was no reply from her; maybe she was too busy studying for her exams.

(POINT #47:- 90% of Indian students know their syllabus just one week before their examination. And they don't practice more than the previous year's question papers.)

Location:- Hostel room.
Time:- 10:00 pm.

I wasn't able to fully concentrate on my studies because there was still no response from Ashwini. This thing was making me nervous. I had my cell phone in my hand so that I could immediately reply when she messaged me.

I was getting negative thoughts in my mind, thinking of rejection. This smart phone creates too much of tension sometimes. Unlike the earlier days, when a letter used to thrill everyone's heart, the same work is done by smart phones in the modern era!

(POINT #48:- Life was sweeter until the day you started to carry mobile phones in your pockets while going to school.)

Location:- College Campus
After two days…

Two days had passed, and there was no reply from Ashwini. I had not seen her online since the day we last met. I tried to call her. But she wasn't answering. I told Vrund and Nishu everything about us.

"She said that she is preparing for her examination; so she might have taken social sanyas in order not to get distracted," said Nishu in order to console me.

"But why is she not answering my call?" I asked.

"Don't worry, Bhavam. All will be well," assured Vrund.

"I guess she didn't like it that I proposed to her," I said with my eyes moist. "Have I lost her as a friend?"

Holding Vrund's hand, Nishu said, "Look at us, Bhavam, despite all the differences, we are one today. Just wait for a few more days. Good girls take time in order to reply."

"Just two more days, and if she doesn't reply, then I will go and meet her personally," I said.

I called Ashwini more than 25 times in one hour, but still she wasn't receiving my calls.

"She is definitely upset because of me," I said.

"Arre, yaar...! Do one thing, call her from a different number," said Nishu, handing over her cell phone to me.

I quickly typed her number and called. It was just ringing, ringing and ringing, but still there was no response!

"What's wrong with her?" I asked desperately.

"Nothing is wrong, Bhavam. You are getting desperate! She said that she is busy because of examinations," said Vrund.

"But I know her. Even though she is busy, she would text me saying that she would talk later. But she hasn't said anything like that presently," I said.

"Don't take unnecessary tension! Let's concentrate on reading, as even we have exams in the coming days."

I repeatedly checked her Hike and WhatsApp. It indicated that Ashwini had been online two days ago.

However, I was not able to control myself, and so I got up and decided to go to the Arts faculty.

"Where are you going?" asked Vrund.

"I'm sorry. I am not able to control myself. I'm going to the Arts faculty. Not because of my fear of rejection, but to check if she is alright or not!" I said.

I ran hastily as Vrund and Nishu followed me.

(*Preksha and I got separated because of confusion and misunderstandings. I never wanted that to happen between Ashwini and me.)

I kicked the gate and entered the campus of the Arts faculty. Vrund saw my madness and tried to stop me, but I was enraged. Like a madman I started looking vigorously at the number plates of the vehicles parked in a queue.

"4651… 4651… 4651… !" was the one which I was praying for.

Nishu interrupted me again and said, "Here's the vehicle number 4651."

I quickly rushed there. Finally my heartbeats were a little calm after seeing that 4651 was parked safely in the college compound.

"What is this, Bhavam?" asked Vrund.

"It's her vehicle," I replied.

"See, I told you that nothing has happened to her. She is safe, Bhavam and is preparing for her examination," said Nishu.

"Wah, brother! You taught us to be patient for our love stories, and now you are getting desperate," said Vrund.

"What can I do? I can bear separation only once, not twice. And Ashwini has started ruling over my heart!" I said.

"Finally you have moved on in your life," said Nishu.

"It was so tough until Ashwini came. Preksha was the only girl before her who ruled over my heart. But she was the one who also ruined my heart!" I said.

"Now forget her!" said Vrund. "But do you wish to know one fact about her?"

"What?" I asked.

"As far as people say, she has completely changed now," said Vrund.

"I don't give a fuck as to what's happening in Preksha's life. I am not her dog. Yes, I waited for her. Waited for four years. But what did she do? She cheated on me," I said briskly.

"If she cheated on you, then someone will too cheat on her," said Nishu, cursing her.

"We shouldn't say that! I don't want something to happen to her," I said, because still I had 0.01% feelings left for her.

"No, Bhavam, she also deserves to be cheated on. She should also feel that pain which she gave you," insisted Nishu.

"And see this Karan will cheat on her too," said Vrund.

"They both love each other. Don't say that," I protested.

Vrund got angry and responded, "Ghanta Love! You don't know guys like Karan."

"I know," I said.

"No, you don't. Preksha is just a source of time pass for him. He is a sexually inclined guy who needs someone to satisfy his thirst for pleasure," said Vrund.

"This can't be true," I said.

Nishu held my hand and said, "This is true! Sorry to say, but they are just in relationship with benefits. The day will come when the consequences will be such that the distance between them will increase, and the benefits will decrease. Their relationship will break down on the basis of cheating and that will be the day when Preksha will truly miss you. She will cry for you, and realize the value of each and every tear which she gave you. She will then be aware of that darkness which you faced alone for last four years, and she will have to pay for everything. Because troubling innocent guys in this world is itself cheating."

I respected the feeling which Nishu had for me, but still in my inner heart, I never wanted to see troubles in Preksha's life, because she was a girl and every girl deserves to be happy with her guy.

I was relieved that Ashwini was there at the hostel only. But still the question remained. Why was she not replying to me? She even didn't receive my calls! What on earth was wrong with her?

This reminds me of the initial days of a relationship. I saw that Vrund and Nishu were walking, holding hands. I smiled from behind thinking that soon, even Ashwini's hand would be in my hand forever. We passed Kamatibaugh. I remembered Heenal. Maybe she was sitting inside the garden. As Vrund and Nishu were there with me, I didn't want to meet Heenal at the garden.

A few things were very strange about Heenal. Firstly she never told me anything about her residence, and secondly, she was mostly at Kamatibaugh.

Yes, she was waiting for her love to come and take her, but I didn't believe that this could be the reason for which she daily visited Kamatibaugh. There was something which she hadn't told me. But I knew that, the next time I met her, I wouldn't be alone. Ashwini would be at my side, holding my hand in togetherness!

Sometimes I think that I didn't even make efforts to save my previous relationship with Preksha. Although she left, I could have been her 'best friend' rather than just 'boy friend', but the fact was that she was mad about Karan that time.

She had the guts to cheat on me behind my back, but she didn't have the guts to hold Karan's hand in front of my eyes. However, I still cannot forget the day when I saw her for the first time after six months of our break-up.

After six months of my break-up with her…

Those days, in order to throw off my emptiness, I would leisurely move on the streets of the VIP road. I entered VIP VIEW complex, where initially, both Preksha and I went for our mathematics tuition. VIP VIEW complex was a building full of tuition classes. Each girl and boy standing outside the classroom reminded me of myself and her. To encapsulate more memories, I entered the complex and headed straight to the bridge, which connected the adjacent sides of the complex.

I used to come early and stand there so that I could see Preksha coming from the front. In those days, it was a rule that girls and boys could not stand together, so girls stood near the class upstairs and boys were allowed to sit on the bridge until the class started. So while standing on the bridge, I used to look at her and she used to do the same. It felt very special because we both did this just for each other's smiles. Yes, those were indeed the innocent days when we used to wear clothes, not of OUR choice but of EACH OTHER'S choice.

Our classes were strict, and so everyone had to maintain a distance with girls. That was how I learnt to respect each and every girl, including my girlfriend, but one day when the change came, it touched Preksha first and everything changed further. Time went by fast, and later on, she preferred Karan's coffee to our innocent staring. Each day after Preksha left me, I loved her even more, but she just hurt me more and more. Each day after she left, I used to wait in the hope that she would come and just hug me and kiss my lips, but it never happened. I hoped that one sweet reply would come from her as an answer to my innumerable messages, but it never came. I desired that even after our break-up, she would call me and wish me on my birthday. Instead, she just wrote 'HBD' and what could be worse? I even cried on my birthday.

Each cigarette I smoked, in order to forget her, and each CCD Coffee she sipped, in order to please herself more!

I know each and every girl has a right to live her own life after a break-up. She can do anything, and she can be everything. But how can she be so rude and self centered that she even forgets her ethics!

First Diwali after break-up

How can I forget my first Diwali after our break-up? In order to make her realize that I still cared for her, I purchased a box of chocolate from the shop and couriered it under the fake name of 'Jalaram Trust' to her residence. It was because, on every Diwali, we used to gift each other something and I didn't want to break that trend.

I checked that courier had reached safely. She might have even eaten the chocolates knowing that they were sent by none other than me, but still there was no response from her side. Yes, I cried on Diwali too!

First Dhuleti without her…

After a few months of our break-up, the festival of colors 'Dhuleti' was even more painful. I got to know that she celebrated each and every festival more happily after she left me.

I was dying to see her at that time. Looking at my pathetic situation, her close friend informed me that, that year, she was going to celebrate Holi with her new friends, which included Karan, at Don Bosco School.

As I wanted to see her, I put on a disguise and colored myself weirdly so that she wouldn't recognize me, even if she saw me in front of her eyes.

I went there and I saw a group of modern students, who had gathered there to celebrate. I termed them as 'modern' because none of them were single and my Preksha was one of them.

The program begin, and they all started dancing to the tunes of Honey Singh's song *'Aaj Din hai Paani Paani Paani'* I considered it my happiness when I saw her smiling at her every dance step. Finally all her friends approached her and colored her with *gulal*. I wish I could tell them that my *gulal*, my sweetheart, my heart was away from me.

A tear came into my eyes when Karan took her in his arms and applied *gulal* on her face. He then showered her with colored water, and at this, she just gave that lovely look to him, which she used to give me when we used to stare at each other, during our oneness.

Yes, I cried on *Dhuleti* too because, just a day before, in front of the hot flames of '*Holi*', I had wished for her happiness, even if it was at the cost of my tears!

Christmas with the approaching break-up anniversary…

It was the month of December, or I believed, 11 months after my break-up, and at this time of year people always wished for something from Santa. I wanted my Preksha back, but I knew the fact that now she was someone's gift! I went to the Red-Church, which was in my locality. There also, my heart had to suffer when I saw the couples who were holding each other's hands. Yes, I was missing her.

Tears came in my years when the Bishop of the Church said a pious sentence from the Holy Bible –

"There is no fear in Love, but the perfect love casts out all fear."

I still remember that, after hearing that sentence, I immediately left the church and ran to Kamatibaugh because it was nearer to the Church.

I sat in the green fields, which looked dark due to the approach of night, and cried vigorously, looking up at the sky and asking, –

"Was my love not perfect?"

At that time also there was no reply.

Uttrayan without her talk…

Her 'modern friends' addressed me as a loser because till date, I don't know how to fly kites, and they were champions at that. I still hate '*Uttrayan*' because that was the black time when she broke up with me. After one year of our break-up, she had become fully 'modern'. She went to Karan's house, maybe for the first time ever. They clicked selfies indicating that they were in a relationship, and what was worse, I cried, not about them, but because of the fact that I didn't know how to fly kites, and so she left me.

There was not a single festival on which I didn't cry. I never showed the world that I was sad, but inside, only I knew what I was suffering!

Time changed both of us. In order to be with Karan, she started lying even to her parents, and they were innocent enough to trust her. I know her parents and they are the best people in the world. It troubled me every single time she lied to them, just to be with him.

She never had to do so when we were in a relationship. The only difference which I see between me and Karan is that Karan always provoked Preksha to lie to her parents, so that she could be there with him. On the other hand, I never told her to lie, because I considered HER PARENTS as MY PARENTS, and I still do, even if she isn't my girlfriend. The break-up not only separated both of us, but it also denied her parents a son like me. Although, my parents were lucky enough not get a daughter like her!

That's why till I got Ashwini in my life, I always used to believe that I was a good ex-boyfriend. I had shared my every chocolate with Preksha, and she made fun of my feelings, sharing it with Karan! Her one close friend, who knew that she was going the wrong way, always reported to me. Once she showed me the screen shot of their chat about me. (This was during *Rakshabandhan*.)

But Preksha, he is so nice. Then why did you leave him?

Fucking nice?
I really don't think so!

But why?

He isn't the man I want. He is narrow minded, self obsessed, somewhat obese and possessive!

Thus, I even cried on *Rakshabandhan*! Those days I didn't have a sister like Heenal, so I had no shoulder to rest my head on and cry! I was alone, while on the other hand, she had everyone and everything! She was a winner and I was a loser. But she was a winner through cheating, and I was a loser because of her happiness! I was defeated. Someone has written beautifully that –

"Loving someone who cannot love you in the same way in return, is not a sign of weakness. It's one of the most courageous things you will ever do. You are putting your armour at their feet and you are saying – I will not fight you ever, I have loved you and that I have already won."

And yes, I won, and as a gift, I got beautiful people like Vrund, Nishu, Dhruvesh Rahul, Ujjwal, Ashwini and most importantly, Heenal!

Sometimes you get the best things if you have the guts to leave the better one!

Chapter 14

Our exams approached, and still there was no reply from Ashwini.

"Yaar, Vrund, she is not replying!" I exclaimed.

Even he looked tense this time and said, "Whatever! Bhai, exams are due. You know we have to clear them, so no distractions!"

He forcefully held my hand and took me to the library, so that we could study.

After exams…

Here were the assumptions of the students of our class after giving each and every paper. (They were bold enough to place it on the notice board.)

Paper	Awesome	Good	Average	Worst
Material and Matter Physics	0%	10%	40%	50%
Mathematics-8	5%	50%	10%	35%
Designing	20%	30%	40%	10%
Computing	0%	0%	60%	40%
Textile Engg.	30%	20%	40%	10%

But I had different assumptions on my mind…

Paper	Pass	Fail	Don't Know
Material and Matter Physics	-	-	100%
Mathematics-8	-	-	100%
Designing	-	-	100%
Computing	-	-	100%
Textile Engg.	-	-	100%

After seeing that, Vrund asked, "What do you think?"

Obviously I had one reply, "I don't know!"

"Don't know?" he asked, confused.

I kicked the wall and said, "Seven days of examination I gave wondering why the hell Ashwini is not replying to me!"

"If a girl is there in your life, there is a problem, and if she is not there, then also there is a problem!" he said.

"Did you try to call her?" he continued.

"I have been doing that since last week. But now her cell phone is switched off," I said.

"I think there is some problem!" suggested Vrund.

Meanwhile, Nishu came and we told her the whole scenario.

"You don't worry, Bhavam. Let's go to her hostel and find out what's wrong," she said.

"As if we will be allowed to go inside the girls' hostel!" said Vrund.

"Who said that you both will go inside? I will go in and check," she said.

Location:- Ashwini's hostel
Time:- 9:30 am

We were anxiously waiting for Nishu to come along with Ashwini.

After a few minutes, we saw her coming with someone.

Vrund tapped my shoulder and said, "Look! Both are coming!"

My eyes were dying to see Ashwini, safe and sound.

But when the vision cleared, I realized that the girl who came along with Nishu was not Ashwini, but someone else.

"That's not Ashwini!" I screamed as Nishu approached us.

"Whoever she is! She's damn beautiful," said Vrund in a low tone.

"Relax!" said Nishu. "She is Himani, Ashwini's roommate."

"Where is Ashwini?" was the first thing which I asked nervously.

"I know you, Bhavam. She talks a lot about you!" said Himani.

"Yes, but where is she?" I asked.

"How can I tell you? It's such a long story!" she said.

"See, yaar...! Seven days have passed and she has not been attending my calls. I am in so much of tension! So please tell me where she is?" I asked.

"It's a very long story, Bhavam. I cannot tell you here right now," repeated Himani.

"Then where?" asked Vrund.

Location:- Fatehgunj, CCD.
Time:- 12:00 pm

(*Why were all horrible things linked with CCD?)

"Now will you tell us something? I beg you!" I said to Himani.

"Is your heart strong enough to listen to what I am going to say?" Himani asked.

"Please! Tell me!"

"Okay then, listen!" she said.

"Ashwini has been my roommate for the last three years. She is my best friend and more than that, she is like my sister. She has shared her every secret with me. Since childhood, she has had a problem in both her kidneys. Twice, major issues occurred and she was operated twice. Thus, this is how she was living. A few days ago, she faced a similar problem. Therefore, she has gone for a checkup. She told me not to say this to anyone, especially you, Bhavam, but I know for a fact that you love her because Ashwini read that poem which you had written for her in that novel," said Himani.

I was shocked as tears flowed down from my eyes.

"You know, after she read your poem in the first page of the novel, she hugged it madly and started crying. She wanted to reply to you that she too loves you a lot, but her ailment stopped her from doing so. Therefore, she wasn't answering your calls," she explained.

"But where is she now?" Nishu asked.

"Wish I knew that," answered Himani.

"What? Then how do you know all this?" asked Vrund.

She took out a part of a letter which was rolled within a keychain.

I was quick to say, "That's Roho and Pruru."

"That's what she left for me," said Himani.

I quickly took that piece of the letter and read it.

My Himani,

Tomorrow morning when you get up, you won't see me in front of your eyes. I have left Vadodara forever, because the due dates of my operation have arrived. I will also not be able to give my exams. I will miss you a lot, Himu! I love you. I am sorry for not saying a final goodbye to you, face to face, because that would have stopped me from going away from you. I never wanted to live, but now, Bhavam has brought a purpose in my life. I know him. He will miss me and the day his patience gets over, he will come to you. But promise me that you won't tell him anything because he has faced so many problems in his life, and I don't want him to get involved in more problems because of me. He doesn't know, but the answer to his proposal was 'yes' since the day he cared for me, along with Roho and Pruru. I love him dearly and he can't even imagine how much in his dreams. He wrote that I am trending in his dreams but he doesn't know that he is trending in my heart. My doctors gave me a call and said that if my kidneys weren't replaced, I have very little chance to live. Therefore, I don't know that if I will get the replaced kidneys of my type or not, so I have not replied to Bhavam. Even if I get the kidneys, my operation is a very risky process. So I don't know if I will be alive or not! So thanks for everything, Himu! Love you...Take care...! And if you get no response from my side within one month, then assume that I have left this beautiful place called Earth. And never let Bhavam know that I love him because, if he comes to know about this fact, he won't trust any other girl ever!

Tears fell on the letter after I read it. I was expressionless!

On seeing this, Nishu snatched the letter from my hand. Minutes later, the expression on her face changed.

Without saying a word, Vrund hugged me and said, "Don't worry! We will save her. We will do anything; we will search for her!"

"Where will you search for her? She has left the city!" said Nishu.

"You guys don't know. Since Preksha left, I have started smoking. This thing should happen to a culprit like me. Why her?" I said in a pathetic voice.

"You can try searching for her! She doesn't know, but I copied the contact number of the doctor whose treatment she is pursuing."

Nishu was quick to check that number on true caller and said, "Dr Priyank Parikh, KTM hospital, Valsad."

"She is from Valsad," said Himani.

"I can't lose Ashwini. I am going there," I said, wiping away my tears.

"You are not going alone. We are also coming," insisted Nishu.

"But you guys…!"

"No, Bhavam! Don't say a word. I have Vrund with me today, and that is just because of you!" she said.

"Correct, you made me realize that Nishu was made for me. Despite all the odds, you completed our love story, and we can't allow you to face your problems in your love story alone," said Vrund.

I just hugged them, because for the first time in life, I realized that you can find soul mates in your friends also.

"I have exams after two days; otherwise I would have joined you all," said Himani.

"Thank you so much, Himani. If you hadn't told me this, I would have never forgiven myself," I said.

Himani hugged me and said, "There is no guy in the world like you. Go, Bhavam, give a life to your love. We all are with you."

Location:- Vadodara Railway Station
Time:- 4:00 pm

Vrund brought the tickets and said, "Vadodara-Valsad Intercity."

"It's an unreserved train. We will have to be quick enough to get in," he added.

Nishu placed her palm on my shoulder and said, "I am very sure that Ashwini will be perfectly alright."

"But she wrote that the operation is dangerous!" I said.

"Life is always complicated, Bhavam, and nothing is without fear. If she is brave enough to face it, you should be strong enough to support her," she said.

"I will give both my kidneys, but I want her to live," I asserted.

"Then how will you live without a kidney?" asked Vrund.

"I just don't care. But nothing should happen to her," I said, as Intercity bustled in, blowing its whistle, on Platform number 2.

Before the train stopped, half the public reserved their seats by throwing their handkerchiefs inside the bogie.

"What was that?" asked Vrund.

"Confused!" said Nishu.

"They are reserving their seats," I said.

"By throwing handkerchiefs?" she asked.

"That's the way seats are reserved in the unreserved trains starting from destination stations. Wherever the handkerchief falls, that seat belongs to that person," I explained.

"Wonder what these people will do if they are in our place, fighting for unreserved education?" asked Vrund.

"Even if the reservation is removed from the education system, the same trend will be followed. Here they throw handkerchief to reserve their seats, there they throw money to reserve their seats," said Nishu.

We somehow managed to get inside the train.

After six long hours we reached Valsad…

Location:- Valsad Railway Station
Time:- 11:00 pm

"Where should we go now?" asked Vrund angrily.

"Why are you so frustrated, jaan?" Nishu asked.

"These unreserved trains! I am never going to travel by it again," he said and moved ahead.

Hearing the word 'jaan', I shifted my attention to Nishu. Her eyes were down as she was feeling shy.

"New city, new feelings!" I said.

"No, Bhavam, the feelings are the same. But this place is something different, so I just said it," she replied.

"That's the beauty of south Gujarat and its people," I said.

"But you see me and you see Vrund. Our cultures are totally different. He is east and I am west. I know I love him and he too loves me, but after he goes to Indonesia, then what?"

"You know, when two people are made for each other, no religion, no barrier, no direction, no cultures can separate them from being one. Hold his hand, whatever comes, you both face it together, but please don't lose your smile because that is what actually separates as well as joins you both," I said.

"You are too mature, yaar!" she said.

"No, I am not. I am just practical. This earth looks like a point when you see it from the moon. Therefore, we should fill this little place only with love, not hatred," I said.

"Wow! So that was the reason why you never showed hatred towards Preksha?" she asked.

"Forget Preksha. I have no respect left for her now. I love Ashwini, because she cares about my love. Just see the reasons of the two persons – Preksha never replied to me because of her EGO, and this girl, Ashwini, didn't reply to me because she never wanted to give me more pain. Such is the difference between the two girls. I wanted to be in Preksha's dream, but then now she is someone's dream and I am too someone's dream now." I said.

I updated my Facebook status with a beautiful poem …

I don't know how to drive bikes,
I don't know how to fly kites!
I don't know how to flirt,
I don't know all those dirt!
I don't drink rum,
But yes…
I know how to rub my thumb,
Over her eyes when they are moist!
I don't know how to impress her,
I do know how to respect her!

(*Yes, I wanted to rub my thumb over Ashwini's eyes because all those smiles were given to me by her. So, in return, I wanted to give her a life in place of the lovely smiles which she had given me.)

"She gave me my smile back; I want to give her, her LIFE back!" I said firmly.

"Don't worry, as you say, it's always good with good people and you are the best, so it's always the best with the best people," Nishu said.

We were standing outside the station, but we couldn't find a single auto-rickshaw!

"That's your South Gujarat!" taunted Vrund.

Finally, after a long wait, we were able to find an auto which agreed to take us to the KTM hospital.

I replied to Vrund's taunt by saying, "That's my South Gujarat. It teaches patience to wait for a thing."

"I am a bit confused!" said Vrund.

"Why so?" asked Nishu.

"KTM - the name itself suggests something related to the sports bike. Then how is it linked with the hospital?" he asked.

The auto driver interrupted and said, "*Poriya*, you are right! Earlier at the same place, there was a show room of bikes, but it didn't work, and the same place was sold to a hospital but the owner didn't care to change the name."

"Fuck! If a doctor is too lazy not to change the name, how will he save my Ashwini?" I questioned.

"Relax! Bhavam. Trust in God," said Nishu.

"As if he will reply to me!" I said.

Vrund nudged the auto driver and asked, "I am sorry, but what is *Poriya*?"

He laughed and said, "You all are *Poriyas*."

"Yes I am asking that only, why are we *Poriyas*?"

"Oh damn it, Vrund! *Poriya* is the same expression used here, which you use as *Baka* in Vadodara."

"Oh I see! I thought of something else," he said.

"What did you think?" asked Nishu in a rough tone.

He was open enough to confess, "I assumed it to be the name of some girl."

"I thought so! That's why you were only interested in knowing what it meant," I said.

Location:- KTM hospital

Time:- 1:00 am

We hurriedly entered the hospital.

The nurse and the security guard stopped us, asking, "What's the problem?"

"I want to meet my Ashwini; she is here!" I said.

"Please let us go in." Vrund said.

"Out!" said the security guard in a loud tone.

"Keep your tone in control," I said roughly.

The guard shoved my shoulder and said in an even louder voice, "And what if I don't?"

"Let me go in. I want to meet my Ashwini," I pleaded.

"Bhavam, he won't allow that. We will be only allowed to visit her during the visiting hours," said Nishu from behind.

"I don't know anything. I want to see my Ashwini," I said as I began entering again.

The guard pulled me from behind and pushed me on the floor.

He lifted his heavy stick and said, "This is the last time. I am telling you to go away or else be ready to face what comes next."

Vrund lifted me up and said, "No, Bhavam! Let's go from here. We will visit her in the morning."

I pulled him aside and said, "My Ashwini is fighting for her life. I need to go."

As I was entering inside, I felt the stroke of a heavy wooden stick on my right leg. It was, indeed, a hit from that guard.

Seeing this, Nishu screamed. This forced the entire night staff to gather around.

Vrund tried to stop all this but Nishu felt insecure, and so she stopped him.

"This is the last time I am telling you. Do you want to book a bed for yourself in the same hospital?" he asked.

I was down due to an injury. Even so, I got the courage to say, "Break me! But I will get in anyhow!"

I was tottering. Due to the injury, blood was coming out from my left leg. Although I managed to get up.

Smashhh!!!! There was a second stroke from the guard, but this time on my left leg.

I screamed aloud in pain. The nurses felt a twinge of sympathy, but the guard was firm.

"Don't come around. He is mental," he said.

I felt another heavy stroke from his stick, this time on my back. He continued to beat me till I lost my strength to get up.

Nishu, who was seeing all this, came and slapped that guard and said, "You idiot. He is not mental. You are dumb! He loves a girl who is admitted here. All he wants is to see that girl, nothing else."

All I remember is that some ward boys lifted me up and took me inside for treatment.

I recalled a saying – "*Love is pain, only if it is true.*"

I got my senses back. The time was exactly 6:00 am.

There was a Doctor who was examining me.

"You will be perfectly alright. But there is so much of nicotine in your body, kid! Not so good!" he said.

My lips were shivering, as I kept saying Ashwini's name.

Vrund looked at me and said, "Bhavam, this is Dr Priyank. We told him everything."

"Kid, get well first. Then we will talk," said the doctor.

"I am alright. I can't wait any more to see Ash...!" I said with maximum energy.

"Take it easy, kid! She isn't here," he said.

"Then where is she?" asked Vrund.

Doctor Priyank took the chair and sat near me. He was a guy in his 50s. He stated, "Look, Beta, Ashwini is facing the same problem which most kidney patients face. But the only difference is that other patients have problems relating to one kidney only, and she has problems in both her kidneys. I have operated on her twice with my own hands. It worked at that time, because she was a child. But now things are bit tough. Firstly, all you need to do is manage the two kidneys, and only then will the operation be possible. And mind you, the operation has only a 5% success rate till date, and secondly, you have to convince Ashwini to take a chance."

"Why isn't she convinced?" Nishu asked.

"Because she doesn't have the money," said the doctor.

"What? Which parent doesn't want to see their child fit and fine!" said Vrund.

"It can't be true. Ashwini belongs to a rich family," I said.

Dr Priyank looked at me and asked, "How long have you known her?"

"For a few months," I replied.

"And I know her since day one. The situation isn't the same now," said the doctor.

"So is Ashwini's family suffering from a financial crisis?" asked Vrund.

"Nope. I will tell you everything. Ashwini is the only daughter in her family. She was loved, cared for and pampered by each and every member of the family. But love changes everyone and it changed Ashwini too. She was in a relationship with a guy. They lived in the same locality but one day, they were caught. Ashwini's father wasn't pleased with her, In fact, he was so angry, that, in order to punish her, he gave her the punishment to stay away from her family, because her family was very close to her heart. She was given the liberty to live by her own rules," explained Dr Priyank.

"But then, why would her dad not give money for her operation?" asked Vrund.

"She had pledged to her father that she would not take a single penny after her education got completed. That's the reason she has no money. I told her that I was like her father and I could operate her for free. But the next issue that came in front was about where the kidneys would be obtained!" explained Dr Priyank.

"But if she is not in the hospital, then where is she?" I asked.

"I really don't have any idea. I forced her to get admitted, but she didn't listen. But you guys find her out soon. We don't have much time. Her case is getting worse, and if she doesn't take proper care of herself, she can collapse into a coma anytime," warned Dr Priyank.

"Didn't she come here?" asked Vrund.

"No," replied Dr Priyank.

"And listen, Doctor, we don't have much money to pay you for Bhavam's treatment because the damage itself was done by your guard," said Nishu.

"Don't worry, girl, I understand. I am a doctor, not a selfish politician," said Dr Priyank and left the ward.

"I can't rest like this," I said, removing all the bandages stuck to my body.

"Stop! Don't you have any idea how much more that can damage you?" ordered Nishu.

"Really, straight people have to suffer more!" commented Vrund.

"Glad you are not! I could have never seen you like this," said Nishu, holding Vrund's hand.

"Where shall we search for her now?" asked Nishu.

There was no reply from both of us.

"We should lodge a police complaint now, I guess!" said Nishu.

"Don't be mad. We can't complain to the police like that. On what basis will we report to the police that Ashwini is lost?" asked Vrund.

"Who said she is lost? We will tell them the real reason," said Nishu.

"If we say so, the police won't do anything to you, because you are a girl, but they will treat me the same way the guard treated Bhavam yesterday," said Vrund.

Chapter 15

After three days…
Location:- KTM hospital
Time:- 7:45 am

"Bhavam, what shall we do now? We have searched the whole of Valsad for the last three days, and still we haven't found her," said Nishu.

I stood up and started walking. My legs were still aching, though I continued my walk.

"Are you okay?" asked Vrund.

I didn't reply. Both followed me.

"But where are you going? At least tell us!" asked Vrund.

"You stay here and call me if you find Ashwini. Now I shall return only when I find her," I said.

"You don't have any proof regarding her. Then how will you find her?" asked Nishu.

"The very first time when I saw her, I was not able to see her face, but her presence gave me a special feeling in my heart. And today I am carrying that presence with me, and I am sure that I will find her," I replied, as I left the hospital premises.

I went into a flower shop and purchased ten lovely red roses.

I plucked one petal of a rose and said, looking up at the skies, "I will search for her in the direction where this rose petal takes me when I release it in the air."

I began my journey. I know that such a thing can only be done by a mad man, but I was ready to do anything for her. She did funny things, in order to make me smile. I was ready to do mad things, in order to give her life.

Every rose petal was taking me on its way. I did not know where I was going. I just followed my fortune.

The final rose was now in my hand. I had been walking for an hour now. My legs were paining because of the injury. I closed my eyes and plucked the final petal of the tenth rose, and it directed me to the left. I went left and when I opened my eyes, I saw a huge building on which it was written – 'Cyber Crime Department.'

Without thinking of anything, I entered the building. It was an enormous building. I was confused about where to go? Again a villainous security guard stopped me and said, "Oh, hero! Where do you wish to go?"

However, he was polite so I replied, " Your head."

"What? We don't have any head," he replied.

I looked confused.

"You wish to lodge a Cyber Complaint?" he asked.

"Yes."

"Okay, then, straight from here, and you will find the complaint section," he said.

I thanked him and moved forward. I was almost tottering because my legs had reached their limit.

A moment came when I dashed to one lady inspector and fell down. She was quick to recover but I was still down. She was gentle and sweet and she helped me to get up. Instead of saying anything, she ordered the officers to lift me up and give me a chair to sit.

"Sorry, mam! That was not intentional," I said with fear, wondering how she would react.

"It's alright, kid! Are you well now?" she queried.

"I am not! I need help! Please help me," I said, tears falling from my eyes.

She saw my hands. They were covered with blood because of the thorns of the roses. She again ordered the officers this time to apply first aid on my hands.

She seemed to be a nice lady, and so I said, "I need your help, mam, please don't go."

"I won't go! Don't worry, but first be all right. Then we shall talk, okay?" she said in a kind manner.

After the first aid was applied on my hand, I was taken inside her cabin.

I saw her name plate on which it was written – Inspector Tanishq Khanna, HOD, Cyber Crime.

Wow! She was the HOD; therefore, she had every power in her hand.

"Please be seated, boy, and tell me your problem!" she said.

I was confused about where to start, but I kept my heart firm and spoke what was true. She was so nice that she listened to me peacefully. I demanded for her help to search for Ashwini by the means of her last cell phone location.

"I respect that, kid, but I cannot do this under such a reason," she said.

"No, mam! Please don't say so. I plucked these ten roses under the name of God, knowing that if couldn't find her, I would definitely find some link which shall help me to find her. And God made me reach your doorstep. Don't close this door on me. Please!" I begged.

"It's in my hand to just give orders, but the work of tracking her location will be done by my deputies. For that you need a very strong reason," she said.

"Someone's life is more important than a reason?" I asked.

"This system runs me; I don't run the system, kid." she replied.

"It's fine. I will find my Ashwini on my own," I said, as I prepared to leave.

"I am sorry, kid!" she said from behind.

She saw me wiping my face with my hands. She was kind, sincere and gentle, but indeed, she was loyal to her job!

She approached me and offered me some water saying, "All right, don't get disappointed. I promise to give you your Ashwini back. Get into my car."

My happiness was in the seven skies. Yes, it's always good with the good people.

I was in her police van.

She asked me, "Tell me her mobile number."

I was quick to respond, "4651."

"What?"

"I am sorry, that's her vehicle number. Her mobile number is 777...." I said.

Indeed 4651 was still ruling my heart.

She turned on the operating system GPS of her police van and called her deputy saying, "A girl is missing. Will you trace her location for me?"

'Yes, sure, mam,' was the reply heard from the system.

She then gave the number details and said, "Tell me her last cell phone location?"

After a few seconds we heard, "Last recognized location of the cell phone is the Ashan Bazaar near Gandhi Chauk, mam."

She drove her vehicle and headed straight to Ashan Bazaar.

"Tell me one thing. How can she be at Ashaan Bazaar, if she is going to die?" she asked.

"She is a free soul and a person who loves life. She was facing a hell of a problem, and still, she didn't say a single word to me," I replied.

My God! Miss Tanishq was lady Singham! She was driving as if she had been inspired from the Fast and Furious movie series.

"A little slow, mam. I want to die after giving her life," I said.

She took out her aviators and gave them to me, saying, "Wear it! It will cast out your fear."

We reached Ashan Bazaar. It was a very humid and crowded place.

She again gave a message on her system, saying, "Can you trace the current location of the girl?"

"The cell is switched off!" was the reply heard.

"Don't get disappointed! If she is here, we will find her for sure!" she said.

Meanwhile I called Vrund and told him to be there at the Ashan Bazaar.

"But where shall we search for her, Miss Tanishq?" I asked.

"You better know your love. You only tell me for what reason she would come here?" she asked.

I closed my eyes and revived every memory which we spent together.

After thinking a lot, my lips muttered along with my heart, "For an ice cream!"

"Ice-cream?" she asked.

"Yes mam, she loves ice cream. She might be here at some ice cream shop!" I suggested.

We quickly entered Bharkadevi ice cream shop which was a little inside the huge Ashan Bazaar.

I looked at the manager and asked, "Did Ashwini come here?"

He looked confused as he stared at my face.

Miss Tanishq pushed me forward and said, "As if he knows who is Ashwini, idiot!"

I got my senses back.

"Do you have a photo of her?" she asked.

I took my cell phone out and opened her Facebook profile picture and gave it to Miss Tanishq.

She than placed my cell phone in the manager's hand and asked in a typical police tone, "Have you seen her?"

The man examined Ashwini carefully as if he was looking at the most beautiful girl of the planet, which she was.

He then asked his servants, "Have you seen this lady?"

One of them was prompt to reply, "Yes mam, she came here a few days ago to eat ice cream?"

Miss Tanishq went near that man and asked, "Was she alone? Answer Yes or No."

"Yes."

"Which flavor of ice cream did she eat?"

The answer in my mind was Strawberry and yes, I was correct as that person replied, "Strawberry."

"Did she pay the bill?"

"Yes."

Lady Singham than turned her attention to the manager and asked him, "Would you mind if I check the CCTV footages of your shop over the last few days?"

The manager was kind enough to stand up and say, "The computer is all yours, mam."

We examined the previous day's footage, but she wasn't there.

Then the footage of the previous days was checked, but we failed to find her.

"Don't worry, the footage is not clear," she muttered.

"You don't have CCTV cams attached at the front door? It would give us a clear vision," she said.

The Manager replied, "No, mam! Robberies generally occur inside the shop, so we didn't find it useful, but just next door, we have a jewellery shop and they have a high tech security system, which might surely help you."

We immediately rushed toward the jewellery shop.

What a coincidence! The name of the shop was Tanishq, and the lady alongside me was Tanishq too.

Seeing Lady Singham entering the shop, the staff turned cautious.

She went near the cash counter and said, "Will Tanishq help this Tanishq?"

"Sure, mam!" was the reply.

She explained everything and what needed to be done. We were inside the control room where everything was monitored.

She instructed the person sitting inside the room to get lost.

"This is the final hope, Bhavam," she said.

She opened that particular footage which just showed the outside view of the shop. I was pleased to see that the footage was much clearer this time.

After two long hours of examining the footages, we came to the conclusion that Ashwini was not there.

I banged my head on the desk and started crying. The lady alongside me looked clueless.

"Wait, we haven't seen today's footages!" she said.

She again rolled the footage of today's date.

A point came where I screamed, "Stop!"

She paused the footage. I examined it carefully. I saw a girl who looked like Ashwini from behind, although her face was not seen at all.

"But you can't see her face!" said Miss Tanishq.

"She is Ashwini, I know. Yes, indeed, she is!" I exclaimed.

Lady Singham minutely scanned her every detail and penned them down on paper. She took a picture of whatever she wrote on her cell phone and sent it via WhatsApp to her deputies, ordering them to trace the current location of Ashwini.

We immediately left the jewellery shop and came down, anxiously waiting for the call indicating the penultimate location of Ashwini.

The day was becoming darker. It reminded me of the similar situation which had occurred when I met Ashwini, for the first time ever. All that came in front of my eyes, as my heart constantly beat to see her.

Miss Tanishq finally received a call which stated that the suspect was outside the 'Sundaram Pan Centre'.

Before Miss Tanishq could react, I ran towards the 'Sundaram Pan Centre' without knowing where it was!

I dashed against a person. He was none other than Vrund.

"Vrund, we just found her. She is at Sundaram Pan Centre," I said happily.

Hearing this, he hugged me tightly and said, "Then what are we waiting for? Let's go."

I turned behind and saw Miss Tanishq waving, indicating me to go there. So I told Vrund to stay there as I went near her.

Miss Tanishq asked, "Do you know where Sundaram Pan Centre is?"

My eyes were down as I said, "I am, sorry mam; I was excited."

"Look, take a left from here and you will see your Ashwini in front of your eyes," she said.

"But where are you going?" I asked.

"I have done my work. Now get to your destiny before it leaves you again!" she replied.

My affection towards Lady Singham was increasing. I didn't know how to thank her so I just joined my hands in front of her and said, "Thank you for everything, mam."

Seeing this, she removed her aviators and said, "Look, kid, once my grandfather wrote me a letter and in that he said, "This world is a beautiful place, and you have been sent here to make it more beautiful and amazing. We all have limited time, and no matter how much we have, it always seems to be less. There is so much to see, so much to experience and so much to feel, that you don't even have time to waste. Opportunities are endless. You can do anything, and you can be everything. You have the capacity to change the world, and so try something new every day. If you have doubts someday regarding your work, remember that it's always better to regret after doing something, rather than regretting not doing it. Fear not from mistakes. Mistakes are done by those who have the guts to try. Take responsibility for your mistakes and try to rectify them, but never throw its responsibility on others. And forgive others, if they ever make mistakes, because you never know what's going on in someone's life. Give as many chances to others for their mistake, as you give to yourself. Treat everyone the way you treat yourself, for that is how you will know how to respect others. Respect everyone, trust few, but most importantly, love everyone. Love is very scarce in this world. I need it and you too shall need it."

The next moment when I blinked my eyes, she wasn't there. Wow! Was she the second version of Heenal, or what?

"Where are you lost?" asked Vrund. "Let's go."

I followed the directions which Miss Tanishq had showed me. A point came when I was able to see the board of 'Sundaram Pan Centre'.

Every step became slower as I moved forward. The dark weather became darker. The winds started to blow from the east. A raindrop fell on my chin, indicating that even God was going to observe the whole scenario which was going to take place. It started raining heavily. This created a huge disturbance in the crowd as people began to hide themselves in search of the shade. My eyes were at the 'Sundaram Pan Centre'. I saw one girl who was endlessly enjoying the rain. She spread her arms open to embrace the rain to hug her. The rain fell faster. Everyone was now away from the road except that girl. Ashan Bazaar was in a small lane, so in no time, water started to cross over one fourth of my feet. The scene was perfect. Only that girl and I were at the centre of the street. The ferocity of the rain didn't allow me to see her face properly. She turned around and looked at me. We both were like dark bodies to each other. I came nearer to her, and my legs were tottering again. They had done their job to make me reach safely till here. I fell on the ground, and on seeing that, she approached me and laughed saying, "Rains are always beautiful."

Yes! The voice was Ashwini's. However, the force of rain was so strong that we weren't able to see each other from such a short distance also.

"But are you okay?" she asked in assurance.

I didn't reply.

"I know that the noise of thunder is mightier than my little voice, but I am asking you if you are okay?" she asked.

I listened deliberately, but didn't reply.

"That is strange. I guess you can't hear. It's all right; no one hears me these days, and life has also stopped listening to me. Then who are you to listen and reply?" she said with mild laughter and turned around to go away from me.

Before she could do that, I held her elbow tightly and responded, "Not this time!"

She turned around with a shock and said, "This voice! It just touched my heart. Who are you?"

"I am the one who loves you and you are the one who loves me too," I said, pulling her nearer to me.

There was a huge peal of thunder and lightning which provided some light in the skies. That fraction of light fell on us and we were able to see each other's eyes clearly. My eyes were full of tears and her eyes were full of cuteness and pain.

"Bhavam…!" she said and just hugged me tightly.

I moved away from that hug and said, "Who told you to go away from me? You know I love you! Then why?"

"You know everything now. I don't have much time to live. I don't want to spoil your life. It was very difficult to make you laugh and smile. I don't want my separation to give you all those tears again," she said.

I took her in my arms, my lips were near her lips, as I said, "You will live. You will have to live. Not for anyone but for me, for our life, for our dreams."

For the first time ever, I saw tears in her eyes, as she said, "I don't have money!"

I wanted to kiss her and tell that everything was going to be alright.

She started crying. I smooched her. Yes, but not on her lips, but on her eyes, and that too in order to drink off her tears.

"They only look good in my eyes, not yours," I said.

Without thinking of anything, she placed her lips on my lips as we kissed each other for the first time ever, in front of all. I kissed her passionately. I felt every pain she was going through. Finally when our lips got separated, she was expressionless. Naturally her eyes were closed after that smooch. It was natural.

But a few seconds passed, but she didn't open her eyes.

"Ashwini...?" I said holding her chin. She collapsed on my chest, losing consciousness, as if she had lost her life there itself.

"No, Ashwini! You can't leave me like that!" I said, holding her in my arms.

Along with the rain drops, my tears were too falling on her face.

I shouted for help and then everyone gathered.

Seeing this entire scene everyone on the street was emotional.

I looked up at the skies and shouted, "I never snatched someone's love! Please don't take my ANGEL away from me. I love her. Please help me."

This time the heavens were not partial enough to reply to me, because after a few seconds, I was able to hear the beeping sound of the ambulance.

It was the ambulance of KTM hospital itself. Ward boys and nurses came down and approached us. They lifted Ashwini in the stretcher. That was the worst sight which I was viewing in front of my eyes. Vrund however, came and said, "Don't worry. If we have found her, then definitely we will be able to save her."

However, we both weren't allowed to sit inside the ambulance, because it was already overloaded.

Location:- KTM hospital
Time:- 4:00 pm

Nishu was standing there, maybe waiting for us.

"Did the ambulance arrive?" asked Vrund impatiently.

"Don't worry! They just took her inside the ICU," she said.

I was down on my feet thinking of what wrong that innocent girl had done! As she faced the pain, which she never deserved.

After a long wait, Dr Priyank came out of the ICU and said, "A few seconds have saved Ashwini from death. Well done, guys, but that is still not conclusive. The damage has crossed its limit and we need to operate her within 24 hours. But for that, we need two kidneys."

"What's her blood group?" Vrund asked.

"B+ve," replied Dr Priyank.

"But how will we manage to find kidneys in 24 hours?" asked Nishu curiously.

Dr Priyank looked up and said, "Just in the same way in which you managed to get her here. Try your best! If God is great, everything will be okay!"

Meanwhile Vrund and Nishu were discussing about on how to get kidneys. I stood up and went near the ICU and saw Ashwini. She was lying peacefully there in the bed with an oxygen pump and ventilator to support her life. I kissed the window and said, "So innocent you are! You never told me anything. You went to face death alone and that too with a smile. With what I faced, I thought I was the saddest person in the world, but in this situation also, you are teaching me how to smile when you get the worst of the pain."

(POINT #49:- When life says 'Fuck you', you say that, 'I fuck you more!" That determines the attitude.)

Nishu placed her hand behind my back. I saw her and just hugged her because I badly needed someone.

"Bhavam, don't forget; we need to get two kidneys before 24 hours," she said.

"I am ready to donate both my kidneys. My blood group is also B +ve," I said.

"Even if you wish, you can't donate both your kidneys, baccha!" said Dr Priyank.

"But what's the problem in that?" I asked.

"Because they are habituated with the smoke of the cigarettes which you generally prefer," replied Dr Priyesh.

I was stunned and at the same time, very guilty. I always thought that cigarettes would take my life away, but now, they had stopped me from giving my life to Ashwini. If something wrong occurred to her, I would die every day in regret that if I hadn't smoked, then maybe I might have saved Ashwini. That is why SMOKING KILLS. Not only physically but also mentally!

"Social media!" exclaimed Vrund. "We will post on social media and appeal to people to donate their kidneys."

"Excellent idea, sweetu!" said Nishu, taking her cell phone out.

Both of them made a sweet and sensible appeal by posting Ashwini's DP on their wall, asking everyone if they could donate their kidneys for her.

I took out my cell phone and started looking at the selfies which Ashwini had clicked with me. I uploaded the first of our selfies and wrote in the caption box…

Tu jahan bhi jayegi,
Mei waha aa jayunga!
Tu jo chali jayegi,
Mei tuje le aaunga!
I love you my angel,
Tuje kabhi na mei bhulaunga!
I love you my angel,
Tuje kabhi na mei bhulaunga!

All of us started receiving 'likes' but no one dared to comment because it was a sensitive issue. My messenger window was covered with messages from most of my friends who sent their prayers and wishes for Ashwini.

Surprisingly Preksha messaged me –

Do you love her?

I did what she used to do! I saw her message, but didn't care to reply to her. After all she was nothing to me now. To irritate me more, she further messaged –

There????

I wanted to avoid her because I was already disturbed due to all this happening around me! And secondly, I never wanted to vent my anger on her because I wasn't like her. So I just went offline.

When all hopes seemed to be dying, I went near Dr Priyank and said, "Sir, please guide us! We are confused as to what to do next."

"I have definitely thought of one option, but that won't work," he said.

I said nothing.

So he continued, "There are a few families striving for money. They are willingly ready to donate their kidneys if you give them some money."

"How much?" I asked.

"The price is too much, baccha!" he said.

" How much?" I again asked

"1.5 to 3 lakh rupees for each kidney. So if you take an average, you need to get 5 lakh rupees for both the kidneys."

I was quiet because I had never had that kind of money.

"I can suggest to you one more thing! I know you are all grown up at 22, but you still don't possess the right to take every decision by yourselves. Get your parents involved in this. Tell them everything and they will support you because, at last they are parents, and they can never see their kid unhappy for a long time," he said.

Dr Priyank wasn't wrong.

When every door of life is closed, the only one which remains open for us is our parents' love.

I was about to give my mom a phone call, telling her each and everything.

But then Vrund came and interrupted me. He was filled with happiness and smiles.

Looking at him, I asked, "Why are you so happy?"

"We got it, Bhavam! Social media's *jaddu* worked. We have got the kidneys," said Vrund.

My word! For a second, I held my breath. Dr Priyank stood up from his seat after hearing this.

"But who is that noble person willing to donate his kidneys for my Ashwini?" I asked.

"You know him; we all know him very well!" he replied.

"But who is he?" I asked anxiously.

"Our friend, Dhruvesh, and he has got one more person who is ready to donate her kidney for Ashwini!" said Vrund.

Respect doubled in my eyes for Dhruvesh, when I heard that he was going to do such a noble thing, only for me.

"But who is that other person?" I asked.

"I don't know about that! But they have left Vadodara, and so, in two hours they will be here. Doctor, you please start the preparations for the kidney transplant," said Vrund and left.

"But firstly, we need to examine if Ashwini is fully fit for the operation or not," said Dr Priyank.

"She is a fighter, and she will never give up!" I said.

Chapter 16

Location:- KTM Hospital
Time:- 10:00 pm

We were anxiously waiting for Vrund who had gone to the Railway Station to receive Dhruvesh and that other person.

After a long wait, the auto rickshaw came to the doorway of the hospital. Vrund was the first whom I saw getting out of the auto. I gave a big smile when I saw Dhruvesh. Indeed my respect for him had increased! But the other person was not coming out of the auto. I went near the auto and said, "Who is inside?"

Vrund and Dhruvesh looked at each other, but didn't utter a word.

"Why are you not saying anything?" I asked.

Again they didn't say anything but just looked down.

Finally I turned my neck inside the auto. There was a lady who was sitting inside. She had covered her face with a duppata, in order to protect her face and hair.

I looked out and asked, "Who is she?"

Again both had no reply.

"WTF! Why are you not saying a word?" I asked angrily.

"Take it easy when you see the face of the girl, and don't get frustrated. She is here to help you," said Dhruvesh.

I held his hand and asked, "But why is she hiding?"

"She is afraid!" said Vrund.

"Of whom?" I asked.

"Of you!" he replied.

"Me? But what wrong have I done to her?" I asked.

"Take it easy, Bhavam! We are going inside! Till then, you convince this girl to come! She is a little frightened," said Vrund and left.

I was in a very odd situation. However, I went and got seated inside the auto. The girl had covered her face in the typical manner in which all girls generally do. Only her eyes were visible. They were sharp and seemed to be familiar.

"Well, I am sorry, but I don't know you. But I am very grateful to you for showing such a sensibility by donating your kidney for my Ashwini," I said.

She looked down but didn't reply.

"Is everything all right?" I asked, looking into her eyes.

She nodded in affirmation.

"Are you frightened by someone?" I asked her.

She shook her head.

"Oh, then it's fine! These guys told me that you are frightened of me," I said.

She just stared at me, but said nothing.

"Can I know your name?" I asked.

She looked the other way, but didn't reply!

"I am sorry! I guess I am irritating you!" I exclaimed.

"No!" she said in a very low tone.

I laughed and replied, "It's so funny that these days every voice, every pair of eyes and every feeling seems to be so familiar to me."

No reply!

With that I left the auto, and she came along with me. It was strange because she was hiding her face in the darkness.

"Are you from Vadodara only?" I asked.

She nodded in a positive response.

"So how much money do you need for your kidney?" I asked.

She stopped for a moment and took out her cell phone. I was confused.

Meanwhile, I started receiving phone calls from someone. When I looked at my cell, it was Preksha, who was calling me.

I looked up at the skies and asked, "Why is she calling me?"

I didn't cut her call and just allowed it to ring.

However, the very next second, I again received her call. The process continued three times. Finally that girl came in front of me and started calling someone. I again received a ring on my cell phone, and again it was Preksha. There was a sudden lightning in my mind when that girl said, "That's my name."

My god! The girl standing in front of my eyes was none other than Preksha! Why was she here? Why had she come here?? She removed her duppata and uncovered her face. Yes, indeed it was she! I was seeing her like that in front of my eyes after a long time. All those memories flashbacked before my eyes when I saw her. Tears were there in my eyes but I controlled them, and to my surprise, she had tears in her eyes too.

"Why are you here?" I asked bluntly.

"For you," she replied.

"I don't need you! Please go!" I said politely.

She held my hand and said, "Listen, Bhavam."

"Don't! Please don't touch me!" I said shoving her away from me.

"I am ready to donate my kidney for Ashwini!" she replied.

Why was she doing so? She had her own life. Then why did she come back into my life again?

"But why do you want to do this?" I asked.

"For you," she said.

"You have already done enough for me, I don't need your debts again," I said.

"No, Bhavam, please don't say so," she said as tears fell from her eyes.

"Please, haan! Don't show me your tears. It has taken me four long years to go away from all this!" I said.

"I am very sorry, Bhavam; please forgive me," she said joining both her hands and crying like hell.

I got hold of her sweet hands, which, indeed, reminded me that they were much sweeter when I was there with her.

"Please don't cry! I can't see tears in your eyes, even if you aren't my girlfriend," I said.

She listened, but continued to cry.

"Why are you alone? Where is your Karan?" I asked purposely.

"He left!" was the reply from her.

Indeed the tables had turned. Karan had betrayed her and now she was alone. She was facing the same pain which I had faced at the time when she left me for Karan.

"How can I explain to you, Bhavam? A few things are left unsolved between us!" she said.

"You left me for Karan and he left you for someone! You guys are experts in all these games!" I taunted her.

She had no reply.

"But why are you here?" I asked roughly.

"Because I know that I have only given you pain. I know you have suffered for these four years and all that was because of me. Finally you found someone who could truly value you, but life again played a rumble against you. Now it is on the verge of snatching that happiness from your life, but I won't allow that to happen. I have come here to save Ashwini, and for that I will donate my kidney," she said.

I had the same question, "Why are you doing this?"

"You even cared for my smile after our break-up. I gave you hell, but still, you cared to secure the smile on my face. I replied to you rudely, and then also you kept on messaging me without any evil intention. So I want to secure the smile, which this girl brought into your life. Therefore, here I am!" she said.

I was speechless. I didn't know what to say, so I just kept moving forward without replying to her. When we entered inside, Vrund, Dhruvesh and Nishu were prepared to see us both. Nishu came forward and asked Preksha politely, "You must be tired? Have you eaten something?"

"Yes, I request you to please eat something from the canteen next to the hospital!" added Vrund.

Preksha wiped off her tears and looked at me again and said, "These people can be your friends only, because they are just like you. Respecting even that girl, who ruined their best friend without any fault?"

No one had a reply to that.

"I know you guys hate me!" she said, as her tears fell on the floor.

I wanted to embrace her and tell her not to cry but I didn't move.

However, the other three went near her and assured her not to cry.

"What's done is done, Preksha. We respect you because you are here to save Bhavam's love," said Dhruvesh.

She looked at me and said, "But he is not talking to me!"

"Four years of suffering is not a small thing. He will take his time," said Nishu.

I was standing there and listening to everything, but I didn't say a word.

"But what is the problem with Karan? Where is he?" asked Dhruvesh.

"That's the thing, Dhruvesh. He is Karan, so he will never come searching for me. He is not Bhavam, who can search for his Ashwini even in a totally unknown city," she replied.

I was standing outside the ICU, looking at Ashwini. I could imagine the pain through which she was going. I was not comfortable seeing her in that situation. Preksha came and stood beside me and said, "She is so sweet!"

I didn't reply.

"I am sorry, Bhavam!" she said, placing her palm over my shoulder.

"Please stop touching me. It hurts!" I said.

"Don't worry! After I donate my kidneys, I will go away from your eyes! Maybe forever!" she exclaimed.

"You went away from my eyes the day you cheated on me!" I said.

"I have never cheated on you, Bhavam, trust me! When I was in relationship with you, I never cheated. All that I did was after the break-up," she replied.

"You wanted him, so you accepted him at the very next second after you broke up with me!" I said.

"It's not so, yaar...! I am ready to explain everything, Bhavam, if you just listen patiently," she said.

"I waited for four years for that explanation, but it never came. Now I am not interested to know why you left me, because

I know that when I loved you, I really did. I also do know that now I love Ashwini and that is forever. If Ashwini never came in my life, I would have died, crying for you every day. But if tomorrow, Ashwini leaves me forever, then I would die smiling for her every day. She has given me the smile which you took away. Do you have any answers to that? She taught me to live; do you have any answers to that? She has stopped my tears; do you have any explanation for that? She taught me to even respect you; do you have any conclusion for that?" I asked.

Tears fell from her eyes but there was no response.

"Don't say anything, Preksha. You have always lied to me and I don't want to hear further lies from you. You please be happy with your future boyfriend. You are attractive, and you will find many," I said.

"Bhavam…Karan left me!" she exclaimed.

"Friends with benefits have no commitments, Preksha! These things look nice only for a few moments. Life works with guts and commitment, not benefits," I said.

"You know his last message for me was…

'A prostitute is better than you!

Good Bye.' "

Nishu felt hurt when she heard that.

"How dare he say that?" said Dhruvesh angrily.

"You don't know how to recognize people, Preksha. I knew that Karan was like that because you were just a number to him. After you, his next target would have been some other girl," I said.

"I feel like dying!" she said.

"Don't die. Your thousands of followers will miss you!" I commented.

"I just don't know what changed me!" she said.

"Time changed you. It even wanted to change me, but I was firm. I stood by my ethics, and as a gift I got a beautiful angel who is resting inside, and fighting the battle of LIFE VS DEATH. Even if I lose her tomorrow, I won't live in regret now that I didn't try to save her. I will live for her, and most importantly, her smile."

Dr Priyank interrupted us and said, "I have checked Ashwini. She is 60% fit for the operation. We will operate on her tomorrow at 12:00 pm."

Dhruvesh went near him and said, "Sir, we are ready to give our kidneys. Kindly operate on us."

My heart came out at hearing the greatness of Dhruvesh. I went near him and hugged him tightly saying, "Thank you, yaar...! I don't know what to say."

"No need to thank me," he said. "You remember, naa, that you have to do my setting with Vish! Bas, that you do in return for this kidney."

I smiled and said, "Damn! For sure."

Both Preksha and Dhruvesh directed themselves towards the operation theatre.

I wanted to hold Preksha's hand and thank her for what she was doing, but I controlled myself from doing it.

They both were taken inside the operation theatre. Dr Priyank and his deputy, Dr Meet, were going to operate on both of them. The red light beamed outside the operation theatre indicating that the operation had started. I kept my eyes closed, hoping that everything would settle well. Nishu was nervous, so Vrund had just taken her in his arms. Later on, Nishu slept, and so he placed her gently on the velvet sofa and approached me.

"You should have talked nicely to Preksha," he said.

"I will slap you, if you say a single word in her favor!" I snapped.

"I understand that what she did was, indeed, very bad, but she has realized her mistake," he said.

"She would never have realized it if Karan hadn't showed his real colors!" I said.

"Now forget everything and be good friends. You have Ashwini, but she is alone, naa." he said.

"You see to your girlfriend, and don't worry about her. She will find someone!" I said.

"Once when a person is betrayed in love, he takes a lot of time to recover. You tell me if Ashwini hadn't come in your life, would you have been the same?" he asked.

"Ashwini is my angel. Preksha is not!" I said.

"Every girl is an angel. The difference is good and bad. See my Nishu, when she sleeps silently on my shoulder, I feel she is a good angel, but when she fights and argues with me, I feel that she is a bad angel. But the fact is that she is an angel!" replied Vrund as he went near Nishu and again placed her in his arms and fell asleep.

(POINT #50:- Every girl is an Angel. She has the supernatural powers to bring happiness, smiles, tears, joy, love and heartbreak in your life.)

After two long hours, the red light of the operation theatre went off. I quickly stood up and told Vrund and Nishu that the operation was over. We all were anxiously waiting for the doctors to come out.

Dr Priyank and Dr Meet were the first to come out. They looked exhausted.

Before we could ask anything, they pointed a Thumbs up, looking at us and indicating that the kidneys had been successfully removed. Wow! The first stage was cleared successfully.

The Thumbs up symbol had played a vital role in my life. Earlier when Preksha used to give me 'Thumbs up' on Messenger, it used to annoy me a lot. I always believed that it was a sign of hatred and pain, but when today, Dr Priyank and Dr Meet showed us the same symbol of 'Thumbs up' with their hands, it made me feel relief in my heart. I realize that I was so wrong in assuming things. I remembered the sentence which Miss Tanishq told me –

'You never know what's going on in someone's life.'

Next day…

The most important day of my life arrived. Yes, Ashwini was going to be operated today. As the doctor had stated earlier, that operation had only 5% of success rate. So it meant that if the operation was a failure, we would lose Ashwini. Tension was running through everyone's minds. No one had breakfast because they were all nervous. However, the two operated people, Dhruvesh and Preksha, needed the utmost care, so I took the breakfast myself into the ward where they both were kept. Dhruvesh was awake. I kept the plate there and asked him, "How are you feeling, dude?"

"Fucking awesome! It feels the same, nothing much. A person can live on one kidney too," he said.

"And how is she?" I asked, indicating Preksha. She was still sleeping.

"You ask her yourself," said Dhruvesh as he began eating his breakfast.

Each and every girl looks cute when she is sleeping. Yes, she looked like the old Preksha whom I had loved, purely innocent.

I placed my hand on her hand in affection. She felt my touch and opened her eyes and smiled.

"How are you feeling?" I asked as my tears fell on her face. "I am sorry for my behavior yesterday," I added.

She rubbed her thumb on my eyes and said, "Look, I am all right and you have the right to tell me anything. I am your culprit."

I placed my hand over her mouth and said, "Don't say anything, please.

You must be hungry. I have brought breakfast for you," I said.

"Promise me you will treat Ashwini like this only," she said.

I nodded.

(*I was thinking in my mind that if I could treat her like this, then Ashwini was totally a different matter!)

She was a little weak, so a saline tube had been attached to her hands. Hence, she was not able to eat the breakfast with her hands. Therefore, I made her eat the breakfast.

With every bite which I made her eat, she was looking into my eyes, but I didn't respond because I didn't want to trouble myself more with her memories.

Finally when everything was over, I said, "Thank you, Preksha! Please take rest. If you need anything, than just tell me."

She didn't leave my hand.

"Bhavam, you are the world's best ex-boyfriend," she said with a smile.

I too smiled and replied, "But you aren't the world's best ex-girlfriend, though you were the best girlfriend."

On hearing this, she laughed as I left the ward.

(POINT #51:- Sometimes a person improves after the break-up and you are again attracted to them.)

The moment finally arrived...

15 minutes were left before the five hour long operation which was going to be performed on Ashwini. Dr Priyank and his team were getting ready for the major task.

He approached me and asked, "Do you wish to meet her before we take her in?"

Obviously I agreed but I had to follow ICU rules, so I had to wear that special green colored attire which the doctors were wearing, and then I was taken inside the ICU room number four in which she was kept.

I entered inside, and noticed that all the things that had been attached to her body had been removed, but her eyes were closed.

Dr Priyank was alongside me, and I asked, "Why are her eyes closed?"

"This is a long operation, so anesthesia was given to her early in the morning," he explained.

I went near her. My face was masked, so I was not able to kiss her, although I hugged her for five long minutes.

I said in her ears, "I love you, Ashwini; please live for me. I want to live with you, be with you forever. Please BE MY ANGEL, please BE MY ANGEL. I know you are listening to me. I know you want to reply to me. I know you want to hug me and kiss me, and guess what? These five hours cannot separate you and me. I was waiting for you until you came into my life and I will be waiting for you again, when you come into my life again."

Dr Priyank consoled me, saying, "We should go now. The time is approaching."

I went out of the ICU. Minutes later, we all saw Ashwini being shifted to the operation theatre. That was, indeed, a very tough moment for everyone.

The door of the operation theatre closed and the red light beamed.

Meanwhile Dhruvesh and Preksha came out from their respective wards.

I was not crying but my eyes were wet, and on seeing this, Preksha approached me and said, "Bhavam, don't worry! Happiness will be yours forever after five hours."

"I am very nervous," I said.

Nishu said, "We are all nervous. Let's go to the temple nearby and pray for her. Where nothing works, prayers definitely work."

Inside the hospital itself there was a temple. We all took refuge there.

I prayed in my mind –

Na usne kisi ka bura kiya,
Na maine kisi ka bura kiya!
Fir kyu mei roj rota hu?
Aur kyu woh roj tadapti hai?
Ha usne mujko paya,
Ha maine usko paya!
Fir kyu mei har daard sehta hu?
Aur kyu woh har daard seh leti hai?
Har manzil meri uski,

Har manzil uski meri!
Fir kyu khafa tu karta hai?
Aur kyu rafah woh hoti hai?
Jaise usne mujko dekha,
Jaise maine usko dekha!
Fir kyu mei aaj tere samne hu?
Aur kyu woh tere bharose hai?

My heart, soul and mind were one when I was praying for Ashwini, because prayers have that magic which no other thing in the world has. Once Swami Vivekananda also said,

I look behind and after
And find that all is right,
In my deepest sorrows
There is a soul of light!

I was hoping for that soul of light to go and give Ashwini the life to live. When I opened my eyes, they were filled with tears and rejoicing just for her. My eyes were diverted to the wall on which it was written –

"Whosoever worships me, for whatsoever desire, I meet him with that."

And yes, my desire was just getting Ashwini back!

The red light was off…

Finally after five long hours of waiting, the red light at the top of the operation theatre was turned off. On seeing this, everyone's heartbeat increased and we all stood up. I was sitting there, expressionless, waiting for the desirable or the worst!

This time, instead of Dr Priyank first, his deputies came out. Vrund and Nishu constantly asked them what was the outcome, but they looked down and didn't reply.

Finally Dr Priyank came out. He took out his specs and wiped his eyes. He looked at me, I looked at him, but no one said anything.

"What happened?" asked Dhruvesh. Even he had tears in his eyes.

"Please tell us that she is fine!" said Nishu, holding Vrund's hand.

Dr Priyank sat on his knees and held my hand and said, "Baccha, I operated on her. Her kidneys were replaced perfectly, and she was responding well, but when we were stitching her, she showed a massive difference in her heart beats, and then she went into a coma, I tried a lot to bring her back but a point came when her heart beats stopped and ultimately, she passed away! I am sorry, Bhavam. We couldn't save her."

After he said so, I lost my senses and fell down. I could only remember that Preksha was the one to hold me. Yes, she too was crying. All were crying. Even Dr Priyank cried.

After a few moments…

"Dr Priyank!!!!!" a shout was heard from the operation theatre.

It was Dr Meet, his deputy.

I was left in Preksha's arms, as all of them rushed inside the operation theatre because of that scream.

"What happened?" asked Dr Priyank.

"The patient's pulse rate is working!" said Dr Meet in excitement.

"What?" asked Dr Priyank in disbelief.

"Trust me, Doctor, when I was covering the body, the patient shivered, moved her lips and said 'H…e…e…n…!' I was confused, and so I checked the pulse rate. It is working," said Dr Meet.

Dr Priyank shoved everyone out of the room and again the red light beamed.

The noise of electric shocks was heard. I fainted, thinking that Ashwini was no more!

After a few moments again…

Yes! This time Dr Priyank came out. I was still unconscious. He caught hold of me and took me inside the operation theatre and said, "Look, Bhavam, she has defeated death. She is yours. She is back."

The words were not reaching my mind because I was still in shock.

In order to revive me, he poured water on my face and said, "Bhavam, your efforts worked. She is back."

I opened my eyes. I saw the machine which measured heart beats. It was beating.

I was shocked. Was she alive? Had she been saved? I was confused.

"Ashwini…!" I said with tears coming out from my eyes.

"No, baccha, no…! Now, no more tears! She saw death, and she faced it. But death surrendered in front of her just because of your love. Adore her, enrich her; she is all yours now," said Dr Priyank.

A smile came on my face as I hugged Dr Priyank.

He went out and shared the same with my friends. There was a huge cheer heard across the hospital! My Ashwini was back. Yes, she had been given one more life by God! And that life was to live with me!

"When will she open her eyes?" I asked Dr Meet.

"By tomorrow. You let her rest now," he said.

When I came out of the operation theatre, my friends jumped upon me. I was down on the floor, enjoying the celebration of Ashwini's life.

"I told you, Bhavam, I told you!" said Nishu, kissing my cheeks.

I kissed her too and replied, "You knew…You knew…!"

I was in the seventh heaven.

"Bro, I told you it's always the best with the best," said Vrund, holding my hands.

"I have a best friend like you; so it is the best," I said, hugging him tightly.

"Bhayya…my kidney worked!" said Dhruvesh.

I replied, "Bhayya, you yourself worked."

We all shared a group hug. My God! Such an awesome moment it was! All the happiness had finally landed in my destiny.

Finally Preksha came and stood in front of my eyes. Without thinking of anything, I hugged her and thanked her for her kidney.

After four years, she kissed my cheeks and said, "Ashwini is all yours now, Bhavam. Live with her."

She joined her hands and said, "I again say sorry for what you went through, just because of me. If it is possible, do forgive me."

"Preksha, I have already forgiven you. Let's be friends again, like we were before getting into our relationship," I said, offering her my hand.

Instead of shaking my hand, she preferred to hug me.

Epilogue

The next day…

I was inside the room without anyone around me, just waiting for Ashwini to open her eyes!

Slowly the time came. Her hands showed a little movement. I had promised myself that I wouldn't cry from now, because I wanted to give her that smile which she had herself revived.

Yes, she did open her eyes. She looked at me and smiled in the same way as she had done, the very first time we met.

Before I could say anything she said,

"I am your angel now,
Love me!
I am your angel now,
Adore me!
I am your angel now,
Just hug me!
I am your angel now,
Just kiss me!"

Without thinking about anything, I hugged her, not very tightly, because she was weak due to the operation. Then I kissed her lips passionately until I was able to hear the knocking on the door.

"Beta, you are perfectly all right now!" said Dr Priyank.

I got up and touched his feet and said, "You are God in form of a Doctor! If each and every doctor is like you, the world itself will be a different place."

"Ashwini is like my daughter, I told you," he said.

"The day I earn, I will surely pay you for this operation," I promised.

"You can pay it now itself!" he said.

"How?" I asked.

"Promise me that you will keep this little girl always happy. Promise me that you won't ever be the reason for her tears!" he asked for an assurance...

"I don't promise; I just commit!" I said, shaking his hand.

After that, my friends entered the room.

"This is Dhruvesh, my friend. He has donated one kidney for you," I said.

Ashwini was deeply obliged as she thanked Dhruvesh.

"And this is Preksha! Without her, we wouldn't have got a second kidney," I said.

Ashwini was a little surprised because she knew everything about me and Preksha, and despite all that, Preksha had still helped me.

Preksha came forward and took Ashwini's hand in her hand, and said, "You are so pretty and innocent. You are perfectly made for this good innocent man."

Ashwini smiled.

Preksha called me, and took my hand and placed it over Ashwini's palm and locked the two together. She said, "Be like this forever. Ashwini. I know this man; he will never hurt you. He will just love you, as that's all he can do! Sometimes you will do things which he won't like, but then also, he won't say anything. I ruined his heart but you made him smile again. I am leaving his hand in your hand. Keep that smile glowing always."

Preksha had the final word as she said to me, "And yes, Bhavam, that's your angel now. If it is possible, do forgive me."

After that, she stood up and started walking off. All were silenced by her act. Again she had gained respect in my eyes. I wanted to stop her, but I didn't, as my hand was locked with Ashwini's.

"You know, a miracle saved you?" said Vrund.

"No…No…! Heenal saved me!" said Ashwini.

"Heenal?" I asked in surprise.

Ashwini looked at me and said, "Yes, Bhavam, she is here. She was there when I was getting operated. She did something which saved me."

"Heenal isn't here!" I said.

"But I saw her, trust me! She was here. I was in deep pain and I know that she came here, and placed her hands over my head, saying that now I will live," replied Ashwini.

I thought it was Ashwini's dream because I knew that Heenal wasn't there here in Valsad.

After 3 weeks…
Location:- Valsad Railway Station
Time:- 3:30 pm

"*Train number 19033 from Valsad to Ahmedabad Junction, Gujarat Queen, is arriving shortly on Platform number 1.*"

"Is this train also unreserved?" asked Vrund angrily.

"Yes!" replied Nishu.

"I told you guys last time that I am not going to sit in an unreserved train," said Vrund.

"Don't worry! We have reserved tickets this time," I said.

We arrived at Vadodara around 7:30 am.

During the entire journey, she placed her head over my chest and slept. We were like those perfect couples, who were determined to enrich their lives with some money after completing college.

"I am telling you that Heenal was there!" said Ashwini.

"But how could she be there? She's here!" I said.

"Okay, come on! Let's go and meet her," she said.

We sat in the auto and it directed us to Kamatibaugh.

Her hand was in my hand, as we entered the garden.

The situation had changed, and now, I was surely never going to visit the garden alone!

I took her to the place where Heenal and I used to always sit and talk!

"What the hell!" I exclaimed.

The place was barren; nothing was there, no benches, no Heenal, nothing!

"What happened?" asked Ashwini.

"There was suppose to be a bench here," I said.

I looked confused. I moved around and shouted Heenal's name, but she didn't come.

We saw that there was a huge stone which was placed in that barren land.

Ashwini went near it and said, "This stone is carved, and some message is written on it."

We both read the message written on it –

"The day I reunite two souls, I will be a free soul."

What was that? I was horrified and so was Ashwini.

"Bhavam, please have a look at the pics which we clicked with Heenal," she said fearfully.

I quickly took out my cell phone and showed her the picture which was taken by the waiter when all of us visited Maji Sainik.

"Oh shit! Heenal is not visible in this photo!" she exclaimed.

I saw each and every photo, but she was invisible in all of them.

Ashwini got a little scared, and she hugged me. I kissed her forehead and said, "Thank you, Heenal!"

I understood everything.

I touched that barren land and held its soil in my hand, and cried a lot over it because I was missing Heenal!

"Don't cry, Bhavam!" said Ashwini. But she was crying too!

"Look, she was, indeed, the real angel, who came to reunite us!" said Ashwini.

I always said that there was 'NO REPLY' when I used to look up at the skies and talk with God. But I was a fool not to understand that he came in the forms of Heenal and Tanishq in order to help me out. He always replied me when I needed him the most and now I was searching for Heenal! Would she ever return to talk with me?

I had many things which I wanted to tell her, so I took the marker and wrote on that stone,

P.S. BE MY ANGEL

Indicating that she would always remain an ANGEL for me.

Then I took Ashwini in my arms and again looked up at the skies and said, "Thank you, Heenal! I Love you!"

This time there was a reply and it was in form of Ashwini's heart beat!

Yeh toe sunna tha ki –
khuda sabi ki kismat likhta hai…
Par,
Ek baar kisi ke aasu mita kar toe dekho…
Ek baar kisi ki hasi lauta kar toe dekho…
Ek baar firse ji kar toe dekho…
Ek baar firse pyar karke toe dekho…

Life is an endless opportunity, NEVER GIVE UP! If there is a story made for Bhavam, there is surely a story made for you too!